Island Bride

*Also by Linda Chaikin
in Large Print:*

Behind the Veil
Captive Heart
Endangered
Golden Palaces
Swords and Scimitars

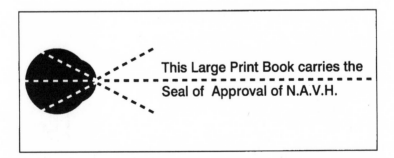

This Large Print Book carries the
Seal of Approval of N.A.V.H.

Island Bride

Linda Chaikin

Thorndike Press • Thorndike, Maine

Published in 2001 by arrangement with Harvest House Publishers.

Thorndike Press Large Print Christian Romance Series.

The tree indicium is a trademark of Thorndike Press.

The text of this Large Print edition is unabridged.
Other aspects of the book may vary from the original edition.

Set in 16 pt. Plantin by Elena Picard.

Printed in the United States on permanent paper.

Library of Congress Cataloging-in-Publication Data

Chaikin, L. L., 1943–
    Island bride / Linda Chaikin.
        p. cm. — (Trade winds ; 3)
      ISBN 0-7862-3120-3 (lg. print : hc : alk. paper)
      1. Pirates — Fiction. 2. Spanish Main — Fiction.
    3. Peru — Fiction. 4. Large type books. I. Title.
    PS3553.H2427 I85 2001
    813′.54—dc21   00-053222

Island Bride

❧ 1 ❧

Encounters

Sybella's carriage waited near the wharf at
Cartagena Bay. She had sent out her guard
with the hope that he would return with
Nicklas. She watched as porters trundled
casks and hauled great wooden boxes and
iron-hooped bales onto tall-masted ships,
elaborately carved and gilded, which were secured to different sections of the crowded
wharf. As the moments passed she became
more anxious and afraid that Nicklas would
not listen to her summons. As she watched
the ship's deck where her guard had boarded
she was relieved to see the two men disembark and walk down the gangplank together.
Nicklas approached the carriage and smiled
as he recognized her. The afternoon was hot
and he wore an open, bell-sleeved white shirt
and breeches, his handsome tanned face
damp with perspiration.

Sybella leaned forward anxiously and put
her hand on his as he stood beside the car-

riage, her voice both soft and hurried. "I must speak with you, Nicklas. I've heard you're loading the prisoners, and that you'll sail to Lima after the wedding."

His gray-green eyes flickered with restrained sympathy. This was the last emotion she wished to evoke from him. "I'm sorry, Sybella, this is not a good time. As you say, we're busy loading."

"I must speak with you, if only for a few minutes. It would be quieter on your ship."

With an inward sigh he stepped back and took her hand to help her down. The wharf was crowded with activity. He led her up the wooden walk-way onto the deck.

"What did you want to see me about?" Nicklas asked, pausing a moment to dip a ladle into the water barrel to quench his thirst.

"We can't talk here. We must not be overheard."

He scanned her, then led her up the quarterdeck steps to his cabin. It had a low ceiling and seemed small, but was neat and fitted with a bunk, closet, chest of drawers, writing table, and some chairs. Maps were nailed to the dark, oak-paneled walls, and on the floor were stacks of leather-bound books.

She turned swiftly to face him. "You're leaving. I can't bear it, hold me . . ."

A light frown creased his brow as he gently removed her arms from around him. "No, Sybella. Do not throw yourself at me."

"I don't care! I don't care what anyone thinks. I love —"

His fingers silenced her lips and his gaze was firm. "You know I'm going to marry Devora in a week. Don't do or say anything you'll be ashamed of later."

"But you can't marry her."

"I'm sorry, Sybella. Whatever there was between us is over. I told you that in Madrid. I don't want you coming to Lima."

"Oh Nicklas, please, I —"

"Hush, Sybella! Someone will hear you!"

"You can't marry her. Not when I love you. And there was a time when you said you loved me —"

"I never told you that."

He had not, but she lifted her chin to try to make him feel guilty, as though he had betrayed her. "You did tell me. Before I was sent to Spain to marry Marcos. Now you'll marry *her*, an English woman!"

A half-smile tugged at his lips. "Are you forgetting I'm half English? Look, Sybella, I've no time. If all you have come for is to engage me in an argument over Devora —"

"I can make you forget." She wrapped her arms around him and pressed her lips to his enticingly. Nicklas firmly loosened her grip and, holding her wrists painfully tight, held her away. His eyes were warm, and she deliberately misread his emotion. "You see? You do want me! You love me!"

"I'm in love with Devora. Please don't make me say anything more to hurt you."

Her rage erupted. She jerked her wrists free, breathing rapidly. She had thrown herself at him and he had spurned her, just as he had done in Madrid! Her eyes searched his. He was grave and distant and walked to the door. "We must go now. You will permit me to walk you to your carriage, or I'll have one of my soldiers escort you."

"You won't get by with this," she breathed huskily.

"I'm sorry," came his gentle reply. "I thought I made it plain in Madrid and Seville that there would never be anything more between us but friendship."

"Friendship," she spat.

Nicklas looked at her with a narrowed gaze. "Favian loves you. You would do well to consider him."

She ignored his unwelcome suggestion. Tears threatened to spill from her eyes but she was too angry to give in. She stood, hands on hips. "You must not go through with this marriage."

Nicklas watched her alertly, studying her, as though something had just crossed his mind. Sybella smiled with satisfaction. "So you remember." She saw his jaw flex, but he made no comment. She sat down on the edge of the desk and lifted a dark brow. "I have the letter from the Spanish governor at Saint Augustine. Do you know what will happen to you, to *her*, if I should turn it over to Maximus?"

She could see he knew very well indeed. It had been sent to the king and would have reached him on the very day that Nicklas was to appear before him to be knighted for sinking heretic ships.

His eyes burned with anger but he remained silent. Sybella folded her arms tightly. "And if you do not send her back to Barbados and marry me, I will have the letter delivered to your father! You'll be arrested."

"You may be lying."

"I have kept the letter since I saved your skin in Seville. And before I lose you, I will use it."

They looked at each other for a long, steady moment before he replied. "Do you now expect to win my heart? You have the wrong approach, Sybella. If you turn over the letter it will profit you nothing. You will only defeat yourself."

11

She stood angrily. "You will be sorry, Nicklas."

"Maybe. But it is a risk I must take. I will marry Devora next week. Letter or not. I cannot see you betraying me to Maximus. You are spoiled and selfish, Sybella, but not innately cruel where I am concerned. Would your vengeful heart be satisfied by seeing me turned over to the inquisitors? I think not."

She glared hotly. "You will see. Before I allow her to have you I would plunge a dagger into your heart."

Nicklas leaned in the doorway. He took a dagger from his belt and offered it to her. "Then you may accomplish your vengeance now," he said gently. "Because there is but one woman I want enough to marry. And that is the daughter of Countess Radburn."

She felt her heart flare up into her face. "You mock me."

"I do not mock you, Sybella. I ask you to forget about us and to return to Seville, perhaps with Favian. Begin a new life."

Her eyes sought his with desperation. His dismissal evoked pain.

"If it weren't for her, you would think differently. You would marry me, I know you would. I hate her!"

He looked at her with both irritation and

12

pity. Then he turned and opened the door. "I'll send someone to escort you back to your carriage." He went out, the door closing.

The sound of his boots ringing on the steps filled her ears with a sinking despair. Oh Nicklas!

A sense of loss filled her mind. With a muffled cry she turned away, her face in her palms as she choked back tears of defeat. In a tantrum, she knocked a book off his desk and took some satisfaction in stomping on it.

The summer sky blurred into a soft twilight of rosy-blue above the Caribbean Sea. Lady Devora Ashby, attired in lavender lace, stood on the wrought-iron balcony of the Casa Valentin in Cartagena, on the Spanish Main. Below, in the tiled patio, a tropical rainbow of frangipani, poinsettia, and crimson bougainvillea overflowed their round terra cotta tubs of Inca pottery. A blue-black mynah bird screeched and strutted along the adobe wall, then flew up to a branch of overripe figs to feast. The day's heat, long baked into the stone, lingered. The air, heavy with the spicy fragrance of tropical flowers, had an intoxicating effect on Devora's senses. She fanned herself languidly with an ostrich-feather fan dyed to match her dress.

Within five days she would step across the threshold of holy matrimony and vow her faithfulness before God to Don Nicklas Valentin, alias Captain Bruce Hawkins. They would then set forth on the long, arduous journey to Lima, to the Peruvian silver mines, where his work for the king of Spain was to begin. Dangerous work, should Viceroy Maximus learn the truth about what his son was planning. Not even Devora fully understood, since Nicklas refused to explain. But she suspected enough to understand that little but the grace of God could save him from his father's wrath if Maximus were to learn of Nicklas' intentions.

Her fan stopped in mid-air. The voice of Maximus drifted up to her from below as he rounded the flagstone walkway with his other son, Don Favian. Favian persisted, as he had been doing for days, in wanting to attack Jamaica for harboring Henry Morgan and the buccaneers after their deadly raid on Granada.

"Jamaica belongs to Spain. Why should that English dog, Governor Modyford, be allowed to protect Morgan a day longer?"

Maximus paused on the walk to light a

Cuban cigar. "You are not using your head again, Favian. Any attack on Port Royal requires the approval of Seville. Unless it is your wish for me to be called to Spain to answer for so rash a move?"

"Since when was I not loyal? Yet, perhaps trouble rising from your own house is not so far removed from fact as you think."

"Watch your envious tongue. What charge do you mean to render against your brother, or is it your uncle you speak ill of?"

"I speak not only of Nicklas or Tobias, but also of the woman you have arranged for me to marry."

"Sybella?" Maximus gave a quick burst of laughter. "That she spurns you is no one's fault but your own. You must let her know that you are a Valentin, and as such, will not permit her to lead you about by the nose. Or do you expect me to propose to her on your behalf?"

"You may mock me, Father, but you will one day see that I am not the whining puppy you take me for."

"Enough of your wounded pride, my son. If there is a spy among us, ferret him out to stand trial. Come to me with proof, or trouble me no more with your idle tongue. Is there an enemy? Simply unmask him. See how your brother Nicklas excels at the work

15

bestowed upon him by the king. Do the same, and you too will be rewarded by both me and Seville."

"I have not been idle. I wish to speak with you about the prisoners. Archbishop Harro Andres is not satisfied with Nicklas' explanation of what happened at Granada, nor am I."

Devora held her fan tightly. She knew the prisoners Favian spoke of were actually members of Nicklas' buccaneering crew. There had already been trouble when Archbishop Andres had insisted the prisoners stand trial as heretics. Only clever intervention by Nicklas and Friar Tobias had thwarted him. She heard Maximus' impatient reprimand.

"Nicklas was wise to commandeer Hawkins' crew of pirates. What more proper way to increase the silver production at the mines than to use the very men who once robbed and plundered the treasure galleons? What news do you bring me besides trifles? I am a busy man!"

"As I said, I've not been idle. Among the few brave and daring Spanish soldiers to survive Morgan's massacre on Granada is a young man sent back by the English ambassador."

"Earl Robert Radburn?"

Devora, straining to hear, leaned closer against the balcony rail and unwittingly dropped her fan. Although the feathers landed silently, Maximus saw it and looked up. Still in his early forties, he was rugged and handsome. His granite features revealed an iron will, while his height and weight suggested a man of enormous physical strength. A scar, long ago healed, slashed his right cheek above a well-groomed, short inky beard.

His mouth twisted into a smile. "Ah, Señorita Devora. Perhaps you would prefer to join Don Favian and me. It may be safer than risking a fall from the balcony."

She retained a demure face. "Good evening, Don Maximus, Favian. If there is news of my father, I would like to hear it, if you please."

Favian was tall and slim, and, though not ruggedly built like his half-brother, Nicklas, or his father, Maximus, was nevertheless wiry and strong. He carried languid airs of unbearable conceit and was always dressed in ostentatious grandeur. He had a sensuous mouth, and his large eyes, which resembled liquid pools the color of cinnamon, looked out on the world of his day with cynical boredom.

He looked up at her. "Your father has

gone on to Tortuga to speak with the French pirate-governor there about Hawkins, but he has sent back a wounded soldier with a message."

"What message?" Maximus demanded.

"He refuses to speak to anyone except you, my Father. The archbishop asks you come to his house tonight. What shall I tell him?"

"Tell him I will come, of course. See that this soldier is there."

Favian looked pleased. Before leaving the patio, he looked up again at Devora and bowed. He turned on a polished heel, but instead of moving in the direction that would lead him to the stables to ride to Harro Andres, Favian walked toward the house.

A soldier from Granada. Did the message her father sent prove dangerous to Bruce?

Maximus walked toward the balcony and stood with hands on hips looking up at her, his black eyes raking her with a glance that was anything but fatherly. "Nicklas informs me I have excellent taste in women."

Devora remained outwardly composed, though his words reeked with pride and arrogance.

"He is pleased with my choice for his bride. From your ready answer after your introduction, I see the pleasure is mutual. He tells me you wish to marry him before the voyage to Lima."

"I have accepted his proposal," she stated briefly, not wishing to give him cause to suspect a previous involvement with Bruce before his arrival in Cartagena. He already knew she'd been aboard the *Revenge* as a prisoner of the infamous Bruce Hawkins. While there was no reason to think Maximus could, or would, suspect his son Nicklas to be the pirate he had sought, she must safeguard every move.

"Your unexpected cooperation came as a surprise."

She pretended to carelessly pluck a blossom from the trellis vine that rambled along the railing.

"I do not see why it should, Don Maximus. It was you who went to great pains to convince me I had no choice except to cooperate with your plans."

He laughed unpleasantly. "And you resisted those plans, Señorita. I knew from the beginning you would prove a thorn in the Valentin side with your opinionated views on Spain's policies in the Indies. Yet now, suddenly, you surprise me. You submit to Nicklas without a peep. Is it so, that my son has — shall we say — swept you off your feet

19

with his goodly appearance and authority from the great king of Spain?"

"Are you now suggesting I am free to resist, to return to Barbados if I choose? I would go at once, Don Maximus, but the countess would hardly approve. You appear to forget I have not only your will to contend with, but my mother's, and now the decision of Don Nicklas. There comes a time when one must accept the inevitable as the foreordained will of God."

"Spoken like a Calvinist, Señorita, but with a little more gaiety than expected from so somber a religion as the Puritans." She sensed by his mocking smile that he didn't believe her. Devora tore her eyes away from his smoldering dark gaze. Maximus made her uneasy. She would have mentioned this to Bruce, but the matter proved embarrassing to her and could also be construed as feminine pride on her part. Maximus, without doubt, remained a robust and handsome man.

"Then the marriage will be in five days. Is so short a time convenient?"

"It will suffice, Don Maximus."

Bruce wanted the wedding held before they set out on the long journey by land and sea to Lima, the chief city of governmental authority on the Spanish Main.

He watched her for a moment longer, then bowed his head, and strode away. She moved away from the rail uneasily, and returned back inside her shadowed chamber frowning. The sooner Bruce accomplished his work at Lima and they departed for English waters, unknown to the viceroy, the easier she would sleep. But that would be six months into the future when the galleons arrived.

Once again she thought of what Bruce had told her about the treasure fleet. It departed Spain from Seville and sailed to the Canary Islands, then on to the Caribbean, dropping anchor south between Grenada and Trinidad, or passing Dominica, one of the few islands which had plenty of drinking water for ships which had run light. The galleons took thirty days to reach the Caribbean from the Canaries, then another two weeks to reach Cartagena.

She looked off toward the harbor where the galleons would winter and where crews would repair the ships for the long voyage back to Seville. When at last the great silver mule train had made its annual journey down the steep mountainous region of Peru, through the Isthmus of Panama, it would be met by the waiting galleons at Portobello. Smaller ships along the Main would bring in their own cargoes of hides, cochineal, and other Indies' goods from the farming colonists, and these lesser treasures would also be transferred onto the galleons. Once the goods and the silver were loaded, the galleons would sail for their last stop, Havana, where they would wait for the other galleons which had wintered at Vera Cruz, and which carried their own rich cargoes, including emeralds. Together the entire *flota* would depart Havana according to a royal *ordinanza* which decreed that they must voyage home in January. If they survived the storms and the buccaneers, the treasure fleet would arrive safely in Seville.

Bruce had told her that when Seville spotted the galleons, a message was brought to the king, "who literally dances with greedy anticipation."

Devora suspected Bruce's secret plans might have something to do with "disappointing" the king by sending his galleons home empty. Even though Bruce had recently been knighted, he didn't serve Spain with sincerity but rather, the cause of England. And Devora had been troubled when she'd discovered that the prisoners he intended to transport to the Peruvian mines were actually his own English and French pirates from Tortuga — many of them mem-

22

bers of his crew when he'd sailed as captain of the *Revenge*.

Whatever venturesome plan he had in mind, she knew it would be bold and dangerous, a scenario that suited him, and that was what worried her. Indeed, while she was apt to shudder over the consequences, Bruce was determined to follow through. On his arrival as Don Nicklas, he had even dared to report to Maximus that he had rid the Caribbean of his father's enemy, the "English diablo," by dueling Bruce Hawkins. Nicklas had added a cynical touch of humor to his daring by bringing Hawkins' sword and laying it at his father's feet.

Thus far, Nicklas' identity remained concealed, but her mother, Countess Catherina Radburn, knew the truth.

"If only I could convince her to return Bruce's pistol," Devora murmured, seeing in her mind's eye the silver initials identifying him as B.A.V.: Bruce Anthony Valentin.

It grieved Devora that her mother was willing to threaten to betray Nicklas' other identity, as revealed by the pistol, in order to gain wealth enough to return to the court of King Charles. Her troubled thoughts were interrupted by a knock on her chamber door. She walked across the cool tile floor and unbolted her lock, mildly surprised to see Doña Sybella Ferdinand. She stood in the corridor, her young face looking like smooth ivory and just as placid, but her dark eyes reflected an internal storm. There was a look of mystery about her, and at once cautious, Devora scanned her.

This was the first time Devora had seen Sybella alone since Nicklas returned to Cartagena and publicly agreed at the governor's palace to the marriage. Even so, there was no reason for Devora to believe Sybella had given up her plans to have Nicklas.

Devora braced herself for the jealous tirade of accusations sure to come.

Sybella smiled, looking almost demure.

Had she decided to submit to the will of the family and withdraw her opposition?

"I would like to speak to you. May I come in?"

Devora concealed her wariness over Sybella's mild tone. "Yes, please do." She stepped back, and the Spanish señora entered with a rustle of inky lace over wide and stiff petticoats. She walked across the room while Devora watched, unsure of Sybella's motives. She wished they might come to some truce over Nicklas, but she remained skeptical.

Sybella moved gracefully about the chamber, her lace hem trailing, distractingly plucking at her fan with slim fingers. She appeared so distressed that Devora's sympathy reached out to her in spite of herself.

"Please, do sit, Sybella. Is all well?"

The young woman of Spanish nobility sank into a chair of burgundy tapestry and fanned herself thoughtfully.

"All is well, if you consider my leaving for Seville a cause for joy. I do not. As for you, Señorita Devora, I think you will be very pleased over my forced departure."

Forced? Devora walked slowly toward her, and stopped. "You're — leaving for Seville?"

Sybella's eyes were softly dark and vulnerable as she cast them down and regarded her black lace fan unhappily. "Yes. Tomorrow."

"So soon!"

"Uncle Maximus insists. I've also spoken with Nicklas. He too tells me that I must go away. He is in love with you. My presence casts a shadow on your happiness."

Devora, not wanting to be unkind, or wishing to be the cause for Sybella's fate, forced a grave face.

"I assure you, your presence is not causing me unhappiness. I'm rather surprised Nicklas would suggest so. I do not consider myself so insecure that you must leave the Caribbean on my account. Not if you wish to stay. If you consider Lima to be your home, it can be so in the future."

"I could wish Nicklas and Maximus felt so."

"I am sure Nicklas did not mean to imply you must leave for my sake. I wish we could be friends, Sybella."

Sybella lifted her chin, showing faint surprise, but she looked away again. "Though we both might wish for friendship, Nicklas would always come between us. I could not bear to see him as your husband, and you will always feel uncomfortable around me, knowing I feel so strongly."

Devora didn't dare tell her that she expected to leave Lima after six months. "We need not live in the same house in Lima."

"I have come to the conclusion Nicklas is right. It is best I leave for Spain. Even so, say nothing of my visit to him, or Maximus. I was told to stay away from you and I wish you no more trouble on my account."

Even though Devora was realistic enough to feel relief over Sybella's departure, she took no pleasure in her sad situation. If Maximus hadn't sent Sybella to Spain to marry Don Marcos, she and Nicklas might have married. Matters had turned out poorly for Sybella. Don Marcos had been killed in battle, and she was left a widow with a small child. Devora found it difficult to fault her for still having feelings for Nicklas. And without faith in Christ and a relationship with her Heavenly Father, Sybella could only view the tragedies of her young life as a mindless set of circumstances that had dealt her an unfair blow. She could not be comforted despite wealth, title, and physical beauty.

As Devora thought of this, she was moved to consider all that she had by the grace of God. Such favor from Him compelled her to reach out in compassion.

"Oh Sybella, you needn't go. This is more your home than mine. And won't Maximus be grieved that you are taking your infant son away to Seville? I have seen the way he makes over the boy, and surely he could be well raised in the Casa Valentin at Lima."

Sybella stood and paced again. "You are gracious to bid me stay, but I sail tomorrow on the *Magdalena*. It may be that I will find a new life in Seville." She paused and looked at Devora. "There is one last thing you can do for me. Actually, what I request is not for me, but Lady Lillian Anthony Bruce."

"Lady Lillian! Nicklas' English grand-mother?"

"Yes. She wishes to meet you. She sent a message early this morning. Cuzita brought it up to my room."

Cuzita was the meztiza servant girl responsible for caring for Devora upon her arrival. Until a few days ago, she had been held by the authorities for breaking curfew, a serious offense in Cartagena. Devora had blamed herself for the girl's arrest. A little over a week ago she had asked Cuzita to bring her by night to the cathedral to speak with Friar Tobias. Though Tobias had not been there, Devora had discovered Bruce's pistol. An unfortunate accident on the way home in their coach had alerted the authorities. Cuzita and the boy driver were held for questioning, and Devora, injured, had survived a concussion in a convent. Later she had been released by Don Maximus, but Cuzita and the boy had not fared as well. And unfortunately, the pistol had ended up in the hands of the countess through her bodyguard, Luis. On her arrival home, Cuzita had explained that Bruce had freed them at Devora's request.

"Cuzita told me that you would like to meet Lady Lillian."

"Yes, I did mention it. How is it you know her?"

Sybella sat down on the red and gold settee, hands in her lap. She sighed. "There is no cause for secrecy. All the Valentins know her. She lived near the hacienda in Lima while Nicklas was growing up. Then some months ago she made the decision to come to Cartagena. She believed Nicklas would soon arrive from Seville. She expects to return to England and hopes that Nicklas — whom she calls Bruce — will sail with her to meet his great-grandfather, an English duke."

Sybella spoke matter of factly, and Devora, who had grown still and inwardly tense at the mention of the name of Bruce, made no reply. It was a relief that Sybella's face transmitted no suspicion over the name.

Devora wondered why Lady Lillian had not returned to England before now. She had learned from Cuzita that the elder woman's daughter, Bruce's mother, was no longer alive. How and when his mother had succumbed remained a mystery to Devora, but she would have expected his grandmother to have returned to England once Bruce had gone off to Spain to the military and riding academy.

"Why did she not send the request directly to me?"

"She thought I should arrange the meeting, since anything you do on your own would be suspect. Though Maximus would object, she feels she has a right to contest him since she will become your grandmother by marriage. She wishes you to come to her house for an 'English' tea. She noticed you with your mother at the processional for Nicklas when he arrived."

The invitation pleased her. Meeting Lady Lillian would provide an opportunity to learn more about Nicklas and his English ancestry. But Devora dared not risk using Cuzita again to help her slip away from the watchful eyes of Don Maximus.

"When can the meeting be arranged?"

"The tea is tomorrow afternoon. It is short notice, but Lady Lillian had little choice. I leave soon, and the wedding is next week."

"Will she come to her grandson's wedding?"

Sybella's lips tightened, then she smiled ruefully. "Nicklas means everything to her. She will come."

"Did she give any details about her reason for wanting to see me?"

Sybella stood with a rustle of skirt. "It is not like her to explain until she meets you. It may be she has a wedding gift, or she may simply wish to see what you are like before she decides to attend the wedding."

Would she like me? wondered Devora. It was odd that no one appeared to take his grandmother's opinion into consideration when his marriage was deemed important for both Maximus and the countess. Since Lady Lillian was the daughter of a duke, she must feel slighted.

"Then you'll come?"

"Yes," Devora said quickly, "but if Maximus discovers what we're doing, he'll be displeased with us."

Sybella smiled wearily. "That's the least thing I'll need to worry about once I'm aboard the ship for Spain. As for you, you have Nicklas to defend you. He is more than a match for Maximus, or Favian."

But Devora was aware that not even Bruce appeared as though he wanted her to contact his grandmother. That morning Devora had attempted to casually ask Maximus about Lady Lillian's health.

"Do not concern yourself," he had said, as he vigorously poured scented olive oil over his eggs. "Have you nothing more important to do with your time with your marriage nearing? Most girls would be busy making gowns and dreaming of their prince. I suppose you wish to gossip with her since all women engage in it." He had lifted his Venetian glass filled with Spanish wine and emptied it, watching her boldly.

"I do not consider an inquiry into Lady Lillian's health to be worthy of a critique on feminine vices."

He waved a strong tanned hand, sudden amusement written on his robust features. "The Señorita easily gets her feathers ruffled. Nicklas' English grandmother does not need to socialize. She is old and tired."

Devora's eyes narrowed slightly over his disregard. "All the more reason to visit her, so it would seem, Don Maximus. However, I saw her at the processional honoring the arrival of Nicklas, and she did not look frail. She must be interested in Nicklas' plans, else she wouldn't have gone out in her coach. It is only right I should be introduced to her, and invite her to the wedding."

Maximus' black eyes boiled. "If there is a wedding." He set his silver fork down firmly and leaned over his plate. "I did not say she held no interest in my son. The important point, which you are overlooking, is that the Valentins no longer hold an interest in her."

"Why?"

Maximus laughed impatiently. "Women! Questions, always questions." He stood and tossed back his chair as though it were weightless. "If Nicklas wishes to invite his grandmother to his wedding, let him decide. He is down at the harbor preparing the ships to transport the heretics to the mines."

Devora too, rose to her feet. "Are you saying he does not wish his grandmother to attend the marriage?"

Maximus' mouth twisted. "The English are a vexing race. They do not seem to know when to take no for an answer. If you insist on knowing the unfortunate details, I shall not deprive you, my lovely Señorita. It so happens she blames me for the unfortunate death of her daughter. It is not so. Nicklas pays no heed and neither should you. Forget this woman. She is old and suspicious. Ready yourself for the journey to Lima. That should provide enough anticipation to occupy any reasonable woman." And he strode from the dining room.

Remembering, Devora frowned, but Sybella didn't appear to notice as she played with her lace fan.

"Lady Lillian's wishes are all that matter to me now," Sybella said. "She is a good woman and I wish to do this last thing for her before I sail. My memories of her when I was a young girl at Lima are fair. She was always loyal to Nicklas." The image seemed to please her, and she smiled to herself as she

33

walked to the door. "I will wait for you to-morrow afternoon in a coach."

"We are bound to be noticed . . ."

"I am not as unwise as Cuzita when wishing to slip away unnoticed," Sybella said impatiently. "I've had much experience in Seville and Lima. The coach will be out of sight down the street. Don't worry, it's only a matter of whether you wish to see her."

"I have told you I do. It isn't so much Maximus' but Nicklas' reaction when he finds out that troubles me. Why does he not wish to speak of his grandmother? Because of her suspicions over the death of his mother, Lady Marian?"

Sybella paused, her fingers on the door knob. Both brows arched. "It is best that Lady Anthony explain such divisions. But do you mean that you believe Nicklas does not wish you to meet her?"

She did, but Devora grew cautious. "Since I've little information, I can only wonder."

Sybella wore a ghost of a smile. "You will soon wonder no longer. When you see her yourself you may ask the reason, if there is one. Unless you are afraid of leaving the house without Nicklas' permission?" A faint mockery appeared in her eyes.

Devora resisted the challenge. "I will meet you tomorrow."

As Sybella set the time and the exact place, Devora wrestled with what Bruce might consider disloyalty if she were introduced to his grandmother without his presence. Yet surely Lady Anthony's request counted for something?

Devora felt she had a right to meet her, to learn about the Anthony and Bruce side of the family before she married Bruce. His grandmother could explain a great deal that Devora may otherwise never know. She could not risk losing this opportunity.

❧ 2 ❧

Lady Lillian
Anthony Bruce

The next afternoon Devora slipped out of Casa Valentin unnoticed. When far enough away from the front patio to escape detection, she quickened her footsteps, keeping to the shadows of adobe walls and pepper trees. Outside the wall the hot afternoon enclosed her in stillness, though the coveted trade wind was rising. The thick palm branches lining the stone street created a lazy shifting sound, disturbing the sleepy heat. Most of Cartagena's populace were indoors for the hottest period of the day, leaving the narrow street deserted.

As promised, Sybella was waiting in her coach. Devora thought of the boy Juan who had handled the spirited horse on her excursion to the cathedral, resulting in a fall and several days incarceration with a concussion, and glanced up at Sybella's driver. There was not one, but two young Spaniards, one handling the reins and the other wearing crossed bandoleers with pistols. She apparently had her own bodyguard of hired soldiers.

Sybella opened the door from inside and Devora stepped up and took the seat opposite her. The smell of heated leather filled the coach. Sybella signaled the coachmen to drive on.

"You're late. I was beginning to think you would not come."

"I had to be certain no one saw me leave. And I had to attend to my mother."

"You said nothing to her?"

Sybella's anxious tone was understandable, since Devora shared her concerns. "The countess is resting. Her feverish condition grows worse in the afternoons."

Sybella nodded, apparently satisfied and relaxed against the leather seat.

The coach turned a corner, passing tightly packed houses, with patios secluded behind more walls and tall iron gates. All the windows were elaborately screened with wrought-iron grills, and Devora vaguely thought about the veiled wives and daughters who lived behind those cloistered bars. How many were there willingly? She suspected most of them were. These women had grown up in a culture adapted from Seville that expected their women to live secluded lives of luxury. Some of the reason for this was the ruthlessness of the age, the violence, and the crime.

The ruffling breeze brought odors of stone and dust and horses. Sybella fanned herself, glancing out the open windows.

"Do you expect to be followed?" Devora glanced behind her shoulder. The street from where they had come was empty except for a boy leading a donkey down one of the narrow, unpaved side alleys. Some pigeons roosted on a roof, keeping to the shade.

"I am always careful. I learned that in Seville. When Don Marcos — my husband — was away at war for months at a time, I soon grew weary of alabaster screens and iron grillwork. I wanted life, people. So I learned to sneak out undetected."

Devora was curious about her. What was it that Sybella wanted besides, like the countess, entertainment, gowns and slippers, and the approval of handsome men?

"Were you ever caught?"

Sybella's full lips curved into a bored smile. "I was. The Ferdinand family was not understanding. They wrote to Maximus."

"He was rather far away to do anything about it."

Sybella's dark eyes turned mysterious.

"He wrote to Nicklas at the military training academy in Madrid. Nicklas somehow smoothed matters over for me with my husband's aunt. He was protective of me in those days. My evenings were at peace after that. In a few months, even my husband's family understood they must look the other way when I needed to get out."

The warm air soothed Devora's damp throat. Had Bruce ever kept her company on those excursions? Devora refused asking the wrong questions. The past was over.

The coach turned onto a pleasant residential street, cool and shady and far from the dust and heated stones. Hearing the tranquil sounds of water splashing, Devora peered out the window and saw a large fountain built on a square carpeted with exotic flowers. Farther ahead, a massive gate stood open and inviting. Devora had a glimpse of green grass, roses, and jasmine.

The guard drove the coach through the gate, and stopped beneath a giant tree whose branches shaded the entire carriageway. Sybella got out first and waited in the lazy shade for Devora.

"This is the house Nicklas bought for his grandmother," Sybella said when she joined her.

So he did visit her, Devora thought,

pleased. "Then he must expect her to stay on in Cartagena."

"She will not stay," Sybella said, and Devora looked at her. What made her so certain?

"This way."

The front door of Lady Lillian's house opened at Sybella's knock. They were not met by a serving woman, but another Spaniard in soldier's garb. His quick black eyes greeted Sybella, then turned upon Devora. He stepped back, permitting the two women to pass.

Devora noted the pistol in his bandoleer. She looked questioningly at Sybella, but she did not appear to make anything of it and instead gestured her forward across the tile floor into another room.

The room was spacious and pleasant, with dappled sunlight peering in through the grilled window work onto more terra cotta tile. Devora's surveying glance touched upon divans, heavy chairs upholstered with leather, and a large wall painting of stampeding white and black horses. Bruce would fit well in such a house. She imagined that the painting of Spanish horses was his favorite since Tobias had once commented that Bruce had tamed wild horses in Lima before being sent to Madrid.

Devora's eyes lowered from the painting to a frail older woman sitting in a wing-backed chair carved with intertwining roses.

Lady Lillian Anthony Bruce wore her silver hair in the style of a Spanish *condesa*, pulled back and netted with white silk. She was gowned in embroidered dark watered-silk, and her small white ruff was laced with silver thread.

For a moment, Devora believed she was gazing into the face of a well-blooded Spanish countess from Seville. But her pale skin with delicate pink wrinkled cheeks convinced her she was indeed English. Nonetheless, the twenty-five years Lady Lillian had spent on the Spanish Main left much of its Mediterranean culture stamped upon the image of the serene-faced woman.

There was no air of blooded authority in her behavior now, only an undercurrent of concern. Lady Lillian appeared to be struggling with fragile health, and her silver lashes batted as if trying to regain her presence of mind. Then at least Maximus had spoken the truth about her health.

Devora gave a brief English curtsy. "Lady Lillian."

Lady Lillian's attention turned to Sybella and her eyes flashed like cool, hard stones. Devora covered her surprise.

"You may leave us alone to discuss the matter," came Lady Lillian's chill tone.

Sybella's countenance had also changed since the carriage ride. "Very well, Lillian, but remember, neither I nor my bodyguard will be far away. Do not do anything you may regret."

Confused, Devora turned to look at Sybella. "What is this about?"

Sybella no longer wore the placid face of a woman surrendered to her future.

"I can imagine your confusion. Lillian will explain everything. May I suggest, Señorita, that you do everything she tells you. There is no time for arguments." She turned to Lady Lillian. "I will return in thirty minutes."

Sybella walked proudly across the room with a swish of skirt, her heels clacking across the tile in a determined gait. The door shut quietly but firmly, but not before Devora saw one of the armed guards taking up a position outside in the hall. Devora turned to Lady Lillian for explanation.

The older woman appeared beaten, but dignified. A sigh escaped her as she leaned her head against the back of the chair.

Devora went swiftly and knelt beside her, looking at her anxiously. "I don't understand what is happening."

"I know you don't, my child, you couldn't. Sybella, like her Uncle Maximus, is a master of deception. She lied to you, of course." She gave an awkward pat to Devora's hand resting on the arm of the chair. "Try to be calm. There is naught else we can do without Bruce to help us."

Without Bruce? "Never mind all else for the moment. Are you all right, Lady Lillian?"

She smiled wanly. "I have survived far worse. Yes, I will be all right. But this is a dreadful thing to happen to you. I have known Sybella since she was a small child, and I can assure you, she was never darkly sinister, or hard and ruthless like Maximus. I don't know what's gotten into her, but her decision has been made. I fear there's nothing either of us can do to talk her out of it."

Confusion swirled in Devora's mind. "Talk her out of what? What decision?"

"Then she's told you nothing."

Devora's fingers gripped the arm of the chair. "Only that you wished to see me, to have tea, to discuss the wedding. Are you saying you did not ask me to come here?"

"No my dear, I did not, but it is not as you think, that I didn't want to meet you. I have wanted to meet Bruce's fiancée from the moment I heard, but not like this."

"I don't understand," Devora repeated.

"I loathe being blunt. I don't want to hurt you. I see by your eyes when his name is mentioned that you do love him."

"Yes," she whispered.

"I suspected that," Lillian smiled. "He would not agree to an arranged marriage if it were not so. However, Bruce must not concern us now, but Sybella. I'm afraid there will be no wedding. Sybella will not allow it."

For a moment Devora was speechless. "Sybella will not allow — ?"

"She has a ship waiting to harry us off to Barbados. At least you will be consoled seeing your uncle, Barnabas Ashby. I've heard of him. Quite a godly man, considering he's related to the countess."

No wedding? She was returning to Barbados . . .

"What ship is this you speak of, Madame?" It was hard to keep her tone calm.

"The *Magdalena*. Sybella has arranged everything. She's very clever, I'm afraid. Should we decide not to cooperate, she will then force us to leave Cartagena. Those men you saw are her personal guards. And there are three more out back waiting to bring us to the harbor tonight when it is dark."

Astonished, Devora tried to take in the meaning of her words. "But how foolish. Does she actually think I will just up and leave without a word to Bruce?"

What made her think Devora would co-operate with such a scheme?

The truth slowly began to settle like dust. All of Sybella's friendliness when coming to Devora's chamber yesterday had been deceit. Sybella wasn't returning to Spain. She had tricked Devora into coming to meet Lady Lillian in secret. All so Sybella might put her aboard a ship for Barbados without anyone knowing. That Bruce did not know, perhaps would never know, why she'd suddenly departed, stabbed at her heart. Who knew what tale Sybella would come up with to convince Bruce, the countess, and even Maximus? As Lady Lillian had suggested, neither of them were a match for Sybella now. They were evidently under guard here until nightfall.

Devora stood, hands clenched at her sides. "She can't possibly get by with this. Why, it's abduction! Bruce will know something is wrong. And Maximus is far from a fool. He knows how she feels about your grandson. He's bound to be suspicious when we both unexpectedly board a ship for Barbados."

But did she believe her own words? Lady Lillian did not look convinced, and her face was still ashen. "So I thought at first. It's not as simple as that, my dear, as you will see. Sybella has managed to arrange for our secret departure. The captain of the *Magdalena* is her acquaintance from Seville. She's left nothing undone. Evidently she's planned this for weeks, even before Bruce arrived. If I had suspected . . ." she sighed. "Alas, I did not." She looked at Devora, her face resigned. "The Spanish captain of the *Magdalena* has arranged to bring us to a smaller ship in English waters which will take us on to Barbados."

"How generous of her," Devora said.

"Yes, Sybella is a very jealous woman. She'll stop at little to come between you and Bruce."

Devora shook her head. "I will marry Bruce. Sybella can't force me to leave." She paced, too restless to sit still and wondered how Lady Lillian could, until she realized that Bruce's grandmother had something wrong with her legs. She couldn't walk.

"Your determination to fight is commendable. I too struggled against the Valentins for years. Until I realized such strivings against Maximus were futile. The man is like iron, unyielding, and his heart is just as cold."

"You resisted Don Maximus? Why didn't you leave for England years ago? I assume it was Bruce who held you here."

A bitter heat caused Lady Anthony's eyes to glow. "Leave? Without Marian?"

"Marian? Oh yes, of course, your daughter. I'm sorry," Devora hastened to apologize as she remembered the name of Bruce's mother. "Yet, she died years ago. Surely . . ."

"She's buried in Lima." Lillian's voice turned brittle. "I would not leave her on the accursed spot. Nor Bruce." She grew reflective, talking quietly, a far-off look in her eyes.

"Both Marian and my husband are dead now. Alexander drowned in the shipwreck."

"Shipwreck?"

"We were caught in a hurricane. Our ship was torn to pieces and only a few of us made it safely to shore using sections of the ship. Marian and I were together, but Alexander was lost from our sight a few minutes after we entered the water . . . we were blown to shore, I don't know when, sometime in the daylight hours. . . . It was a wonder any of us survived. There were sharks, many of them." She closed her eyes as if remembering. "It was dreadfully vile. We did make it, but only to find Spanish authorities waiting. Don Maximus, for one." Her voice grew taut. "He was a soldier then, an important one, looking for advancement. He took us in — Marian and I and several others . . ." she shook her silver head wearily, as though it were too painful to remember. "I do not know what befell them. I was never able to find out. I think they must have been made prisoners and sent to the silver mines. But Marian — Maximus took her. . . ." She dropped her head.

Devora stood still, only her breath dispelling the silence.

"She died soon after the birth of Bruce. She named him Bruce Anthony, after my family and her father's. Maximus refused to accept him as a son. He would not give him his name."

Devora's throat was dry. She sat down weakly. "But why wouldn't Maximus receive him?"

Lillian's eyes raised and were as hard as green gems. Devora had seen that same hardness in Bruce's eyes.

"Maximus never married my daughter." Her voice came cold and bitter. "He treated her as a slave. He treated me little better. I think he would have let me die back then had Tobias not intervened. I was injured in the shipwreck and I've never walked since.

It was Bruce who was able to elevate me to the status I've enjoyed these past few years."

Devora was beginning to understand Bruce. His anger, and his almost consuming desire to shame Maximus and ruin him. Bruce had not forgiven him for what he did to his mother and his grandmother.

"Was Bruce treated roughly?" Devora managed after a moment of silence.

"To say the least, my child. Cruelly, indeed. Emotionally, physically — for years he lived near the mines unwanted, forgotten by Maximus. Had it not been for Tobias — well," she shook her head in thoughtful dismay. "God was good to us after all. I think we both would have perished. But Tobias taught him about God — we both did. That's why Bruce is of the Reformed faith. But whatever you do, say nothing of that! We all three could end up before the inquisitors should we escape Sybella's plot. Not that I believe we shall."

"How did he manage to rise in the ranks where he is today, knighted by the king of Spain, and in command of the silver production at Lima?"

Lillian relaxed into her chair, looking weary but wearing a brief smile. "Ah, Bruce is very clever. More clever than all of the Valentins, including Sybella. From the time he was a boy riding and breaking horses near the hacienda he planned to survive this, to prove Maximus wrong. He did prove him wrong. Favian is little more than a spoiled dandy, but with distorted ambitions. He has an innate jealousy of Bruce and a desire for Sybella. He would do anything to defeat Bruce and win her." She looked off, musing. "Bruce studied hard. And whatever he did, he out-performed Favian, whether it was handling horses or in warfare for the king. The rest is history, my dear. Maximus cares for little except power and glory. And Bruce offered him more reason to be proud of the Valentin name than Favian ever did. So Maximus eventually made Bruce his legal son and named him Nicklas. He sent him to Spain with Favian to the famous riding and military academy. Again, Bruce excelled because he had to — he had plans."

Devora was silent, thinking. And all this time she'd mistakenly believed that Maximus had favored Bruce. Yes, he had bullied Favian, but only because he was proving an embarrassment to the Valentin name. And what would Maximus do if he learned the truth?

Several moments must have elapsed before Devora stirred from her musings and looked again at Lady Lillian. "Does Sybella think she can be rid of us both by sending us to Barbados? We can simply refuse to let her bully us. Guards or no guards, as you say, you're the grandmother of the great and notable Don Nicklas Valentin. Would anyone dare hold you against your will?"

Lillian's hands shook with weariness. "The answer is no, they would not dare, but there is, as I said earlier, something you do not know. I'm afraid we must cooperate willingly with Sybella."

Devora stood, feeling indignation. "Willingly? I won't."

"Please, my dear, you'd better sit down. This is the most painful part."

Devora's heart beat anxiously, for as she stared into the face of Lady Lillian, the harbinger of defeat stared back, convincing her that somehow this fragile woman, though dedicated to Bruce, knew something she did not.

Lillian leaned forward in her chair. "Sybella has the means to see Bruce arrested if she wishes."

"Arrested? She wouldn't!"

"I'm not as convinced. Sybella is a woman who will destroy what she cannot have."

Devora's hands were cold. "Maximus would never arrest Bruce," she protested with feeble bravado.

"I think we both have genuine doubts about that. When Sybella first came to me with her ultimatum, I too scoffed, but I'm convinced otherwise now. She has information that, if turned over to Maximus, or anyone else in authority in Cartagena, would mean the end of Bruce."

Devora watched her, fear placing its icy grip about her heart. She wouldn't be afraid. That was the response Sybella was planning on. There was the Valentin pistol with the initials "B.A.V." Had Sybella managed to take it from the countess? How could she have? As long as she believed she could use it to obtain what she wanted in silver bullion, the countess would guard it with care.

A look of dismay washed over Lady Lillian's face. She reached beneath the silk-fringed shawl across her lap and produced not the pistol that Devora feared, but a document.

"This is a copy of a letter from the governor of Spanish Florida, Don Octavio Sanchez."

Slowly bits and pieces of the past came to Devora's mind. Her hand shook as she spread open the sheet Sybella must have carefully copied from the original. Favian had also mentioned Florida several times. Always in light of a particular incident —

52

perhaps more than one — which did not broach well for Bruce's supposed loyal reputation as a soldier of the Spanish king.

Each time Favian had brought the matter up, Maximus had rebuked him and ended the conversation. Devora had asked Bruce about his days in Florida, but he had diverted her, obviously not wanting to discuss it.

The letter was dated nearly a year earlier in Florida to His Illustrious and Most Catholic Majesty, King Philip of Spain, from Governor Sanchez. Her eyes skipped over the official greetings and details until they stumbled across the incriminating charges. . . .

I have suspected for some time that Capitan Don Nicklas was too lenient on the Seminole Indians who more than once have attacked His Majesty's soldiers and threatened the town of Saint Augustine. I reported this earlier to Commander Demetrio. Now, grave information reaches me on Don Nicklas' behavior in these waters.

Disturbing evidence, Sire, coming from a notable eyewitness who has come to me swearing that this same Don Nicklas Valentin fought and killed Commander Demetrio on the night of June 5th on the

53

Florida beach near Saint Augustine. If this were not enough to call this man into question before the Seville tribunal, there is evidence that the cause for this was that Commander Demetrio had claimed that Valentin had not sunk an English ship off the Florida coast as believed by His Majesty and first reported, but rather a Spanish galleon. When Commander Demetrio discovered this nefarious treachery he sought Don Valentin's arrest and was murdered in the ensuing fight.

It is my humble duty to recommend that Capitan Don Nicklas Valentin be held for questioning and trial in Seville when he appears before your illustrious throne . . .

There was more but Devora could not read on. The letter slipped into her lap. It was several moments before she could raise her anguished eyes to look at Lady Lillian.

Lady Lillian was grave. "I fear for Bruce that Sybella may turn the letter over to Archbishop Harro Andres if we do not leave Cartagena."

"She wouldn't! If she wants Bruce for herself, would she risk him to the inquisitors?"

"Perhaps not, but then. . . ."

Was Sybella bluffing? Devora didn't know

her well enough to judge. At least not well enough to take the risk. If this information were delivered to the authorities, it would mean the end of Bruce. Who else knew about this information beside the governor of Florida and Sybella? Certainly not Favian. Not yet.

"How did Sybella get hold of this?"

"She says she intercepted it when in Madrid. She saved Bruce at the time, but as you see, she has kept the letter as a bargaining tool. I suspect she has done nothing yet because she truly believed he cared for her, and that he might refuse you in the end. When she saw her hopes dashed, she made plans to use the letter."

Devora tried to stand but her knees were like water. If Maximus learned about this . . .

"Sybella wouldn't betray Bruce," Devora insisted. "She couldn't. Not if she loves him enough to force me to leave Cartagena."

Lady Lillian considered gravely. "One never knows with Sybella what she will do. She is volatile. I believe her desire for Bruce could just as easily turn to revenge if he married you. She is a proud woman, a Ferdinand. She will not accept the shame she feels is hers by losing Bruce to an English woman."

Devora shut her eyes, pressing her knuckles to her lips. Yes, she could see Sybella doing something rash in a terrible moment of rage. And with the wedding in five days. . . . Sybella might indeed lose her self-control and turn against the one man she claimed she wanted.

"We cannot take such chances, my dear, for Bruce's sake. We must leave tonight. Once we reach Barbados we shall try to contact him, or Tobias. There must be something we can do to let him know what has happened."

Devora managed at last to stand. "If only I could get word to Tobias, he might warn Bruce."

"I thought of that. And I have a maid who might be sent secretly to try to locate him, or contact Bruce. But she is being held somewhere in the house under lock and key. I don't suppose you told anyone at the Casa Valentin you were coming here?"

Devora sat down again. "No," she said weakly. "I trusted her. What a fool I've been."

"Do not berate yourself. I doubt whether it was ever possible to thwart her. She has power on her side, and the letter. Sybella has thought of everything."

"Even if we leave for Barbados, she still

56

has the letter," said Devora, frustrated.

"Yes, but she'll have no reason to betray Bruce once you're gone. She'll come up with some reason why you did not wish to marry him after all."

"He won't believe it!"

"Ah, a woman never knows what a man may believe when he is hurt. And Sybella has ways to make it all quite convincing. Your consolation is that you may be able to contact him once you are in Barbados."

"But perhaps not," Devora said glumly. "Any letter I send may be swiftly confiscated by her if she is able to become close to Bruce. Somehow I must warn him of the danger he is in. Sybella will always have this letter to hold over him. And there's the pistol as well."

"The pistol?"

"There's no time to discuss that now, Lady Lillian. We must think. Once we sail, once we are left ashore near English territory, yes," she said hopefully, "perhaps then something can be done to warn Bruce, to let him know we did not leave willingly."

Devora gripped the letter with frustration, staring at it. Her fears loomed like insurmountable mountains. What if the worst happened? Bruce would be angry and hurt. He might actually believe Sybella's lies. She might never see him again.

Cool reason returned. She must not allow her emotions to run rampant. There must be something she could do to warn him that she was being forced to board the *Magdalena*. The guards . . . was it possible she might offer one of them her jewelry to warn Bruce? Or someone on the ship —

Ultimately her hope was in God. She also knew that Bruce was not easily deceived. Would he suspect treachery when he discovered his grandmother too was missing? He would then begin asking questions.

The door opened and Sybella entered the room. "Come with me," she told Devora. "It is necessary to separate you from Lillian until you are at sea."

"I won't leave Nicklas' grandmother. Can't you see she's overwrought? She's not well, and you're the cause for her anguish —"

"Enough. She is quite able to see her way through this, as she has all other disappointments." Sybella turned to Lady Lillian and Devora took heart when she saw a look of concern, even subdued guilt, written in Sybella's countenance. "I am sorry, Lillian, there is no choice in this matter. If you and the Señorita do as I say there is no need for alarm over Nicklas' safety. The letter from Florida is safe with me."

"For how long?" argued Devora. "Such a thing cannot be hidden forever. Keeping information such as this is like keeping a viper in your room. You never know when it will reach out and strike you."

"I am quite able to handle secret information. I have done so many times in the past. Once Nicklas and I are married I will destroy it."

"You forget Don Favian. I heard him speaking to Maximus yesterday. He searches for something to bring down Nicklas. Do you think he will stand by and allow you to marry his brother?"

Sybella seemed unconcerned. "Never mind Favian. That child shall pose me no problem once I have him sent to Vera Cruz — perhaps as governor. He will soon forget all about me and Nicklas."

"I think you underestimate him," protested Devora. "He wants you as much as you want Nicklas."

Sybella smiled indulgently. "Like any little puppy, he may be comforted by another."

"You'll arrange that also, of course?" came Devora's cool response.

Sybella raised her brows. "I must, to survive. And now you will come. This way, quickly."

Devora turned to Lady Lillian with a look of despair, but the older woman nodded her silver head with sad resignation. "Do as she says, my dear. I know Sybella far better than you."

Sybella smiled. "Thank you, Lillian. Come, Devora." And she led the way from the room to a stairway.

Devora went before her until Sybella gestured to a door. "In here."

The chamber was cool and richly furnished. The windows were barred with grillwork. "I will come back for you tonight. You might as well rest. You have a long voyage ahead of you." She turned to leave.

"Sybella, you could still change your mind and we'll forget this ever happened. I'll say nothing to Nicklas."

"But I have nothing to gain by that."

"But Nicklas will never believe I've run away of my own will."

"Don't you think I know that? I know him better than you. We grew up together in Lima. When he was only a boy he was in love with me! I filled his vision, his heart."

"Genuinely touching. But a boy grows up and becomes a man and his dreams often change. And he may realize that you have grown into someone very different than his previous vision. The only world he knew

60

back then was Lima, the horses, the mines, the injustice with which Maximus treated him."

"You know of that?"

"Yes, Nicklas' bitterness toward Maximus may destroy not only his father, but also himself. I can deter him from the plans he makes that will ruin his life. If you would arrange for Nicklas and me to be sent away you will be doing more for the man you say you love than you will by keeping him here on the Main."

"I already have plans . . . for him and for me. They are better than anything you can provide him. And in the end, he will believe you have left willingly. You must realize that this is necessary for his own happiness . . . and mine, as I must have his heart."

"Do you think you can outwit him? You can't. He'll know you've done something to tear us apart. Oh Sybella, you are a wealthy and beautiful woman. Why can't you accept the truth about Nicklas and find someone else?"

"You speak as a fool. Do you think I could ever be content with 'someone else'? Do you think I'm so childish that I have not thought through what I am doing? I am a daughter of Spain!"

"Does a daughter of Spain have no princi-

61

ples? If you were a woman of honor you'd care enough about him to walk away and leave him in peace."

Sybella's eyes flashed. "You are a foreigner. You have no right to Nicklas, nor to Lima! Go back to the English — to your heretic religion!"

"If it is heretic, then why do you desire Nicklas? He believes as I do. If you are not one with him in the most important area, how do you ever expect to have his heart?"

"Simple. I will fool him. Men are easy to deceive. I will become whatever he thinks is necessary for his ideal wife. As long as I have him everything else will matter very little."

"And how long do you think he will remain deceived? You say that you must have his heart, but do you think that you can win it without him eventually coming to know yours?"

"Perhaps. And after many years we may come to see things alike."

"In this, Sybella, you deceive yourself. The years will only reveal your true heart. If it is not yielded to our Savior you cannot be of the same mind as your believing husband."

"That is for me to discover. Enough of your talk. I did not bring you here for a compromise."

"I will not surrender him to you so easily. Somehow he will learn what you have done. What then do you think he will do? He will loathe your dishonor. Whatever affection remains in his heart for you will surely die."

Sybella turned pale, her eyes like two gleaming dark pools. For a long moment she was silent, her chest heaving. Devora thought she might strike her, but at last she lifted her chin. "I assume you are anxious to return home where you belong, among your own people. Therefore the Valentins will keep you no longer a prisoner in Cartagena. My guards will escort you to the *Magdalena* as soon as night settles."

Is Bruce at the harbor? Was there any way she might —

Sybella's lips turned. "Do not try anything foolish. I warn you. I will turn against Nicklas if you do. Since you boast so much of honor — now is your opportunity to show it. For his sake — go in peace. You may have the comfort of knowing that I will do him well. I have already arranged with the king of Spain to call him back home to Seville. There he will serve with great honors."

"You have arranged . . . ?"

"You forget, Señorita, that I am a Ferdinand. I am here in Cartagena only because I wish to be. Because of Nicklas. It

63

was never my intention to stay. Nor is it now. I will return and make plans for advancement in the palace itself. And that is where Don Nicklas belongs — not with an English woman in Barbados or England. And now —" She flicked her fingers abruptly, turned on her black satin slippers, and walked out of the room.

Devora stared after her in restrained anguish. A moment later, alone, hearing Sybella's footsteps fading, she sank to her knees before the divan and held back her tears, praying. "Oh Lord, You alone are my hope, my expectation. Unless You come to my aid, all is lost."

❦ 3 ❦

The Treachery of Favian

The night wind softly rustled the banana leaves on the fibrous trees secluding the patio. Sybella stood on the patio steps, her flowing gown moving about her feet. The house behind her was silent, reminding her that she was alone. Her two prisoners would be out to the Caribbean Sea by now on a voyage to rendezvous with an interloping English ship headed back to Carlisle Bay, Barbados. She had done the wise thing, Sybella told herself, ignoring the uneasy prick of her conscience. If anyone knew what was best for Nicklas, it was she. She had laid her plans carefully, and now she must proceed. The most difficult part was yet ahead — convincing Nicklas when he came to her that she was as surprised as he by their disappearance. She was sure she could convince him. She had deceived men close to the king of Spain. She could deceive Nicklas as well.

Her long lashes flicked upwards. Foot-steps. She had told the guards she wanted to see no one for the next two days unless Nicklas came. She didn't expect him yet. There was no way he could know that either his grandmother or Devora was missing. She turned quickly to face the doorway as the steps slowed. She sped to a drawer in the desk and felt for her pistol. Had one of her guards turned against her, for jewels perhaps? She lifted the pistol, her eyes narrowing steadily as the door opened and was cautiously pushed aside.

"Ah, my lovely white rose," Favian mocked, "with a pistol in her tiny hand. Would you kill your devoted querida? Such a pity."

Sybella met the hungry smirk on his lean handsome face, showing clean, even white teeth beneath a ribbon mustache. He was garbed in a tight-fitting black suit with pristine white lace. His black hair was oiled and curled, and a gold ring was looped in his left earlobe. Her alarm subsided, but irritation flooded in to take its place.

"So it is you, my cousin. One day I shall accidentally shoot you and then what will I tell Maximus?" she mocked in return.

"I am confident you will find a ready answer from your bag of tricks, sweet Sybella."

66

"Softly," she gritted. "Your silken tongue does not please me. Come in and shut the door. How did you get past my bodyguard?" She lowered the pistol and set it on the desk. Favian shrugged gracefully and shut the double doors, leaning against them, arms folded. His dark eyes scanned her, then circled the room, focusing on the open doorway down onto the patio. "Close it tight. We must talk and I wish to take no chances. Your sharks may be loitering near the wall."

Curious over his seriousness, she did so, then turned and faced him.

"How secretive you are, Favian. Have you yet found the spy who betrays Uncle Maximus and the grand Valentin family?"

"You mock me, but like father you will learn that I have grown."

His confidence alerted her. She masked her concern but watched him. "Into what, a jackal?"

Favian smiled, stroking his mustache. "If I am a jackal, then we are of the same pack. What have you done with Señora Lillian and the English rose?"

Careful. "What have I done? What do you mean?"

"Ah, Sybella, you underestimate me. Ah well, it is all to my advantage. There is usefulness in having my opponents think they have outsmarted me."

"You talk in riddles," she said scornfully, moving about the room as though he didn't matter. "I am weary and wish to retire. I could have the bodyguard arrest you now for sneaking into the house."

He tapped his sword. "That would be most unwise. There are few better than I with this blade."

She whirled. "Did you come here to threaten me?"

"To threaten? That all depends on your cooperation."

She was searching her mind frantically, trying to imagine what he might know without revealing her secret.

Favian's smile vanished. His eyes were cool now, flicking with determination. He left the door and walked toward her, stopping in the middle of the room.

"I know everything."

Her heart quavered, then pounded. He couldn't. Not about the letter. No one knew of it except herself, Lillian, and now, Devora.

"What is there to know?"

"Yesterday when I spoke to my father in the patio, I left him to deliver his message to Harro Andres. He thought I did. But I had seen you earlier. You looked distraught as you came into the house. Asking the servants where you had come from proved an easy task. 'From the harbor,' they told me. Now who was at the harbor you might have gone to see? Nicklas, perchance?"

"You seem to know everything. You tell me."

"You went aboard his ship. No doubt you went to plead with him not to marry the English señorita, but he turned you down. It must have hurt to have him do so in so kind and gentlemanly a manner. His sympathy, his pity, it upset you terribly. So you came up with a plan."

"You don't know what you're talking about." She turned away, but her alarm increased. Perhaps she had underestimated Favian.

He came up behind her. "In the house, I followed you up to Devora's room. I was careful enough to overhear your conversation. Such a touching story, Sybella."

She walked away stiffly. "You are a Spanish dog, Favian."

"I followed your coach this afternoon when you brought Devora here. Do you wonder how is it your bodyguard did not stop me from entering the house just now?"

Sybella's eyes narrowed, but she kept her back toward him in silence.

69

"It is because my own soldiers now have them held under pistol. They have told all, dear heart. How upset Nicklas will be should I tell him his love sails aboard the *Magdalena* homeward bound to heretical Barbados. And dear Grandmother Lillian with her."

Sybella turned, pale and angry, her eyes spitting venom. "Say a word of this and I'll . . ." she stopped, breathlessly.

Favian smiled slowly, arching a brow. "No, no, my querida, do not speak so bitterly to one whose heart beats only for you. Are we not to be married according to the will of Maximus? Since we shall share the same room, and raise our sons and daughters, do control yourself or you will break my poor heart."

Sybella gave a gasp of rage and hurled a vase of flowers at him, but Favian stepped aside, laughing.

"Ah Sybella, we shall make a such a wonderful match."

"I'll kill you first," she gritted.

He backed away in mockery, palms forward. "You frighten me."

"It is good I frighten you, you pig, you jackal, you — you —"

"Husband? Lover?"

"Never! Never!"

"Ah yes, the letter from the Florida governor. Have you forgotten? Refuse me and I shall go at once to Maximus. Do you think I won't?" He came toward her now, all somber and eyes flashing. "Oh yes, I know of it."

"You may know of it, dog, but you will not have it. Do you think I will let you harm Nicklas? He is twice the man you are. Coward! Worm!"

"I have heard that all my life. I am sick to death of hearing it. It will be a great pleasure to have him arrested and carried away just to see Maximus' face when his hero is unmasked. Do you think I do not know now that Nicklas is the spy that father seeks? And Archbishop Andres . . . one word from Andres to the king and Nicklas will find chains wrapped about his neck!"

Her eyes widened with alarm, for she could finally see his internal rage boiling over. She rushed to him, trying to soothe, to appease him, to tell him she hadn't meant to insult the gallant Don Favian.

Favian, in a rage, pushed her away. "There is time enough in the future for your embrace, your kisses. It is Nicklas who will fall from his pedestal now. Ah yes, I will have both. You will be my devoted wife, and Nicklas will be arrested. I need make no bargain with you."

Sybella, horrified, tears rushing to her eyes, fell upon her knees before him. "Don't do so wicked a thing, Favian. I beg of you."

"You beg me? You who would have brought the letter to Maximus had Devora not gone willingly," he scoffed.

"No — no, I wouldn't have —"

"Yes you would. You could not bear to see her in Nicklas' arms, bearing his children. You would have been willing to harm him. Your love is selfish, as mine is for you. Neither of us know anything of devotion. Look at you! On your knees before me to save his life. Don't you know I despise you for it? In begging and fawning before me you only tell me how much he means to your selfish heart."

He turned on his heel and stalked toward the door. Sybella scrambled to her feet.

"No, Favian!"

"I do not need the letter. I know the truth now. I can notify the authorities in Seville to send a messenger to the governor in Florida."

She stared, stricken, at the door. She looked over at the pistol and rushed to the desk and picked it up. She turned, her eyes wide and started to follow him. But in horror she stopped, and her emotions cracked. She dropped the pistol with a clatter and her hands flew to her mouth. How could she think of shooting Favian? Murder. . . . Her legs weakened with emotional shock and she sank to the floor in bitter tears. Ruined, everything she had fought to attain, had planned for, prayed for —

Prayed? How could she profane that word. How distressed Tobias would be if he knew she had actually prayed to accomplish a matter harmful to someone else?

It didn't matter now. She must save Nicklas.

She stumbled into the alcove where she had set up her images of the saints, much to the distress of Lillian. Sybella, with trembling hands, lit a candle before the Madonna and fell to her knees, tears streaming down her cheeks, her hands clasped before her breast. Her lips moved urgently.

Within fifteen minutes she had fled out the door to find and warn Nicklas. She would need to ride a horse. Where would Nicklas be at this hour? She suspected he was still at the harbor readying the ships for the voyage to Callao, the harbor near Lima. What a mockery! That the *Magdalena* had sailed with Devora aboard within his very sight. Sybella knew he would hate her for what she had done, but his hate would be something she must carry for the rest of her life. Better his hate than his death at the hands of the archbishop.

She had no notion at the moment that she was responding with the very self-sacrifice that Favian had just accused her of lacking.

4

The Unraveling Begins

The trade winds had not yet risen, and the heat was intense from the blazing tropical sun reflecting off the calm surface of the green water of Cartagena Bay.

Bruce, who was in command of the galleons and brigantines that would voyage to Callao Harbor, Lima, pondered his personal mission known only to Tobias and members of his crew from Tortuga. With each passing hour the sense of foreboding increased. Archbishop Harro Andres was suspicious. So was Commander Cristobal. And Favian's resentment toward him was growing more open, and had, perhaps, become dangerous.

Bruce was anxious for the week to pass when he would, with Devora aboard, leave Cartagena behind. He had given orders for the commander to transport the "heretic prisoners" from his flagship, *Our Lady of Madrid*, to the brigantine, *Del Carmen*. At his request, Tobias had arranged for weapons to be hidden aboard the *Del Carmen* for the buccaneering crew of prisoners. He had also spent long hours subtly arranging for just the particular Spanish soldiers and officers he wanted to command the *Carmen*. Men who would prove an easy match should a mutiny by his crew become necessary. The decision to mutiny would be left to Tobias, who had agreed to sail aboard the *Carmen*. If anything went wrong on the voyage, Bruce wanted to make certain his men had a chance to break away from the convoy and sail to Tortuga. Keeping them aboard his galleon would be a death trap, since its Spanish crew were of the best soldiers and officers on the Main.

In order to make a good show of presumed Spanish pride and arrogance, he was clad after the fashion of high Spanish nobility, in black, coupled with a dash of silver lace, a silver-handled sword sheathed in a silver-embroidered baldric, and a broad hat with a sweeping plume. He rode his horse along the crowded wharf as slaves and common seamen moved quickly out of his way.

Ahead, he saw Lieutenant Hernando being harassed by soldiers serving under Commander Cristobal. Hernando was no match for them, so Bruce rode up, interrupting impatiently, deliberately putting the two soldiers on the defense.

"Where are the heretic prisoners? Why do you stand about doing nothing? You are worthless! Did I not command that they be brought immediately to the *Carmen*?" He looked at Hernando, who mopped his sweating face. "And you, Hernando, is this how you repay my trust in you? I have made you lieutenant to the capitan of the *Del Carmen*. Yet you stand about idle."

"Trouble, Señor Capitan. Commander Cristobal questions moving the prisoners from the Spanish guard aboard the *Our Lady of Madrid*."

"I do not take orders from Cristobal. He takes orders from me." Bruce gestured to the two soldiers under Cristobal. "Tell your commander I shall have him removed from his position if he does not act on my order immediately!"

They saluted and ran down the wharf. Bruce turned toward the round-bellied Hernando, who was sweating profusely. Bruce smiled. "Easy, amigo. You need not worry about your old commander. You report to me now."

"A pleasure, Don Nicklas, but I do worry about the Dominicans."

"We both do," he said softly, wryly. "What of the supplies? Did you get them aboard?"

"Yes, last night, Capitan. We worked late." He suddenly stopped and paled, as though he remembered something. "Alas, my transgression, Capitan! I forgot — I also have a message from Friar Tobias. He came aboard last night very late!" He reached hurriedly beneath his jacket and removed a sealed letter, fumbling as he did so, and dropping it to the plank. As he stooped down to pick it up, Bruce smiled. But when Hernando straightened to hand it to him, Bruce wore an appropriate scowl. He snatched it.

Before Bruce could open and read it, voices were raised further down the wharf. The two guards were returning, and the burly Pizzaro, captain of the guard aboard Bruce's galleon, was with them.

Bruce waited, looking grandly austere. Pizzaro saluted. "Capitan!"

"Why this ineptitude, Pizzaro?" Bruce demanded in the tone of his father. "I gave you an official order and document to remove the prisoners from my ship and transfer them to the brigantine. Is it too much to ask you to carry it through on time?"

Pizzaro threw back his shoulders and saluted. "A thousand pardons, Don Nicklas. I assure you, the prisoners are coming now."

Bruce, with secret relief, saw them herded onto the wharf from the smaller boats. They were shirtless and barefoot, and other guards were prodding them along in Bruce's direction.

"What took you so long? I wanted them aboard last night."

"The order to desist transfer came from Don Favian —"

"You dare follow his orders instead of mine?" *Favian. What is my brother up to?*

"No Capitan, but —"

"I could have you removed from your command at once!"

"Yes, Capitan! Patience, I beg, see — I have heeded your command, even though his Excellency the Archbishop raises questions to the viceroy about such a needless move at this time . . ."

The Archbishop Andres again.

"I follow the orders of the king of Spain. Not even the archbishop must interfere, is that clear, Pizzaro?"

"To me, Capitan, yes, very clear. But to . . ."

Bruce lifted his hand. Pizzaro fell silent.

"Get the prisoners into the hold of the *Carmen*," Bruce gritted.

Pizzaro saluted, turned on his heel, and

was half-running back toward the prisoners when Hernando whispered, "Capitan, look! I fear there is trouble . . . my old Commander Cristobal comes, a Dominican with him."

Bruce sat still in the saddle, fingering the horse's reins as he watched the two Spaniards approach.

Commander Cristobal stopped on the plank before him and saluted crisply with a haughty face and manner. He wore a neatly trimmed black mustache and pointed beard, and his vibrant eyes scanned Bruce. There was a lithe, easy movement about him, which spoke of trained muscles. They had clashed from the moment they had met on his arrival. Bruce understood that he'd get little willing support from Cristobal. The Dominican was another matter. Bruce saw his gaze seeking for a crucifix about his neck. Bruce had carefully worn one this morning for just such a confrontation. The Dominican looked away toward the *Del Carmen*.

"Don Nicklas Valentin," Commander Cristobal greeted stiffly.

"Commander," Bruce said amiably.

"May I ask, Señor, who has ordered that the English pirates be brought aboard the *Del Carmen*?"

Bruce smiled slowly. "I have."

Cristobal's eyes sparkled and a muscle in his square jaw tightened.

Bruce lifted a dark brow. "You object, Señor?"

"The Archbishop Andres objects, Don Nicklas."

"Then with all respect, Señor, tell him his revered king in Seville has placed me in command of the mission to Lima and the silver mines. If the archbishop protests his Majesty's decision, let him voyage to Seville and present his complaints to the king."

The Dominican glanced at him, but Commander Cristobal lifted his head. "Be assured, Don Nicklas, that I will convey your exact message to his Excellency Harro Andres, new archbishop to Lima."

Cristobal gestured to the nervous Hernando, who averted his eyes. A look of irritation flicked across the commander's haughty face. "And *this* particular soldier — has he also received orders from his Majesty to place him in a position of command on the *Del Carmen*?"

Bruce saw the sweat stand out on Hernando's forehead.

"No, Commander Cristobal," Bruce said cheerfully. "That wise decision was entirely mine."

Cristobal drew in his muscled chest. "I object, Señor!"

"On what grounds?" Bruce removed his hat and checked the plume, removing a speck of lint from the black brim. He settled it again, cockily. "Not jealousy? Did you wish the lieutenancy for yourself?" he asked with a trace of innocence.

Cristobal turned a ruddy color beneath his tanned skin. "I object on grounds of ineptitude, Señor."

"You jest, Señor! Ineptitude?" He held out an arm toward the quaking Hernando. "This brave soldier of the proud flag of Castile? He who has served as an honorable seaman of Spain these ten years? Why Hernando and I go all the way back to Seville. We served his Majesty together in Spanish Florida."

Commander Cristobal looked uncertain. He turned to Hernando. "Is this true?"

"It is, Capitan!"

Cristobal looked up at Bruce with marked suspicion. "Why is it I have never heard of his courage?"

"It is enough to satisfy me. If you have further objections, Commander Cristobal, you will draw them up according to military rules and send them to me aboard the *Our Lady of Madrid*. Although a busy man, I promise to look them over when I have a moment of time to spare." Bruce raised his sword to his hat brim and saluted Commander Cristobal.

"Adios," he said. Turning the reins of his horse he rode past to where the prisoners were being placed in small boats to be rowed out to the *Del Carmen*.

Cristobal and the Dominican would cause him trouble, he knew that.

Once aboard the *Del Carmen*, Bruce removed Tobias' message from his jacket and read:

H.A. has sent F. to summon M. to his residence.

Bruce destroyed the message. Musing, he looked out toward the sea. Did Harro Andres want to speak to Maximus again about the prisoners, or was there more?

A restless spirit settled over him. He'd gone aboard the brigantine to make certain all was in order and the prisoners were brought below. Once alone, confident he was not being watched, he made certain Tobias had secured the weapons. They were there, hidden under foodstuffs beneath several loose boards: swords, cutlasses, pistols, ammunition, and powder.

Satisfied, Bruce went to the hold to look at the prisoners. He wore a hard countenance as the guard led him along the aisle, crowded on both sides by men whom he pretended were animals, expendable for the mines. He had already informed them aboard his flagship where the weapons would be stored. When Digges ventured a glance in his direction, Bruce laid a hand on his scabbard. Digges got the message and averted his eyes, as though afraid he might give away his excitement. After a look around, without speaking, Bruce left the Spanish guard and went up on deck.

Now that the sun had set, the sweet evening twilight offered its benediction over the sea, and the gentle swells of Cartagena Bay were reflecting a red sheen. The warm trade winds moved through his dark hair like caressing fingers. The front of his shirt was open, but he had retained the nearly insufferable Spanish jacket. Spain was a purist for grandeur and display, so he tolerated the uniform even aboard the brigantine lest anyone wonder why the newly knighted Don Nicklas was not pleased to be strutting his colors.

Bruce enjoyed the wind, and stood with hands on hips looking ahead across the bay to the other vessels at anchor. Things appeared to be going well. But the restlessness continued to dog his steps. One ship in particular had caught his interest, the *Magdalena*. He leaned back against the rail, his boots crossed at the ankles, his gaze following the *urca*, a tubby, flat-bottomed storeship, bringing last minute cargo to the *Magdalena*'s hold. He held out his hand to Hernando.

"My telescope, bring it."

"Right here, Capitan." He watched Bruce. "The *Magdalena* sails for Puerto Principe, Cuba."

Still analyzing the bigger vessel, Bruce drank from a waterskin, plugged it, and handed it to Hernando.

Hernando followed his gaze. "You are troubled about the merchant ship, Don Nicklas?"

"Only curious, Hernando. Last night I happened to speak to its honorable capitan. He assured me the *Magdalena* was not commissioned for a voyage to Cuba until next month. He spoke of a great need to careen the vessel. See how she sits low in the water? Her voyage will be a slow one."

"You are very observant, Don Nicklas. Would you have me find out more?"

"Find out when she intends to sail. Tonight, or at dawn."

Hernando turned to carry out the order and looked toward the wharf. "A cockboat. This one moves quickly. It looks like your uncle, Friar Tobias."

Bruce moved toward the quarterdeck steps. "Send him up to me when he arrives."

Bruce's rugged form, solid with muscle, took the steps to the high aftmost deck to the taffrail, the curved walk over the stern. He braced himself and fixed the small brass telescope upon the *urca,* slithering across the water. Unfortunately, the shadows concealed recognition of who was aboard. He squinted curiously but saw nothing unusual. His concerns made him too suspicious. He noticed several silhouettes were seated on the bundles of cargo in the *urca,* but otherwise it was too near nightfall to see. "Convenient," he thought. "Just as I would do if I did not wish to be seen."

He lowered the glass. Perhaps the sun had gotten to his head today and he was making much of nothing.

He turned and looked out across the bay to the towers crowned with cannon. Cartagena with its stone walls looked disdainfully down upon him, daring any to trifle with its mastery. He surveyed the other gates and towers on the seaward entrance facing the ever-darkening but silvery waters of the bay, crowded with galleons and vessels of varying size. His eyes took in the flag of Spain which beat proudly in the wind. It seemed to dare Henry Morgan or any other notorious buccaneer to attack.

Bruce looked off toward the Fortress Lazaro, and the strong hill that appeared to mount up out of the water. The Cathedral *La Popa* gazed down with sleepy eyes on a city united in religious fear to its rule. His eyes hardened as he looked at the separate outcropping in the bay, the *Tenaza*, where the holy inquisition trials were held. He frowned, as though his heart heard a quiet warning.

Bruce was still considering when sandaled feet plodded heavily up the steps. He looked down to see his uncle, Tobias Valentin, a Franciscan Friar, coming up, his loose brown robe flapping in the wind.

Tobias was a husky man, as round in the middle as he was across the chest, with thick gray hair. A swatch blew across his wide forehead above a rugged brown face. His sharp cocoa-brown eyes sought Bruce out. The silver cross about his thick, muscled neck caught the last ray of sunlight and twinkled a response toward the heavens.

Bruce always knew when a matter caused his uncle agitation, though Tobias moved as calmly as a leopard in the South American jungles. So he waited until Tobias had joined him at the taffrail. He looked out to sea as though enjoying the vivid rays slowly submerging into the water like a great fiery ship going down. When Tobias was apparently satisfied they were alone he spoke in a low voice.

"Defeat stares us in the face, Nicklas, but I don't see what can be done to avert it."

"Don't even suggest failure, my uncle. I don't intend to lose what I've so carefully planned for these last months. We've been in tight places before, you and I. We'll get out of this too."

Tobias cast him a disapproving glance. "Unfortunately, you may already have lost. I warned you even in Seville what your fate would be if the truth is discovered. Now my worst fears are unfolding before my eyes and I'm helpless to stop it!"

Bruce glanced below, his eyes sweeping the deck, taking in the Spanish soldiers and seamen. He saw nothing amiss. "Say on."

"Andres possesses enough information to stop your departure for Lima. He will certainly call you to an official inquiry before the authorities."

Bruce recalled his meeting with Harro Andres on Granada during Henry Morgan's raid. Then again, here in Cartagena, over the crew of Bruce Hawkins standing trial. He had elicited the help of both Maximus and Tobias to save them for the Peruvian mines, but he would not be at rest until the ship was under sail for Callao. That was still a week away. He had learned in other tight situations that seven days could be an eternity in which anything could go wrong.

"You paint a very dark picture, Tobias."

"Of necessity. If called, do not go. If you do, you may not walk free again."

Bruce's gaze lingered below on deck. Any one of those Spanish soldiers would turn against him in a moment if they knew who he was. Even the mild-mannered Hernando, whom Bruce liked.

"And the information?"

"An incriminating letter from Earl Robert Radburn."

Devora's stepfather, the English ambassador for King Charles to the Spanish Court.

Tobias looked out toward the *Magdalena*. She was setting sail in the twilight, her canvas billowing against the red and gold sunset.

"Earl Robert! He'd throw his own mother to the hounds to save his skin!" Bruce said, thinking of how he had permitted Devora to

89

be sent here not knowing her fate, or what kind of man he himself was.

"Yes, and how much more readily a son of the viceroy who sailed as Hawkins."

"He doesn't know that," Bruce insisted.

"Doesn't he? Radburn decided to land at Barbados to pay his respects to the governor before going on to Tortuga. He didn't count on your English uncle Lord Arlen Anthony being in Bridgetown."

"Don't tell me Arlen moved against Radburn now!"

"It has its ironic side. Radburn had barely stepped from the ship when Lord Anthony slapped him with an arrest for treason. 'Spying for Seville,' is the charge. Radburn and Anthony will soon be on their way back to London. It looks as though the señorita's stepfather will languish in the Tower."

"Devora's not likely to think well of a bridegroom whose uncle arrests her father a week before we voyage to Lima. Radburn is likely to be hanged and quartered for treason. But how does this give information about me to Harro Andres?"

Tobias frowned. "Radburn's trying every trick possible to keep his head in place. Someone in Bridgetown, most likely a sympathizer of the Spanish Peace Party in London, helped him smuggle out a letter. It arrived yesterday for Andres. In the letter Radburn pleads for his intervention by appealing to Seville on his behalf. Furthermore, his wife, the countess, has been notified of her husband's ordeal and has taken a turn for the worse in her illness. Need I remind you she holds your pistol? If she thinks either Maximus or the archbishop can save Robert from execution, she may use the weapon to buy their support."

Bruce had already learned from Tobias that he had thought his room at the Casa Valentin a safe place to store the weapon until Bruce returned. Why it was that two Dominicans had been on their way to his cloister to detain Tobias when Devora had hid there was yet unanswered. Bruce's sword, on the other hand, from the Anthony family in England, had not been detected in his chamber at the house and was now back in Bruce's control.

Bruce suspected Favian of searching for the pistol, and perhaps even alerting the Dominicans, but he had no proof yet.

"Even Radburn's denial of spying for Spain is likely to stir up a controversy in England," Tobias said. "Especially if the countess is sent back to London in tears and ill health begging King Charles for mercy and denying her husband was a spy."

"If that's Robert's plan it won't work. The countess is as guilty as he is. I don't think she'll risk her head for him or betray the pistol to Maximus. She is a selfish and spoiled woman, but her attitude toward her daughter has been changing recently. I think she's almost sorry she brought her here."

"I pray it is so. But we still have Radburn to contend with. He's offered the archbishop critical information about you in exchange for his help."

Bruce looked at him. He thought he knew what that information was. "Granada?"

"Yes. The letter was delivered by a Spanish soldier who survived the attack by Morgan."

Bruce remained silent. Even so, there was no way for the soldier to know he had worked with Morgan.

"The soldier swears you were congratulating Morgan on his success. A grave situation for us both, as you can see."

"The soldier is here now?"

"He arrived yesterday, but I only learned of the matter this afternoon. That's the reason Andres summoned Maximus yesterday." Tobias glanced at him. "And they'll be demanding your appearance before the tribunal before they ever allow this convoy to sail for Lima. Andres wants to know why

92

Don Nicklas Valentin appeared so friendly with the rascally pirate from English Jamaica."

Bruce didn't need to be told what Maximus would demand to know. He reprimanded himself. This was all the archbishop needed to strengthen his resolve to question the prisoners and put a hold on his plans. Now what! He must think! First, Devora must be gotten safely out of Cartagena. He could take no chances leaving her here should he find himself under arrest.

"You say Andres called for Maximus yesterday, yet neither of them have approached me for answers. There was trouble over transferring the prisoners here to the brigantine, but it was solved easily enough. If Maximus or Andres had wished to arrest me, they could have done so by now. That's what disturbs me."

"Nor have I seen Maximus all day. He hasn't been back to the house since he left yesterday to keep the appointment. He's either mulling it over in his mind somewhere, or he's still with Andres. If it wasn't that the Señorita Devora was away with Sybella visiting shops, I'd urge you to slip away tonight."

Bruce frowned. "Devora is with Sybella?

They are not friendly enough to visit the Mentidero together."

Tobias looked at him thoughtfully. "Yes, so I thought, yet that is the word I received at the Casa Valentin. More and more I do not like what is happening."

A silence fell between them. Bruce became more agitated and walked slowly along the taffrail, his mind seeking some way out. He could not run. It would be a sure sign to Maximus that Earl Robert's letter had credence. Yet, if the authorities arrived with papers demanding that he release the prisoners for questioning, or request his own appearance before the Cartagena authorities, he would have no way to resist. If he went, matters could easily get out of hand. Once he began to lose control the entire plan would unravel.

He must be prepared to fight if all else failed, but with his crew here on the smaller brigantine the cannon aboard his flagship did him no good. In frustration he tossed his hat aside with scorn and removed the jacket, letting the wind cool him as it blew through his shirt.

"There may be a trap waiting aboard my ship by now."

"What of the Spanish soldiers aboard this ship?"

Bruce glanced toward the two helmeted and cuirassed sentinels on guard who patrolled the upper deck where the twilight cast a reddish glow on their steel.

"That problem can be dealt with," he said, his voice coldly efficient. "Find Devora, but don't bring her here. If it comes to it, I'll need to fight. I won't surrender the men. Before it's over this ship may go down with all on board."

"If I thought it possible to convince you, I'd ask you to slip away alone. I'll bring Devora to you. We'll make for the village where I first borrowed the horses. From there we can make our way into English territory."

Bruce's eyes glinted flecks of hot green. "And live the rest of my life remembering how I ran out on them? Leave them below like sheep to be sacrificed? No, Tobias. It is not my way."

"If you stay for honor's sake there will simply be one more for the inquisitors."

"They trusted me with their lives. If we go down to defeat, we go down together. Fighting. They will have it no other way. And neither will I." He took Tobias by the shoulder. "Look, my uncle, if you can do anything else for me, take care of Devora. Go now. If God permits, I'll find her in Barbados."

Tobias looked at him fiercely, starting to protest, but Hernando came up the steps and they quickly moved apart.

"Capitan, you have a visitor. Doña Sybella Ferdinand. She says it is urgent she speaks with you. She waits in your cabin."

There was only one woman on his mind. "Is Señorita Ashby with her?"

"No, Capitan. Doña Sybella came alone. She says it is most urgent."

Bruce exchanged glances with Tobias.

"Tell the señora I will be right there."

Hernando hurried off. Tobias turned to Bruce with concern etched deeply upon his hard brown face. "She comes to warn you."

"Yes," Bruce said grimly. He loathed saying what he thought. That Maximus may have taken Devora. He would use her as a ransom to force him to surrender.

Tobias gestured his head. "Sybella may have the answer."

"Come with me then. Perhaps it is wiser to first hear what she has to say."

❦ 5 ❦

". . . it's your destiny I fear for."

Sybella was pacing the cabin floor when he opened the door and entered with Tobias. After one look at her wild eyes and frightened face, he gritted back his concerns.

"Where is Devora?"

Sybella's eyes locked upon his as she rushed toward him like a frightened bird, her cloak floating behind her.

"Aboard the *Magdalena* with Lillian."

"The *Magdalena*! To Havana?" He took hold of her, giving her a shake. "What happened? Why are they aboard?"

Tobias laid a restraining hand on him. "Easy, my son."

"No," she cried, shaking her head. "The destination's been changed to Barbados. Nicklas, listen to me. There's no time to explain everything now. Devora and Lillian are all right. They will be safe. It's you who are in danger." She grabbed him, her eyes wild. "Favian knows of the letter. You must escape *now*. He's on his way to find Maximus. This will bring on your arrest. Go! Go now!"

Bruce took note of her paleness. "Tobias has already warned me of the letter. I will do what I can. But first I must know why Devora and Lillian are on board the *Magdalena.*"

Her face contorted with sorrow as she cast her eyes downward and clasped her hands together. "Because . . . I put them aboard."

His suspicions were immediately awakened. "Explain! Why, Sybella?"

Her lashes fluttered upward and her eyes were full of agony. "Because she has no right to you! I arranged for them both to voyage to Barbados. I was going to tell you they went willingly, but it no longer matters. Everything has turned against me, against you. Your safety is all that matters to me now."

"And Devora is what matters to me. Who else is with her and Lillian? Favian?"

"No, no one —" She took hold of his arms. "Nicklas, escape while there's time! Favian knows of the letter from Governor del Campo in Saint Augustine. Once Maximus reads that letter . . ."

She turned away, knuckles pressed against her mouth.

Tobias stepped toward her. "Sybella, do you speak of the letter sent to Spain by the governor of Saint Augustine?"

She nodded. "I — I intercepted it in Seville. I saved Nicklas then, but I kept it . . . I didn't mean —" her voice could not go on.

Tobias shot a glance at Bruce. "With everything else we know, this is the bell toll of death. You *must* escape tonight by horseback."

Bruce thought again of the letter from Governor del Campo. Bruce had been returning from a secret raid against Spanish shipping when the general he served was waiting for him on the beach. The general had discovered the truth. A duel between them had cost the great general his life. Tobias had watched from the palm trees on the white beach and later told Bruce that the general's captain had slipped away before he could stop him. The captain's report had undoubtedly become the source for the letter from the governor of Florida. Recently Favian too suspected something but, until now, did not have proof.

Bruce looked at Sybella. He remembered their last emotional meeting here in the cabin only yesterday. That she had arranged for Devora and his grandmother to be sent away was making sense.

"What did you tell them to force them aboard the ship?" he demanded, his face hard.

Sybella lifted her chin. "I confess I did a foolish thing. I threatened them with the letter. I know that my apology will not remedy the circumstances. But you still have time to save your own life, Nicklas. You must try! Devora is safe. So is Lillian. I've arranged for them to be placed aboard another ship that will rendezvous with them outside English waters. They will be brought to Bridgetown. Leave now! Both you and Uncle Tobias. I will try to deter Maximus."

Tobias came between them, his eyes burning. "She is right, Nicklas. We have a short time. If Favian brings news of Florida to Maximus, we will soon be overrun with soldiers!"

Bruce walked over to his desk and taking a key unlocked a drawer.

"What are you going to do?" Sybella whispered.

Bruce took out two pistols, loaded them, and shoved them into his leather bandoleer. "I am going to defend this ship," he stated, "then I'll go after the *Magdalena*."

"Go after —" she breathed, eyes wide.

Bruce looked over at Tobias. "There's no way to carry through with my original plans for Lima. Once Maximus knows about Florida he will not rest until he delivers me to Seville."

Sybella turned away in despair. Tobias was grim.

"What do you want me to do?"

Bruce appeared calm — he was not. His anger at Sybella boiled. He had one plan left. "Send Sybella ashore," he told Tobias. "I intend to release the prisoners and arm them."

Sybella whirled and looked at him.

Tobias scowled. "We'll never fight our way out, Nicklas."

"Neither I nor the crew will be taken willingly. Go, do as I ask, Tobias! Each man has known of the secondary plans since Granada."

"What of the Spaniards aboard?"

"I'll take care of them. First, the crew is to be loosed." He walked over to Sybella and took her arm, pulling her toward him, his green eyes like granite. "Go back to Cartagena. If you would do anything for us, try to delay Maximus from coming here. I need to get the *Del Carmen* out of the bay and into the open sea."

101

"The fortress cannon! You'll never get out of the bay. Leave with Tobias now. I'll stop Maximus and give you time to get horses."

His cool gaze fixed upon her as he gently removed her clutching fingers. "You and I do not see things the same way, Sybella. It is not my way to deal treacherously with those who trusted me. If the *Carmen* is blown to bits, then I go with her. Your life I give you. Though you may have destroyed mine, and Devora's."

Sybella, white and stricken, sank back against the desk as he released her. She leaned there with a look of defeat while he turned to the peg on the wall and removed his bandoleer and fighting gear.

Tobias gravely took her arm. "Come, Sybella, you must get off the ship." He moved her toward the door.

Tobias escorted her down to the main deck and she followed him like a child guided by her father. "Do not show alarm," he whispered. She squared her shoulders and lifted her head. Tobias walked her calmly past the Spanish crew to where the ladder waited. Her boat and two rowers waited below in the dark water that glinted in the moonlight. Tobias glanced around them and saw they were alone. He spoke in a low voice.

"My child, like seed we plant in the ground, our disobedience too will produce a harvest. Christ will forgive our sin, but He does not promise to stop the harvest. I suggest you go to Him, ask His forgiveness, and beg Him for mercy. The one you least wanted to hurt, Nicklas, is the one who will bear the most danger and pain before this is over." He felt her shoulders tremble with silent tears. "But it would be something if you are able to delay Maximus."

He helped her over the ship's side and watched until she climbed down the rope ladder, the rowers guiding her into the boat. Tobias watched until the oarsmen pushed away into the water, then he scanned the watery expanse between the *Carmen* and the shore, but did not see any suspicious flurry of activity on shore or in the fortress where the cannon looked down upon them. Would Favian follow through on his threat to betray his half-brother to Maximus? Was there any hope that honor and blood ties, however strained, would prevail to silence him?

Tobias turned again, and this time looked out toward the open sea where the *Magdalena* was now gone from sight. He sighed. A foreboding veiled his heart, and he thoughtfully fingered the silver cross that lay against his chest. *Father God, in the name of Thy Son Jesus, have mercy on us all.*

Tobias wondered why Maximus hadn't returned to the Casa Valentin last night. Twenty-four hours had passed since Favian first brought him word that the archbishop wished to see him. Twenty-four hours to make plans, if that is what Maximus had chosen to do. But had he? If only Maximus had learned his lesson about treating Bruce so poorly as a boy, rejecting him, scorning him. If Maximus would lay his viceroyalty on the line now for Bruce and intercede for him, asking forgiveness and mercy from the archbishop — Tobias doubted, however, that Andres could be appeased. But he believed that the breach between Bruce and Maximus could be bridged, even mended. There was time for that if Maximus would yield his proud heart and iron knee.

Forgiveness, mercy — all precious gifts from the Father above made possible because of the Holy One who bore the guilt and shame of the world's transgressions. If only Maximus could reach out for that grace. If he did, Tobias was almost certain Bruce's own bitterness and resentments would melt like snow in the tropics. If only.

How hard was the human heart. How full of pride. How unwilling to dispense even a small drop of the same mercy that the Father poured in an abundance upon us! Tobias' eyes moistened. He touched the cross beneath his rough, masculine fingers, but in his heart he touched the broken body of Jesus — *broken for my sins*, he thought tenderly. He envisioned himself kneeling beneath the Savior's cross as a drop of blood fell upon him, washing away the guilt of every sin. The precious blood ran from the Roman soldier's piercing wound . . . that brought forth blood and water . . . water? An absolute proof of the death of Christ — the blood had separated into its component parts — the long-awaited Lamb of God had accomplished His work.

If only Maximus, the ruthless father, and Bruce, the offended son, could somehow understand the depth of God's forgiveness.

Tobias sighed again, but it came out as a groan from deep within, and he lifted his eyes toward the purple gloom of twilight.

Tobias' heart grew as heavy as a stone. There was no pain like the pain that came from knowing the remedy but also knowing that the cure would be rejected by those who needed it so desperately.

Footsteps, and Tobias turned his head. In the moonlight he saw Bruce garbed for battle. His handsome face was hard, his eyes flickering with determination. He came up quietly, laying a hand on Tobias' shoulder.

"You've got to leave the brigantine. We can't afford to let Maximus find you with me. Kitt must be informed or he'll arrive at the Isle of Pines months from now thinking our plans are all intact for the mule train."

"I'll warn him when the time comes. Now . . . it's your destiny I fear for."

Bruce reached inside his shirt and drew out a letter. "For Devora, should I not make it. See it's delivered to Ashby Hall in Bridge-town."

Tobias sighed. "I'll do as you request. My prayers are with you. Go with God, my son!" He gripped Bruce by the shoulders, then turned quickly as emotion welled in his chest and he went to the side of the ship.

❦ 6 ❦

Duel in the Bay

"Hernando," Bruce called, and the lieutenant came hurrying toward him.

"Yes, Capitan?"

"It's necessary that we talk alone. Let's go down to the hold of the ship."

Hernando looked curious, but did not appear to question the order.

Bruce lifted the hatch. Dim lantern light arose from below. "After you, Hernando." Bruce gestured.

Hernando went down the ladder, and Bruce followed him into the ship's hold, pausing at the bottom.

In the glow, the faces of Bruce's old crew turned toward him. The Spanish guard, patrolling casually, was completely unaware of what awaited him, and looked at Bruce expectantly.

"Hernando, take the guard's weapons and store them over there in the corner out of reach. Then shackle him to the rowers' bench."

Both Hernando and the guard turned to look at him with amazement. "What?"

"Quickly, amigo. It is important."

While Hernando rushed to obey the order, Bruce calmly drew his pistol and held it on the guard, who was swiftly stripped of his weapons and shackled to the bench. Hernando turned to look at him, sweating, his eyes wide. "Now what, Capitan?"

"Now," Bruce said cheerfully, "remove your own, stash them, and sit down quietly."

"Capitan!"

Bruce arched a brow as he lifted his pistol.

Hernando swallowed and obeyed.

"Good lad. Behave yourself and all will be well. I am doing this for your safety — and," he sighed, "we will need new rowers to take the place of Hawkins' crew. If we manage to sneak out of Cartagena Bay without being blown up by the fortress cannons, I promise you all will be unchained and released to the Main." He shackled Hernando, then proceeded to loose his men. They all kept their heads and spoke not a word. They went immediately to confiscate the stashed weapons. As planned, Hakewell, Bruce's lieutenant from the *Revenge*, and Kirby struggled into Spanish garb and slipped quietly up the steps while Bruce quickly unchained the others.

In a few minutes all the men were released and beginning to make their way onto the waist of the ship to melt into the shadows.

By now, Bruce expected Hakewell and Kirby to have disabled the two Spaniards above who guarded the storeroom. The floor boards would be lifted, and more pistols, swords, and cutlasses would be passed one by one to the silent crew.

Bruce loosed the last of his crew from his shackles. The man grinned with satisfaction as he rubbed his wrists, then followed after the others. A moment later Bruce followed to lead the final undoing.

Before the moon had fully risen in the cloudless sky the *Carmen* was secure and in the hands of Bruce Hawkins and the crew of the *Revenge*. "Anyone injured?" he asked when all were assembled on deck.

"Kirby here got 'imself a wounded arm," Githens said, "but he'll be awright."

"An arm injury's nothing, Capt'n." The red-headed Kirby assured him. "The Spanish dog got worse."

"Where is he?" Bruce asked.

"Dead, Captain," said Hakewell.

"Anyone else?"

"Nae, all the papist curs is below, chained to the oars wheres they belong," Githens stated gleefully. He was a lank and wiry man with gray brows that stuck out like a cat's whiskers.

"Neither man nor devil will stop us now, Capt'n," Kirby stated.

Bruce glanced toward the distant cannons on the Fortress Lazaro. "No, but a few forty pounders could blow us out of the water. You all know, as well as I, that our chances of slipping past the cannons are one in ten. It's either that, gentlemen, or a sure escort to the Tenaza."

He knew they had all heard of the dark fortress outcropping where the inquisition trials were held.

"We'll take our chances, Capt'n," Lieutenant Hakewell said darkly.

"Better fish bait than roastin' on coals," Githens said.

"Then every man to his post."

Bruce stood on the quarterdeck emotionally prepared for the inevitable, any moment expecting sea-shaking, thunderous booms to halt their escape. The silence encircling them came as a canny bewilderment when the cannons remained lifeless. The Fortress Lazaro stood above them against the hill peering down, dark and still. Bruce sensed it was the ominous stillness before the certain storm. Slowly the *Carmen* edged toward the Caribbean sea. Freedom teased and beckoned in the warm trade wind, in the glitter of winking stars, in the surge of water beneath the belly of the ship.

Maximus should have attacked by now. *Like a ravaging hawk,* Bruce thought. Was it possible Favian had not gone through with his threat? Or had Sybella been able to stop him, or even Maximus?

Bruce tensed. His hopes were short lived. He peered ahead at the opening into the sea and was confronted by the looming silhouette of a great Spanish warship drifting almost motionlessly on the moon-filled water ahead of him.

He had taken heart too soon. He knew that ship without being told. It was the flagship of Viceroy Don Maximus Valentin. *He wants a fight,* Bruce thought. *He knows he can blow me to bits. Or else he wants to shame me.* The flagship *Santa Maria* waited like a vulture about to swoop down upon them at the very door of freedom. It was what he would expect of Maximus. The fortress cannons were too easy. His father wanted him to suffer for shaming the Valentin name. Bruce could envision him, relentless, furious, his handsome, proud face as immobile as stone. In a flash he remembered his childhood and saw his father's hand come out like lightning to wallop him across the face. "You dare insult your father? Ah, I know those English eyes of yours, the blood of your mother. You've a heart of betrayal!"

For a brief moment fear and anguish gripped Bruce and he was nothing more than a quavering boy again, longing for love yet so angry at the cold man who scorned him that he could hate him as well. He broke out in a sweat as he looked at the great ship. It represented everything he had loathed from the past. His father had power, cannons, authority — and Bruce had nothing to fight back with but a few fifteen-pound cannons and some pistols. He knew, somehow, that Maximus would not sink the *Carmen*. He would seek to shame him first.

"I'm sorry I got the crew into this, Hakewell. Bottled up here, we're done for. One broadside can blast us to bits."

"If we coulda only gained the open sea, we mighta had a chance."

There was no chance of open sea now. The harbor had become a deathtrap. Bruce knew even better than Hakewell what the weaponry of a Spanish ship of the line could do. The galleons were mounted with basilisks and long culverains that could comfortably keep their distance and lay on a broadside with sixty-four pounders.

Whereas the brigantine had only the fifteen-pound roundshots.

Hakewell gestured toward the mouth of the Boca Chica where war vessels formed a blockade. "He's not alone either . . . looks like he's been waitin' for you, awright."

Bruce's eyes slowly fired with temper. "The wounded bull wishes to stomp me into the ground a bit before the final blow." The will to resist Maximus to the bitter end washed over him. He had thought himself clever in moving the crew onto the brigantine. Had he left everyone aboard the *Madrid* they might at least have put up a worthy fight. There was no chance of that now. Bruce was still staring at the four Spanish galleons at the mouth of the Boca Chica when Kirby came running up, his bare feet sturdy on the deck.

"Begging the Capt'n's pardon, but if you'll allow, the crew of the *Revenge* would like to say somethin' to you, seeing our situation ain't good."

Bruce lifted his telescope to focus on his father's ship. He knew what they wanted to say. They wanted to surrender and take their chances in the dungeons.

"Say on, Kirby. Any captain who asks his crew to go down fighting can at least hear the men's complaints."

"Nay, you got it wrong, Capt'n. No complaints. Not one. We all voted to go down with the *Carmen*. We're with you all the way. That's what they wanted me to tell you. There ain't a one of 'em who's willing to surrender, just to be hauled to the dungeons." He cleared his throat. "What we're asking, Capt'n, is for you to lead us in an honorable fight, though we know we don't have equal guns. Then you abandon ship — before the viceroy boards. We'll cover for you. We know he'll board, but if he's got any kind of heart he ain't going to kill his own son. No use you going down with us, sir."

Bruce was moved more than he would show. It hurt all the more because they had entrusted their lives to him. He'd gotten them into this daring raid. *This is all my fault, Lord. All because of my bitterness toward Maximus.* He studiously avoided Kirby's gaze. But as he looked at the *Santa Maria*, he found that his anger only welled up inside of him. Maximus too was to blame. Maximus and his pride. If his father hoped he would come crawling to ask for mercy, he would be disappointed. He'll need to remember he sent his half-English son down to the bottom of the sea.

"You may tell the crew we're in this together. When this ship goes down, your captain will be going with his men."

"But Capt'n —" began Hakewell quietly.

"That's an order, Hakewell. We'll wait for darkness, then make our move."

"Aye, Capt'n!"

When Kirby went down to the waist, Bruce took the steps up to the forecastle, and Hakewell followed. Bruce held to the taffrail and squinted out at the line of ships. "If it's a fight he wants, then I wouldn't think of disappointing my father." His jaw set. "He'll need to sink us to the bottom of the bay before I surrender. That will give him something to haunt his dreams."

The pale blue evening sky lingered, then darkened to violet until it became a royal mantle of purple deepening into darkness. The Caribbean stars and planets burned white. Bruce thought it might be the last time he would see them, but even as he looked at them it was the loveliness of Devora that crowded into his mind and heart. He hadn't told her strongly enough that he loved her for who she was. His kiss and embrace had spoken of love, and more, but he should have told her with words too. Slowly the minutes dragged on.

Above the palm trees bending in the trade wind, the great yellow moon was climbing. Maximus and his galleons crept through the water like sentinels, guarding the entrance to the open sea, to freedom, to the *Magdalena* and Devora . . .

He looked up at the glittering stars.

Hakewell sighed with a far off look in his eyes. "I was thinking of the farm in England . . . where I grew up . . . and my mother. She was a godly woman. She did her best to raise a batch of kids after our father died. She never wanted me to leave for Bristol and the sea. The sight of her praying still comes to mind."

"Does a boy ever forget things like that, Hakewell? Despite Maximus, we had our good times, you and I. I've never forgotten."

"Don't think so. I shoulda listened to her, but I thought there was more to life than farmin'."

"I remember something else . . . horses," Bruce admitted softly. "Their eyes like flames, their muscled bodies glinting like silver. I can smell the heat-sodden earth, taste the dust, and feel the sweat as we rode."

Hakewell stirred, his eyes hot in the night. "Maybe ye should seek your father out, Capt'n. Maybe he'll yet listen to you. Ye could take a longboat, bring a white flag and torches —"

"No, Hakewell. It is too late for that. Do

not let the emotion of this hour woo you with false hopes. You know the manner of man the viceroy is. He will never forgive now. He knows I am Bruce Hawkins, that I willingly harassed him on the Main. And he must know I returned to ruin him even further. What angers him now is knowing this truth will spread among his officers, throughout all Cartagena, and beyond. He is too proud of the Valentin name to ever accept such a bitter cup. In his own mind he tells himself he is obligated. He has no choice. His honor requires him to see me dead or sent to trial. I choose death. Let us speak no more of it."

Hakewell was silent for a long moment. "Aye, I'm thinking you're right. It's a night like this when old memories come pleasantly on the wind that gets them embers stirring to life again. We wish for impossible things."

The darkness deepened. Now was the time for action. He knew the Spaniards better than the English and French buccaneers he commanded. They were seamen, and they were men of honor in a battle, though the buccaneers would rarely admit this at Tortuga, so strong was their hatred for anything from Seville. Those Spanish ships would sink them in a matter of hours.

Once those long culverain were in range, they could pound the *Carmen* to pieces at a safe distance, and Bruce could do nothing about it.

Bruce leaned over the carved rail. "Ho, there, Kirby!"

He turned. "Crack on all sail," he ordered. "Gunners to their stations. Stand by to repel boarders!"

In a moment, the brigantine that had seemed to doze lazily in the water bustled to life. The winches of the *Del Carmen* were cranked to free the anchor from the deep night waters of Cartagena Bay. Then followed the creaking of blocks, and within minutes Bruce saw the sails unfurled beneath the yardarms, giving a spine-tingling snap as they dropped downward until the trade wind bellied them out. It was a beautiful sight. On the mainmast, the fore-and-aft sail swelled like a mammoth white moth's wings on a dark, ghostly silhouette. The helm was put over hard, and while the chief gunner was receiving Bruce's final instructions, the trade wind was moving the ship through the shiny, rippling sea.

Out there Maximus and the Spanish war ships waited in the silvery moonlight. The *Carmen* moved silently down the Bay of Cartagena, heading southward to the Boca

Chica channel leading out to the open sea.

"Hold your fire," he told them, "until we are too close to miss. We will take one of them with us before we go down. And," he stated, thinking of Maximus, "I want the *Santa Maria*."

"Aye, Capt'n!" came the satisfied growl. "We'll give her to ye before we gulp seawater!"

"Helmsman, keep us in the shadow of the hills, away from the moonlight."

"Aye, Capt'n."

The brigantine crept precariously near to shore so that before the galleons noticed the smaller vessel the *Carmen* was among them. Bruce identified Maximus' ship and the helmsman slid into line.

"The flag of Castile!" shouted Bruce.

At his signal, all of the brigantine's port guns blasted, rumbling like thunder. On the recoil, the guns jolted back tightening the breeching ropes. Bruce steadied himself. Every shot had made contact. He watched with satisfaction as his father's masts teetered, then came crashing down, bringing with them the flag of Seville in a tangle of sailcloth and ratlines. He could hear an uproar on the *Santa Maria*. Spanish voices shouted.

"Point-blank range!" Bruce commanded.

The English gunners swiftly used their hammers to drive the quoins from beneath the gun trucks. As the hardwood blocks came free the guns lowered and the barrels were pointing straight at the waterline of the *Santa Maria*.

"Fire!"

The broadside boomed and exploded, shaking the bay. Again Bruce gave the signal to fire. He heard the crash of the galleon's timbers, the shouting, the screams of his father's elite crew. A glow of fire sprang up amidships of the *Santa Maria*. Voracious flames ran upward into the broken rigging; in minutes the fire spread into a blaze. Boats were being lowered and men were fleeing down ladders, others jumping into the bay. In amazement he saw Maximus on the bulwark abandoning the sinking ship. A cheer went up from Bruce's crew, and they commenced firing with muskets and pistols. But the firelight also illuminated the *Carmen*. Immediately the other galleons opened up with their great cannons, splitting the night asunder.

The slow, rolling bellow from the cannons reverberated across the bay and into the hills. White geysers stood up like momentary columns all about Bruce. A blinding explosion of water and wood filled the air not far from where he stood. Four of his best gunners crumpled to the deck, the planking running red.

The Spanish galleon *Santa Rosa* had come into parallel line with the *Carmen* and her demi-chasers swept the deck with a hail of small, deadly shot. When she passed, half of the brigantine's crew were wounded.

The galleons continued to fire small shot. Hakewell was hit, and fell. Bruce already had several wounds, and rivulets of blood mingled with his sweat as he pulled his dead helmsman from the whipstaff.

Bruce heard the shudder and crash of a broken mast, followed by another, and he knew it was all over. The *Carmen* sat helplessly like a great bird with broken wings. Not all the trade winds of the sea could aid them now. He crawled toward Hakewell, who though injured, was bending over Kirby.

The glassy blue eyes looked up at Bruce. "We . . . got the proud . . . *Maria*, Capt'n . . . the devilish flag came . . . down . . ."

"You fought honorably, Kirby," Bruce told him, resting a bloody hand on his head.

Hakewell looked up, his arm limp at his side. "They'll soon be boarding, Captain! But the men aren't able to fight!"

Bruce struggled to his feet, nearly losing

his balance. "Do your best, Hakewell. . . ." Bruce staggered toward the rail, and with blurred eyes slowly climbed the steps in full view of the oncoming Spaniards and Maximus, making himself an easy target as he held his pistol in one hand and his sword in the other. His shirt was blood-soaked and he tried to focus. Maximus had deliberately lengthened the spectacle. He suspected his father was in no mood to end it quickly now, either. Bruce would not bend the knee to Maximus. He swayed dizzily on the steps.

It was several moments before the deepening silence registered on his mind and he realized the gunfire had finally ceased. Bruce squinted and saw the giant bulk of a galleon drawing closer, saw helmeted and cuirassed soldiers with the grappling hooks hurling into place. He heard each thud as the hooks latched hold of the *Carmen*. Bruce managed to lift his sword — vaguely wishing it were the sword of the English house of Anthony.

He saw Don Maximus, splendid in a coat of mail, climb down to the *Carmen*'s decks followed by Don Favian and a score of soldiers with swords drawn and guns in hand.

The moonlight glinted blue-silver on their armor. Maximus' eyes burned hotly, like two black coals in his swarthy, handsome face. The firelight reflected on his brow, glistening with sweat. He scanned Bruce, taking in the blood-soaked shirt, the sword that he still gripped, the pistol in his other hand. Maximus removed his helmet and hurled it across the deck with such ferocity that it bounced. He stood, his chest heaving. He whipped out his pistol and aimed it steadily at Bruce's heart.

Bruce was trying to concentrate. He deliberately managed a goading smile. "Welcome aboard, my Father." He gestured to the deck littered with the dead and dying. "A regret I've so few men left to greet you in style!"

"Curse you," Maximus gritted with passion.

Bruce offered a deep bow. "Captain Bruce Anthony Hawkins at your service!"

Maximus' fingers gripped the pistol tightly, a muscle in his cheek twitching. He climbed the steps to the quarterdeck. For a long moment he looked at Bruce. Bruce stared back evenly.

"I ought to kill you here and now. I ought to string you up on the yardarm like a common pirate for all to see!"

"Words! Do with me as you wish. Do you think to frighten me? That I'll wallow at your boots and whine? My life means nothing to me now. Go on, hang me! Get it over with! Call Favian, he will surely want to watch! Or have you no stomach for it after all, *Father?*"

Maximus' clay-colored face twitched.

"Maybe my dear brother Favian will do it for you?" Bruce looked down at Favian, who stood below, silent and grim. "Come, my brother, you have long wanted to show Maximus how you excel. He needs your help now. Can't you see? Or do you hold back for fear Sybella will hate you? Does that matter to you as long as you have her?"

Favian turned his shoulder toward him and walked away. "What, Favian? You too disappoint me. Then you must leave it to one of your soldiers, Father, as you leave most of your foul work."

"I do not need Favian to hang you," Maximus growled. "And I'll silence your tongue, you son of an English dog, but I'll do it my way." At the insult to the memory of his dead mother, Bruce raised his fist to smash into him, but his strength was gone. Loss of blood had left him weak, and he realized he had only lifted his arm.

Maximus snatched the pistol and sword from Bruce and backhanded him on one side of his face, then the other. Bruce fell back against the rail.

Githens rushed forward, his face contorted with rage. He fired his boarding pistol with a cloud of pale gray smoke, but his arm shook so from his wound that the shot smashed harmlessly into the deck. One of the Spanish soldiers nearby used the flat of his sword against the back of his neck and Githens toppled.

Maximus' burning gaze had not once left Bruce's face. "Take this pirate to our ship," he ordered a soldier. "When I am through with this wild jackal, he will at least learn the lessons of the bit and bridle." He wheeled on his heel, and went down the steps.

Maximus walked to the side of the ship and caught a rope thrown to him from a Spaniard on the *Santa Rosa*. Maximus swung himself over with agility, landing steadily on his feet.

A moment later Bruce felt the firm grip of several soldiers leading him away to board the *Santa Rosa*. As Bruce reached the side of the ship, he glanced back. He saw Hakewell being rounded up by the soldiers. The others, perhaps two dozen, were being brought out of hiding, and the wounded were being left to die. Bruce looked at Favian. Favian lifted his head, the wind moving against the white plume in his broad castor. He walked away, his boots ringing on the deck. He had at last conquered.

🌿 7 🌿

The Galley Slave

The sun was rising, sending shimmers across the wide-open Caribbean Sea. The wind came warm and steady, yet Devora wondered if the ship were even moving. Only moments ago she had awakened to the shrill sound of the bos'un's whistle. Strange . . . had the ship set anchor? Where were they? Surely not in English water, not so soon?

She sat up in bed, grabbing her wrapper, and slipped her bare feet into sandals. She hurried across the cabin floor to the little gallery connected to her cabin near the upper deck of the *Magdalena*. Cautiously she gazed out across the sea. Today the water appeared one huge glittering sapphire —

Her eyes narrowed. Her heart slowed, then beat quickly. A ship! A great and tall Spanish galleon was approaching and signaling to the *Magdalena*. The galleon's flags whipped in the wind and the colors of Spain rode high and gloriously. Beside her rode two smaller ships that looked to be escorts.

Did they intend to board? She felt no fear, since the *Magdalena* was a Spanish vessel. As the galleon came closer she could make out the name: the *Santa Rosa*.

She turned away and went quickly to dress. She had no notion how Lillian fared since they'd been given separate cabins and were kept apart. Devora believed that once they were transferred to the English ship heading to Barbados she and Lillian would be able to see each other. Devora hoped she was doing well, since she had been ill when they first boarded. All her questions to the servingman when he came to bring her meals went unanswered.

Devora's heart took on new hope as the galleon anchored not far from them. Perhaps Bruce had discovered the truth of her departure and sent a ship to come after her and his grandmother. Perhaps Bruce himself was on board.

It was with a light heart that she answered the knock on her cabin door some forty-five minutes later, expecting to be summoned to meet Don Nicklas Valentin. As she was escorted above to the deck of the *Magdalena*, Don Maximus and Favian stood waiting wearing full regalia, the wind whipping Maximus' shirt sleeves. She glanced about curiously and saw the sober faces of the ship's crew. Lillian was nowhere in sight. Keeping her concerns under tight control, Devora turned to meet Maximus as he walked toward her. He wore a smile, but she noted the bitterness it reflected. Again, she was struck by the alarming thought that Maximus reminded her of one of the statues of the conquistadors she had seen upon arriving in Cartagena. This time he was not missing the steel armor and plumed helmet, and his height and weight were intimidating. His handsome but ruthless granite features told her plainly that he could not be resisted. *Does he think I chose to run away? Just what had Sybella told him? Surely not the truth.*

The sleeves beneath his black steel-like doublet billowed. He walked toward her with an air of ownership that caused her to step back before she realized her response. He saw her flinch, and his dark eyes mocked her. A scar, long-ago healed, slashed his right cheek above a well-groomed, short inky beard.

"It is well we overtook you, Señorita. Your mother and I have been sadly grieving over your hastened departure."

At once alert, she scanned him. He and the countess, but he hadn't mentioned

Bruce. Why? Her chest tightened. She was reluctant to ask.

"I do not suppose your niece has explained the reason for our hastened departure? You do know Lady Lillian is aboard?"

"Yes. No need to disturb her. She will be going on to Barbados."

"Does Nicklas approve of this?"

His mouth tipped down. "You may ask him that yourself. He is aboard my ship."

"Nicklas — here?" her hopes recovered. She glanced toward the galleon overshadowing the decks of the *Magdalena*. "Where is he?"

"Injured. We came upon his brigantine, which was in shambles. He is alive. I shall bring you to him."

"Seriously injured?" came her anxious voice.

Maximus' dark eyes flickered. "You shall see him for yourself. Did you not once tell me you had studied medicine with an uncle in Barbados? Good. Your presence will cheer him. We would miss your loveliness too much, Devora, to let you return to Carlisle Bay."

Her heart cried out to rush to Bruce, but something mocking and even a little ruthless in the face of Maximus repulsed her and held her back. She glanced toward Favian.

There was something different about him. What was it? Satisfaction? Or was she mistaking his haughty expression for gravity?

She had no choice but to respond to Maximus' orders. He gestured toward a soldier who came to bring her to the *Santa Rosa*, then called orders to one of the men to secure her belongings and bring them aboard.

Devora had to climb down to a boat that was rowed out beside the hull of the great galleon. She seemed to be rising and falling as she reached to grab hold of the rope ladder. She climbed up the ship's side until a soldier helped her over the rail and onto the deck. She looked around, hoping against hope to see Bruce, but more Spanish soldiers in full uniform waited, along with the dignified captain with a short, pointed black beard.

Maximus appeared. "I understand your interest in medicine was used on slaves in Barbados on the countess' sugar plantation?"

Ashby Hall Plantation belonged to her Uncle Barnabas, but it seemed a small matter to set straight when her soul quavered with unease. "Yes. I was helping Barnabas treat the slaves."

"I was counting on that, Devora. Your fair

hands are now needed below. You'll come of course?" His dark eyes challenged her, as did his small smile.

"Yes . . . of course. I'll need a chest of medicants —"

"Naturally. We have them below. Come."

He strode to a door that opened onto a flight of steps that led down into the hold of the ship. She hesitated at the rank smell. Then she went down, hearing Maximus' boots coming behind her.

There were torches glowing, and a dreadful stench. She wanted to recoil. A burly Spaniard met them, shirtless, sweating from the heat. She saw the hard face and lifeless eyes that flicked past her to Maximus. Again, Devora stopped, horror stealing over her. Could she even bear to look at these pitiable galley slaves? Maximus came up beside her. She felt his strong hand take hold of her arm. As his fingers enclosed about her forearm her eyes rushed questioningly to his. A slow sense of panic and horror welled up in her throat. *Bruce.* . . . His sober gaze held hers and appeared to answer her wordless question.

Devora tried to pull her arm away as anger burned within her. Had he brought her here to taunt her — or to taunt Bruce? He had him chained as a galley slave!

131

She wanted to scream, but stopped herself. Her response would only place more anguish upon Bruce. Apparently that is what Maximus wanted. She must not panic, weep, or fight against him now.

She tried to swallow, but her throat was so dry she couldn't. Sweat ran down her back and dotted her forehead. Maximus steered her forward into a ghastly dimness. The ship creaked and groaned at its moorings, like the voices of a thousand men in everlasting chains. She saw them — how many? Fifty? A hundred? The narrow walk between the aisle reeked with stench. The men were chained to their oars; their condition was worse than beasts. Their hair was long and snarled, their flesh was marked with healed whip lashes and bloody gashes. Their eyes seemed blind as they looked at her and no one made a sound as Maximus steered her down the aisle.

Devora stiffened, knowing whom she would see. *Please Lord, give me a measure of Your grace, Your strength. I cannot bear this. Oh God, why, why?*

Her footsteps matched the groaning of the wood, and then Maximus stopped, but held her arm firmly.

"This is the one, Señorita."

Devora held her breath, and glanced

down. Every hellish fear came true. Bruce was there, chained, asleep so it seemed, his head back. She winced, but held in the sob when she saw the dried blood streaking his chest and arms.

"Can you do anything for this slave?" Maximus asked.

Devora turned her head away, unable to keep back the tears.

"Wake him up," Maximus ordered the guard. The guard picked up a bucket of water and threw it across Bruce's face and chest. Some of the foul water splashed on Devora.

"Ah! He wakes at last. Well, Captain Hawkins, I've brought you a visitor," Maximus said. "Do you recognize her? Ah, I see by your face that you do. The lovely English señorita you expected to marry next week. A shame it will not be. But do not worry. I have rescued her from the *Magdalena*. She will not go to Barbados but to Lima. You may find her at the Casa Valentin, but I don't believe you shall come to visit her. Our good friend Archbishop Andres has plans to see you stand trial in Lima."

Devora kept her face averted, trying to silence her tears.

"What?" said Maximus. "You have

nothing to say, Captain Hawkins? Then let me explain. I wouldn't want your journey to Callao Harbor to upset you. We are on our way now, and you will help us get there. Your fellow crew of pirates will come in another ship. They are still destined for the mines. But you, for trial. We would keep you strong and well, so I have brought you an angel of mercy to bind up your wounds." Suddenly Maximus released her arm and Devora nearly fell. The burly galley guard caught her.

"You have five minutes," Maximus said, and gestured abruptly to the guard. The Spaniard brought a chest and set it down on the wet deck.

"Come now, Devora, tend to your patient," came the voice of Maximus.

With that, he strode away, and the guard left them.

Devora turned, her face wet with tears and dropped to her knees beside him, her hands grasping him, unaware of anything else or caring that she knelt in filth.

"Bruce, darling . . ."

"Devora . . ."

Her hands caught his face as she looked up at him, and she pressed her trembling lips against his, kissing him gently at first, then desperately.

"I'm sorry," she whispered. "How did it happen? Did Sybella deliver the letter to Maximus?"

"No time," he rasped. "Listen — Maximus is only doing this to trouble me. Expect him to make advances toward you . . . try to delay him . . . somehow, I'll get free again . . ."

"Yes, yes," she soothed, "you will, my darling. God will help us. I shall pray for you every day. I shall go to sleep at night with you in my heart, your name presented before His throne of mercy."

His eyes burned like molten lava. "Tobias is aboard. Both of you will need to be cautious. When he has opportunity he will try to get you safely to Barbados . . . until then, do nothing to rile Maximus. Do what he asks, but hold him off."

Tobias is aboard! Thank God, she thought. And seeing that the guard was returning, she quickly rummaged through the wooden chest for a salve to smear on his wounds. As she rubbed it in she whispered: "What about Kitt? Is there any way I can get a message to him?"

"Isle of Pines . . . but not for months . . . not till the silver shipment . . . leave that for Tobias to handle."

Their eyes met and her hands grew still.

His gaze went to her lips again but the guard stood over them and he turned his head away. "Is there any wine . . ." he asked instead.

Devora glanced cautiously toward the guard. He scanned Bruce, then Devora, and then went to a barrel. He lifted the lid and dipped in a tin cup. He brought it to Devora who held it to Bruce's lips. When he had finished it, the guard grumbled, "You must go now, Señorita."

"I shall try to see you again," she whispered, but Bruce shook his head. "Maximus won't allow it. This brief time was only to torment me, and you. Remember what I said . . . I shall find you again in Lima . . . if God permits . . ."

"May He be our strength."

The guard's big hand touched her shoulder, and she got to her feet, and with a last lingering look at Bruce, she turned away and walked down the aisle, keeping her head high, her eyes on the steps up to the deck. Maximus waited against the sunlight, a masculine figure in black, the wind tossing his hair. As she came up the steps, her eyes met his. She could see he watched carefully for her reaction. Yet unlike the mockery with which he had heaped upon Bruce, there was a new look in his eyes, a bewildered look as his eyes swept her, and she actually saw a glimmer of something like respect.

She brushed past him breathing deeply of the fresh sea air, feeling the wind in her hair and cooling her soaked skin.

"Your belongings are in your cabin," he told her. "One of the soldiers will bring you there."

Devora turned away to follow the soldier, but Maximus caught her arm and whirled her around to face him, his dark eyes searching hers again. She met his gaze evenly, unflinching, though her repulsion was evident. His jaw flexed.

"He has shamed me."

"As if that is an excuse. He is your son! No matter what you do to him, or how much you seek to hurt and humiliate him, nothing will change that. Nor will it destroy him. He remains what he always was — the best you have ever sired. Buccaneer or not! You drove him to it! You and your ruthlessness, your —"

Her breath caught as he jerked her against him with an iron grip, his eyes burning. "Easy, Señorita. I do not take well to the lecturing tongue of a woman." His eyes dropped to her lips and she stiffened when she saw a tiny flame leap into his eyes. She jerked her head away.

He slowly released her. Devora turned with outward calm and followed the guard, her heart thumping. Lima! How long? Weeks? Months? She must endure, she must be strong, not just for herself, but for Bruce.

❦ 8 ❦

The Captain's Table

Devora lay awake that night grieving. Each move of the ship as it progressed through the water only reminded her that Bruce was below in the galley, where a guard patrolled with his whip. She envisioned him chained to the oars, thirsty, feverish, denied rest while his injuries worsened. All while Maximus slept in a comfortable cabin, drinking wine and devouring roast meat and fruit!

Unable to sleep, she threw her coverlet aside and paced the cabin floor. What awaited in Lima? Could she and Tobias do anything to rescue Bruce? She wrestled with her deep and growing hatred toward Maximus. What kind of a father was he! What kind of a man! Her hands clenched. She couldn't treat a stranger the way he was treating his own son! She hated him —

She stopped, realizing the danger of the path her emotions trod. Hatred led to all manner of vice. She must not allow it to control her heart. Vengeance belonged only to God. Prayer was her one weapon. On her knees she could enter the very throne room of the Most High God. What an awesome thought. There, before Him she could plead her case, ask for His intervention, His will to prevail in their lives. She was not helpless.

This was not her first battle with bitterness. She had grown up resenting her mother, Countess Catherina Radburn, for abandoning her as a child. All so that her selfish, immature mother could indulge in entertainments and doting men without the complications of caring for a child. Even so, her anger toward Maximus exceeded even the feelings she had battled with over her mother all these years.

She placed her trembling palms over her face. The emotion she struggled with was like a canker that ate away at her insides and destroyed what was honorable, truthful, and pure. Hating him would do nothing to solve the problem. She couldn't even think clearly when she was full of rage. It would rob her of strength to pray on, to have hope for the future at Lima, to trust in deliverance from the Lord. He was the God of all flesh and nothing was too hard for Him, she solaced her bruised heart. He who was full of compassion had heard her cry. She could wait on

Him to face the trials surrounding them.

Tobias, too, was here! Was this not an act of God's mercy? As angry as Maximus was with Tobias he normally would have refused his presence aboard his ship.

No, she was not alone in her quandary. Leave this injustice to the wisdom of God to handle, she kept telling herself again and again, as new floods of anger swelled within her heart. But loving Bruce as she did made her resent Maximus all the more. She would be able to handle her anguish far better if Bruce was not being mistreated, she thought. Finally she sank back to the bed and prayed fervently, trying to fill her mind with all the Scripture verses she could recall. At last she must have drifted off into a fitful sleep, for the next thing she was aware of was the brightening sun.

That morning no one came to her cabin, nor was she allowed to leave it to walk on deck. When she opened her door a guard patrolling the companionway refused her liberty. "My orders, Señorita."

Her meals were brought, but she hardly touched them. Then, toward late afternoon as the sun was dipping in the west, there was a knock. Favian entered, looking pleased with himself, and it was all she could do to be civil to him. Maximus was ruthless, but she usually knew what to expect from his temper. Favian, on the other hand, worked his schemes in secret.

"Maximus requests that you dine with him at the Captain's table."

"You may tell your father I do not care to have company," she said stiffly.

"He will insist. I suggest you do not rile him any more than you have."

" 'Than I have,' " she protested with mild indignation. "May I likewise 'suggest' it is the viceroy who troubles us all?"

He sauntered about the cabin and finally leaned against a chest of drawers, removing the flower from his lapel to smell, and watched her thoughtfully. "You rile him, Señorita. I have not seen a woman do so for many years. You have power over him."

She folded her arms and icily met his stare. Had Maximus sent him to suggest this to her?

"I wish nothing of the viceroy but the release of Nicklas and my own freedom."

"That is what riles him, that you wish nothing. Other women would rush to make gain of his interest."

She turned away so he wouldn't see her embarrassment and walked to a small chair where she sat down.

"Does he think I will come begging to him to release Nicklas?"

"He is so angry at Nicklas that not even your begging would change his fate. However, it is your fate that might be changed."

Her eyes searched his cautiously and she did not like what she saw. "I shall trust my 'fate,' as you call it, to the hand of God rather than to the whims of your father."

"You have that liberty. I say these things only out of friendship. I have seen the way my father looks at you. I have not seen him look at any woman with respect in years."

"And of course, it is honor toward me and Nicklas that prompts such *unexpected* emotions from Don Maximus," she said wryly.

Favian tapped the flower against his chin. "Pursue my unfortunate brother and you will have neither man."

She was surprised Favian would even say this to her. He straightened. "I would advise you to come to dinner. My father is not a man to be refused."

Bruce had told her not to rile Maximus, but neither could she allow him to think there was a chance she would respond to his carnal appetites. He must not think she might in order to save her own skin, or Bruce's, no matter what.

"Your father's pride naturally resents a refusal of any sort. Nevertheless, you may tell him I have no interest in his dinner. I wish to be alone to grieve over the injustice that he, a man of political authority, has heaped upon his son Nicklas."

Favian showed a spark of contempt. "Pray tell, Señorita, why should my father treat a common English pirate as anything more than what he is?"

"Because Nicklas is more than a common pirate as you both know."

He smiled coolly. "Yes, a very clever one to be sure, to deceive the court of Seville and my father too. But a pirate nonetheless, Señorita. The letter from his Excellency Governor Sanchez of Saint Augustine is proof he dueled and killed General Don Demetrio because the general discovered Nicklas was secretly attacking Spanish ships in the Florida Straits."

"Perhaps he is not telling the full truth. Governors are known for such things," she said.

"General Demetrio's captain saw what happened on the beach and informed him. He arrived on the Main recently as a witness."

"Why did he come here? Why not go straight to the king of Spain?"

"For a payment, Señorita. He thought to

receive much from me — but what he did not realize was that I, above most, wish Nicklas' downfall. He not only has robbed me of my father's favor, but holds the key to Sybella's heart. I confess to being a very jealous and sometimes vindicative man."

Her breath drew in. "You betrayed Nicklas to Don Maximus?"

"No, to Archbishop Andres. You see, I did not even fully trust my father. You do not understand him as I do. While he is willing to chain him to the oars and humiliate him, he secretly holds to favoring him still."

"So you did betray your brother."

Favian sniffed the rose. "It gave me no great pleasure. It had to be."

"Is your brother's blood worth the new favor you receive from Maximus?" she asked bitterly. "Beware, Favian; his favor is like the mist beneath the Caribbean sun. The first time you disappoint him he will cast you aside even as he has now shackled his other son to the oars. If you were wise, you would seek the acclaim that comes from obedience to what is right and good in God's sight and not the applause of sinful men."

Favian frowned. "I cooperate with him for Sybella's sake. Maximus has promised she will be given to me in marriage at Lima.

Even so, I take no particular pleasure in seeing Nicklas suffer, but it is either Nicklas, or me, who will prevail. I will not lose Sybella."

"Maybe. Then again, it is also true that what a man gives his soul to attain he often loses anyway. Then what will you have?"

He walked to the cabin door, tossing the rose aside. "If you are wise, Señorita, you would think of your own good favor and not worry of my fate." He opened the door. "Again, the viceroy expects you at dinner."

"Where is Tobias?"

"What would Uncle Tobias be doing aboard this galleon but prowling about among the soldiers? Everyone knows he favors Nicklas. He practically raised him. Tobias is looking to help Nicklas escape. It was a mistake to allow him to sail with us, but Maximus is not always wise in everything he does. He makes mistakes. Tobias is one of them."

"And I suppose you'll be quick to try to convince Don Maximus to turn against Tobias even as he has Nicklas."

"He knows my opinion. You have been a witness to how often in the past he has scorned it. He is little more inclined now to listen than before. He puts on a bitter face toward Nicklas, but he mourns his prized tiger in traps and chains below. He fools me not, Señorita! As for Uncle Tobias, he may one day be the ruin of Maximus."

Devora tried to conceal her alarm. Favian understood too much. "You exaggerate, surely," she said in a bored voice.

"Do I, Señorita Devora? One day Maximus will know that to trust Uncle Tobias is to play into the hands of Nicklas. The reverent friar has more on his mind than an interest in the fate of the Inca Indians at Lima."

When Favian left, Devora considered his words. He was more clever than anyone thought. Little did Maximus know that Favian was right when he said Tobias favored Nicklas, and that he was working for his escape. It was to everyone's benefit that Maximus held Favian's counsel at arm's length and to some capacity continued to confide in Tobias.

The captain's table faced windows displaying the amethyst sky and rippling Caribbean. Normally Devora would have found the beauty calming to her emotions after being confined to her cabin since the day before. As it was, she could only think of Bruce below in the foul-smelling hold chained to his oars. She sat immobile at the white-clothed table set with Peruvian silver and crystal, and covered with an abundance of food and drink fit for the king of Spain. Maximus was resplendent in Spanish garb, with manners fitting a viceroy. Jewels, as eye-catching as the sea, sparkled on his strong hands.

Don Favian wore claret-red velvet with cream lace, his thin mustache oiled, his thick black hair curled meticulously and framing his lean, haughty face. He was dangerous, and his reputation with the sword was respected. His slim hand tossed back inches of lace at his wrist as he plucked purple grapes and popped them into his mouth.

"Señorita Devora is pained over the chains that hold my pirate brother to his oars." He looked at Tobias, a hint of suspicion in his eyes. "Perhaps you, my Uncle, should call for Nicklas to join us now." He lifted his wine glass. "We may all toast the glories of Spain — how our illustrious king was so highhandedly made into a fool by the heroic don he knighted in Seville!"

Devora wondered at his audacity. Thankfully, she saw that Tobias merely appeared bored by his nephew's remarks.

Maximus, however, shot Favian a scalding rebuke while slamming his strong hand on the table, causing the glasses and plates to tinkle. Devora winced.

"Perhaps you, Favian, wish to take your traitorous brother's place at the oars?"

Favian's sleek brows humped above his aquiline nose. He clicked open a snuff box made from a large pearl. "I!" He proceeded to remove a pinch of Cuban tobacco. Calmly he sniffed the weed up one flaring nostril, then the other. "Hardly, Father." He coughed discreetly at the tobacco's sting. "Alas, you need me now."

"You flatter yourself," Maximus said dryly.

Favian was not to be put off. "I was never built for manual work like a donkey. The art of warfare fills my mind and my great sword hand."

Maximus' dark eyes slowly heated in the candlelight. "You deceive yourself, and your chattering is wearisome."

Favian grew sullen. "Where is my honor? Was it not my investigation that identified Nicklas?"

"You, of course, find that treachery commendable?" Devora quipped, unable to keep silent.

Maximus smiled wryly as he scanned her. Aware of Tobias' glance in her direction, she silenced herself, holding down the emotions that churned within.

Favian went on with a wave of his slim, graceful fingers. "Had I not trailed the true betrayer, the sweetly treacherous Sybella, and discovered her plot as she cajoled you, Señorita, to board the *Magdalena*, the real treachery would still exist." He looked soberly at his father. "And who would know she had confiscated the incriminating letter from Governor Sanchez? You, my illustrious Father, would be the most deceived of all! Deceived by the feigned diabolical loyalties of your prized Nicklas!"

Devora's breath paused in her throat. She expected to witness his hand across Favian's mouth, but the quick, steadying hand of Tobias on his arm stopped him as coldly as ice in his veins.

"Did I not say to speak no more to me of that pirate?" Maximus snapped.

Favian lapsed into sullen silence.

"If mention of Nicklas is distressing to you, there is yet hope for you," Tobias said flatly.

Maximus stood angrily. When Tobias calmly went on eating his dinner, Maximus glanced at Devora, then sat down again. He abruptly gestured to the slave to fill his wine glass.

"If you've come aboard the *Santa Rosa* to

harass me all the way to Lima about showing leniency toward him, you are mistaken, Tobias. Do you think I don't remember how you sailed with 'Captain Hawkins' on his *Revenge?* From the hour he sacked the Isle of Pearls, you've protected his identity. I could have you arrested as well —" he waved a hand of dismissal. "Once at Lima he will stand trial with the others. That will be the end of it."

The thought of seeing Tobias or Bruce turned over to the inquisitors sickened Devora.

"Enough of this. I fear we disturb Señorita Devora," Maximus said. "Or perhaps she is pale at the prospect of seeing a certain thief and pirate face justice for his treachery. Perhaps she approves of the name Hawkins?"

"You have broken your own law, Father. You have mentioned him."

Devora looked up at Maximus from her plate, troubled by his glibness. "If he took the name Hawkins, perhaps it is because you took too long to make him a Valentin. As for justice, he will not receive it, Señor."

Maximus smiled unpleasantly. "How it pains my heart, Devora, to see you rush to defend this half-English dog."

"Dog? Only days ago he was your lion!"

"Perhaps it will also please the archbishop to know you approve of the sinking of Spanish ships and the death of General Demetrio."

"Leave the Señorita in peace, Maximus," Tobias warned. "I fear you show evidence of a jealous heart."

"Jealous? I? Don Maximus Valentin, viceroy of all Peru?"

"Yes," Tobias said wryly.

Devora felt her face flush and said quickly, avoiding the subject — "You have no proof Nicklas murdered this renowned General named Demetrio. All you have is the accusation of the governor at Saint Augustine. Perhaps he tells less than the truth," she said calmly. "And as for this capitan, who supposedly witnessed the duel on the beach, it is only his word against Nicklas'. Why should the king of Spain believe *him* over a knighted warrior of Castile?"

There was an awkward moment of silence as though her simple denial had taken them by surprise. Favian frowned, but Maximus looked as though some new thought stirred his mind.

"She speaks with simple wisdom, Maximus. In the end, this matter of the duel may come down to the capitan's word against Nicklas'."

"Yes, a proven soldier of Spain," Devora added.

"And, now, a pirate," insisted Maximus, "since he admitted before witnesses that he was Hawkins. That in itself is enough to hang him."

Devora persisted. "A man may say many things when under cannon fire by the flagship of the viceroy. He was wounded and feverish when I attended him. It is cruel not to let me attend him again —"

"So you can coddle him? He is man enough to endure chains and the oars!"

"Did you not fire on him at the mere word of Earl Robert and the soldier from Granada who claims to have seen him with Morgan?" Tobias asked.

"He fired on my flagship first — and sank it. A matter worthy of the dungeon in itself. Enough of this worthless talk. One would think I, as viceroy, am the man on trial! Nicklas has admitted to being Captain Bruce Hawkins, who is wanted for piracy by Spain. There is nothing more to be said."

"I think the duel was most likely forced upon him by General Demetrio."

"Ah, the steadfast love of a woman," Favian said. "If only Sybella should love me as much."

"Perhaps you, Devora, are willing to go to

153

Seville with him to bear witness of this to the king of Spain?" Maximus asked with an edge to his voice.

Tobias gestured for the servingman to take away his plate, and turned to Maximus. "If Nicklas is actually Bruce Hawkins as you suggest, there are more fitting ways to punish him than sending him to Cadiz. Once in Cadiz you will lose full command over his destiny. I assume you still wish some control."

Maximus made no reply but raised his wine glass.

"As I thought. . . . Then as long as your son remains in Lima —"

"He is no longer a son of mine."

"— you control the chains that bind him. You have your revenge, and Nicklas retains his life. That is what you really want, isn't it, Maximus?"

Devora held her breath. She thought she knew what Tobias was doing, but would Maximus see through it and refuse?

Maximus bit the end of his cigar, lounging back against his chair, one arm over its back. She saw that he watched her, rather than Tobias, as though meditating on her response.

It was Favian's tense voice that broke the silence.

154

"All this talk means nothing. It is law that a pirate and heretic be turned over to the ecclesiastics."

"Keep silent," Maximus ordered. "Go on, Tobias. Say what is on your mind or, should I say, your heart?"

Devora held her glass stem tightly, careful not to interject her own feelings and perhaps provoke Maximus to reject Tobias' words.

"The solution seems simple enough," Tobias said. "Did he not insist on sending the prisoners from the *Revenge* to the Peruvian mines? Since they intended to pirate the treasure fleet before it could reach the Canary Islands, is it not also fitting for their buccaneering captain to be sent to the mines with them?"

Favian showed interest. "Then you think Nicklas brought them here for that purpose, to attack the treasure fleet?"

"Why else? The amount of silver heading back to Spain would be more than that devil Morgan ever looted."

Devora glanced at Tobias. From his frown one could hardly guess that he counseled in favor of Bruce.

"That is so," gritted Maximus. "He also knew what the loss of those galleons would cost me before the king. The title of Count of the Realm was within my grasp. Yet he deliberately planned to mock me."

"Yes," Tobias agreed. "I will admit as much, Maximus. I warned you when he was only a boy what your rejection would do to his loyalties."

Maximus angrily tossed his cigar down. "Let him go to Cadiz."

"Is it not more fitting that he should mine the very silver he came to steal from under your nose?"

"Mining is too good for him."

"Think what it will mean to you to have foiled him, to see that silver sent to Seville, something he loathed. And the irony of having him and his crew producing the bars."

Maximus looked at him gravely.

"It will shame him," Tobias continued. "That's what you want more than his death, isn't it? What good will his death do you? But years of service in the silver mines — where he was *born*. Sentenced back to the very lowly place where Lady Marian gave him birth — ah, that will sting, Maximus, long and hard."

Favian shot an anxious glance at Maximus. "I could oversee them. I could make certain they produce."

Maximus silenced him with a lifted hand,

his eyes never leaving Tobias. "Why do you say these things? You, who first pleaded for his release, his pardon?"

"Why? Out of concern for his life. I would rather see Nicklas a prisoner in the mines than sent to Seville. Is there another choice? He is a prisoner in chains. Escape is impossible. I choose the lesser of two evils. Because despite everything, I love him as a son. This is no secret, Maximus."

Favian began to rub his empty glass between his nervous palms. "Perhaps he has something, Father. No prisoner has ever escaped the mines. And we are too far inland for any raid by Tortuga pirates. Years in the mines will be harder on his spirits than hanging."

"At least you admit you are trying to save his life," Maximus told Tobias.

"If it is revenge you want, and irony, you have it," Tobias told him. "He who came to oversee an increase in the silver production, with secret plans to attack the fleet on its return, is now sentenced to dig it from the great mountains."

Maximus' face revealed nothing of what he thought. Devora's heart was pounding. Was Tobias giving too much away? Or was he doing the one thing that might buy them time?

Favian's eyes glowed with excitement. "He is right, Father. The irony of it all will be a bitter cup for Nicklas. But your plan lacks one important factor. It lacks a man to replace Nicklas in service to the king."

"You, my ambitious nephew, should be that man," Tobias said easily.

Favian turned anxiously to Maximus. "Give me the command of the mines just until the treasure fleet arrives and I'll see that the quantity of silver bars is produced, even if I must use every prisoner and Indian I can round up for the royal task!"

Maximus looked at him wryly. "Yes, you would. And in that lies your greatest value at the moment."

"Anything for the glories of Spain, and the Valentin name."

"And do not forget the king," Tobias warned. "He sits on his throne, expecting Nicklas to fulfill his duty. If that silver doesn't arrive in Seville, he will be most displeased, whether Nicklas is hanged for piracy or not."

"I shall consider," Maximus said. "It is weeks before we arrive at Lima. By then I will have made my decision."

Devora carefully avoided showing any relief. As silence fell, and each of the three men withdrew to their own thoughts and plans, she used the opportunity to excuse herself and go up on deck.

The Caribbean moon was full and pale yellow, the trade winds warm and fragrant. She hadn't expected Maximus to be bold enough to come after her, but he overtook her and, taking her elbow, he led her along the deck while soldiers and crew gave them wide berth. She recognized his great importance in the Spanish way of rule, and knew that a viceroy was something of a king here on the Main. Maximus guided her to the ship's side.

"You are upset," he said.

"Can you blame me? I am unaccustomed to the cold cruelties which Spain so commonly orders in peoples' lives."

"As if no injustice prevailed in England or on Barbados!"

"At least it is done under the cover of civility."

"And that makes all the difference?"

"Of course not. But you wondered why I was upset, Don Maximus."

"At Lima, things will be different."

She didn't know why he said that, but did not wish to ask. "Favian tells me we will soon dock at Nombre de Dios."

"Yes, by dawn." There was no pleasure in

his voice. "The *Valencia* will be there waiting for us."

"The *Valencia*?"

"The galleon bringing Sybella and the countess. From Nombre de Dios it is only a short distance to Portobello."

The news of her mother's arrival brought some cause for cheer. Except for Tobias she had no one to confide in, and while her mother was to blame for their being in this situation, the past began to matter less and less in these trying circumstances. She longed to see Catherina and to feel her arms about her. Perhaps it was time for healing to begin in their relationship.

"Tobias wishes me to transfer you to the *Valencia* to be with the countess."

She thought of Bruce. Did she wish to leave him? She was almost certain Maximus would not permit her to see him again, even if she remained aboard the *Santa Rosa*.

"I would prefer her company, yes. If she is ill, she will need my help on the rest of the voyage."

"Then Catherina can be brought aboard the *Santa Rosa*," he said contrarily. "You will stay aboard my ship until we reach Panama. From there, we will all journey together to Lima."

"As you wish, Don Maximus." She turned

to walk past him, but he blocked her way.

"I am very tired and wish to go to my cabin."

Maximus' handsome face mocked a brief smile. "You are afraid of me, Devora."

"Do you expect me to feel otherwise?"

For a moment he said nothing. "I could wish it otherwise."

Her fingers tightened on the rail as she looked out across the rippling water shimmering for miles in the distance. "I am sorry, but it cannot be different. Not as long as you hold Nicklas in chains."

"Your fear of me, is it because of Nicklas or something else?"

"You have given me little reason to trust you."

"I am bringing Catherina aboard. I could, if I wish, rid everyone from this ship except you and I."

"That would do you little good, Don Maximus. Not if it's my trust you want."

"Maybe I am willing to ignore such weighty matters as trust and take what I wish."

"Then your earlier words of wishing it differently were not spoken in truth."

"I did speak in truth."

"Then you will not ignore the weighty matter of trust."

"If I find there is cause to hope, you may find me a reasonable man, Señorita."

Devora trembled and looked up at him, and for a moment she saw something of Bruce in him — the way the wind ruffled his dark hair, the slight smile on his mouth, the strong, handsome, masculine features.

"I am in love with your son, Maximus. I will always love him."

She was not prepared for the flinch of anger that creased his face. "You deliberately taunt me. I warn you, do not play lightly with me, Devora. I am not to be manipulated in the hopes of getting Nicklas released from his just due!"

"That is not my way. Has it occurred to you that your implied accusation is a most vile insult?"

He laughed shortly.

"I have never given you reason to think I might care," she persisted in a low voice. "Nor do I play dangerous games with any man, including Nicklas. Must you hate him? Must you hate us both?"

"Hate him?" He looked for a moment actually stunned. "I do not hate him. I was proud of him until he betrayed me. As proud of Nicklas as I would have been of myself in his place."

"Perhaps that is part of the problem. You

expect too much of him, because you want him to excel at all the things you find glorious. You should have simply loved him as your son."

His face hardened in the moonlight. "I do not want your speeches. Go to your cabin. I have not yet decided what to do with you."

Devora looked at him, pained by the emotional moment, then turned and walked away briskly.

🔥 9 🔥

When Hope and Love Die

The next day they sailed the short distance from Nombre de Dios to Portobello. The castle of San Felipe, known as the Iron Fort, stood guard at the entrance to the mile-long harbor. Devora looked upon the outline of tall, crenelated towers topped by a flag staff. Below it were eight-foot machicolated walls flanked at their corners by little martello towers or stone lookout boxes.

As the *Santa Rosa* sailed proudly into the harbor displaying the flag of the viceroy, drums and horns sounded a grand welcome for Maximus on shore. Devora stood on the forecastle with Tobias looking below at the throngs of Spaniards, Indians, and African slaves on the wharves in front of the vast customhouses. There were two other forts, San Geronimo and Triana, protecting the city.

Tobias pointed down the harbor. "That is

the *aduana*," he explained, "where the silver bars from the mines are stored along with much gold, emeralds, and jewels until the treasure galleons arrive."

"Have you ever seen the mule train?" she asked, musing at the sight.

"Ah yes . . . I saw two hundred mules enter the city once with nothing but silver bars. You can tell when the mules arrive; they tinkle with a myriad of pure silver bells."

Devora shaded her eyes and looked toward the inland jungle mountains. "Is that the Gold Road I've heard so much about?"

He smiled. "The great Camino Real — the soldiers follow it across the Isthmus from the City of Panama over here to Portobello. That mule train is a sight to behold." He sighed. "One that awakens the greed in each of us I fear, Señorita. There are times when the silver is stacked several feet high on the streets, glinting in the sunlight while being guarded by soldiers loyal to the king of Spain."

She tried to imagine such a sight and shuddered, thinking instead of Bruce's plans, now foiled. She glanced at Tobias and whispered, "Will Kitt be warned not to come?"

"Do not even whisper that name here. It is too risky. Until I can be alone with Bruce, no further plans can be made. Our friends know what to do if something should go wrong, but our enemies are a cause of great concern."

With good reason, she thought, seeing Maximus walk out on deck in full viceroy regalia, Don Favian with him, looking proud.

"We will disembark the *Santa Rosa* here at Portobello tomorrow," Tobias was telling her. "From here we will journey by mule train across the isthmus to Panama City. New ships will await in the Gulf of Panama to carry us on the Pacific to Callao Harbor near Lima. The land trip will be trying. It will not be easy for you or the countess. Sybella has traveled it before, so she knows of the hardship."

Catherina was reportedly quite ill and Devora's concerns were compounded. *If Maximus had any kindness he would send her to Barbados,* yet, even as she thought this, she also knew that her mother would not pay heed. Imprisonment could await her if Earl Robert admitted to Lord Anthony that she had been privy to his spying for Spain while he served King Charles as his English ambassador. "It's not my only reason for staying," her mother had written her in a note delivered the night before. "For once in my life I've made the decision that mother

166

and daughter will stay together. This time I won't abandon you."

Her mother's feeble, but brave, gesture, though accomplishing little, had brought tears to Devora's eyes.

Now, standing on the forecastle, Devora looked at Tobias worriedly. "What about Bruce and the other prisoners? What will Maximus do with them now?"

"They also must travel by land. There is no other way to reach the Gulf of Panama."

Devora's excitement grew as she thought of seeing Bruce again, even for a few minutes.

"If only . . ." she sighed.

"If I could only get away long enough to send a message to the Isle of Pines . . . but Favian watches me like a hawk. I think he is suspicious."

"Oh Tobias, be cautious. You are the only man that can aid Bruce now."

"We will both be cautious. And it grieves me to see how Maximus' emotions have become entangled over you. This was the last thing I expected to happen, and perhaps the worst."

Maximus walked over to the rail as his captain called: "A boat comes, Excellency."

"From the *Valencia*?"

"From the Fortress Geronimo. Soldiers — and Archbishop Andres is with them."

Maximus leaned over to the side of the ship to gaze below. Devora noticed that Tobias frowned as he removed a small telescope from his belt and focused on the boat plying toward them.

"Is not the archbishop an ally of Maximus?" she asked, concerned.

"Nay, not since that hour in the Cartagena square when Maximus sided with Bruce. Maximus refused to hand over the prisoners to Andres for interrogation. He has not forgotten the affront."

"But Maximus is head of the viceroyalty."

"True, but there have always been confrontations of power between political and religious thrones. Even now certain kings in Europe wrestle in disagreement with the pope over who has final authority. It is no different here on the Spanish Main."

Devora wondered whether Bruce was aware of his father's dilemma. Maximus, who was enraged over the shame Bruce had brought upon him by siding with England against Spain, was now in the awkward position of refusing to turn him over to the authorities. Maximus had succeeded in having Bruce chained to the oars, but neither son nor father was free. Bruce's behavior was slowly tightening the noose around both of their necks.

Devora, displeased by it all remained a bystander, unable to affect the outcome. She hadn't approved of Bruce's buccaneering ways, but neither did she approve of Spain's cruelty, or Maximus' vengeance.

"It's Andres all right," Tobias murmured under his breath. "I think we are in for trouble . . . there is someone with him . . . some official from Portobello . . ."

Devora watched as the Spanish soldiers boarded the galleon in their cloaks and scarves of blue, green, and scarlet. The sunlight reflected off their steel head pieces and breast plates. One officer in particular, wearing a vermilion cloak embroidered generously with silver lace, turned to assist the archbishop to the deck of the *Santa Rosa*.

Devora's uneasy gaze stumbled over Andres' stately figure in handsome black and crimson. His silver hair glinted as brightly as did the soldiers' helmets.

Devora and Tobias came halfway down the forecastle steps and paused when the boarding soldiers stepped aside to admit a high-ranking military officer. She was sure she recognized him from Cartagena as Commander Cristobal, whom Tobias said had disagreed with Bruce over the prisoners. Evidently he had sailed on the *Valencia* with the archbishop.

"Excellency!" Commander Cristobal was addressing Maximus. "When we arrived this morning a report was waiting from the military at Panama. It concerns the English pirate, Captain Hawkins, and his crew. General Alfonso de Aviles from Panama is here to speak with you."

Maximus returned Cristobal's salute, but it was clear from his expression that he was not pleased as he turned to the general from Panama.

An iron-faced Spaniard wearing as many medals on his exquisite uniform as did Don Maximus, stepped forward with an official document. "I bring you greetings from the viceroy of Panama, Don Juan Perez de Guzman!"

Viceroy? Devora's fingers tightened on the rail. Was not Maximus viceroy over all the Main? What had Tobias told her when she first arrived, about there being powerful viceroys in the various provinces, but that Maximus was the greater in the extent of his authority?

Had she only imagined General Aviles' slight pause when he mentioned the name of de Guzman, as though emphasizing its importance?

170

The general's face was grave, but Archbishop Andres wore a satisfied expression on his tawny features as his cool gaze confronted Maximus. Tobias had been right . . . trouble.

General Aviles, the emissary from Viceroy de Guzman, was speaking.

"Archbishop Harro Andres has informed the authorities at Panama City that you carry aboard this ship the diablo Bruce Hawkins, the infamous, traitorous dog who has troubled the Spanish Caribbean for years! He has not only attacked and plundered the Isle of Pearls, but recently fought with Morgan in the sack of Granada. He has also murdered General Demetrio on the sands of Florida! Not to mention the sinking of many Spanish ships and the aiding of heretics."

Devora's alarmed gaze darted to Maximus. He turned to confront Archbishop Andres as though accusing him of betrayal by going above his head to the viceroy of Panama.

"Yes," growled Maximus, "that is why I have captured him and placed him in chains. You may tell Don de Guzman that Hawkins will stand trial in Lima."

"You are to be commended, Don Maximus. His Majesty will hear of your success." The general deferred his head, his dark eyes hard, adding: "But we are to bring this prisoner to Panama. Viceroy Don Perez de Guzman will escort him to Seville aboard his flagship." With a bow, he handed Maximus a sealed document.

Maximus stepped forward and snatched the document. He read it in silence.

Heart in throat, Devora glanced at Tobias. He was grave. *Dear God,* she prayed, *do not let them take Bruce!*

"I have come for the pirate Hawkins and the members of his murderous crew, your Excellency," the general stated in a calm but deliberate voice. As Maximus finished reading the official letter, the general spoke again, "Bring the galley slaves up on deck and prepare to transfer them to shore."

Devora caught Tobias' arm. "We must do something!" she whispered in a tight, frightened voice. "If he leaves this ship it will mean his end."

"Courage, child. There is nothing we can do yet. Any move would be futile under the power of such men. Perez de Guzman is one of the most powerful dons on the Main. Only Maximus can hold him off, but his anger at Bruce may have weakened his will to contest. We shall see. In the meantime I'll do what I can, but we must be careful. Any overt act now will quickly unmask me. A Franciscan friar is no match for an archbishop."

Devora glanced across the deck to see the ecclesiastic. He looked displeased that Maximus had not immediately yielded to General Aviles.

Devora's hopes, like coals, were quickly turning to ash. Maximus would not choose to confront the authorities at Panama. He risked being called to Seville to explain to the king. That would not be pleasant, seeing that he was the father of the English pirate.

Devora felt her greatest fears being realized. She drew back as soldiers returned bringing a line of prisoners dragging their chains. Her anxious eyes sought for Bruce, yet she feared to behold him in such straits. It was all over, she told herself in a swell of defeat. Bruce would stand trial in Panama, and she was doomed to belong to Don Maximus in Lima.

Belong to Maximus. Unless. . . . Her busy mind revived as she glanced in his direction, the breeze whipping his cloak. He emanated strength, a will that would not be easily defeated by the political plans of others. If she could appeal to that will, if she could urge him to save Bruce —

But would Bruce want her to do so? He

had warned her to be careful of Maximus, with good reason. She knew that Bruce would rather be consigned to the dungeons or even be sent for trial in Seville before he saw her surrender to the plans of Maximus. She saw Bruce then, among the prisoners, and as she had expected he emanated a strength of purpose equal to his father. There was no sign of despair or defeat. Nothing in his strong build beneath the torn, blood-stained clothes offered satisfaction to his gloating enemies. His dark head was held high as his eyes deliberately sought out Maximus rather than avoid his father's gaze. A faint smile touched his lips as he held his hands together, bound with chains.

Maximus stared back evenly before turning his head and barking an impatient order to the soldiers to get the pirates lowered into small boats.

Devora loitered on the steps, on the verge of moving toward Bruce, her heart in her eyes, the warm sultry breeze ruffling her satin dress. She must have his attention if only for a moment, to exchange a look as strong as any embrace.

Bruce, her heart cried out. She faltered, coming down the steps, and skirted the edge where the soldiers stood. He noticed her movement. Their gaze met and locked. She saw a quick flash of brilliance in his gray-green eyes, but it turned to visible pain. She winced, feeling the strong grip of Maximus on her arm. He drew her beside him, and there was a possessiveness in the action. She knew it was deliberate, to hurt Bruce. He was moving her forward across the deck toward the bedraggled line of prisoners. Knowing what he intended, she tried to break free without causing a scene, but his hold was too strong, his fingers digging into her flesh.

"So you wish one lingering gaze, do you?" Maximus hissed in a low voice. "You shall have it."

"No, Maximus —"

He forced her to walk with him past the line of galley slaves who cast their tormented eyes to the deck. One of the buccaneers made a move as if to help her and a soldier backhanded him. "In line, dog!"

Maximus stopped in front of Bruce. "She wishes to say something to you, Captain Hawkins," came his cold voice. "There is no understanding a woman's heart. Despite your treasonous, murderous ways, and the shame brought to my name —"

"The shame brought to the Valentin name was done by your unbridled lust when you shamed my mother, Lady Marian

Bruce! As for murder, she is buried near the mud hacienda near Cuzco, the victim of your selfish brutality! Do not speak to me of honor. I cast aside the Valentin name of my own free will. I am, and always have been, Bruce Anthony!"

Maximus, his strong features clay-colored, backhanded him. Bruce, unsteady on his feet from previous injury and being chained to the oars, stumbled. Guards rushed at him, pushing him back into line.

Devora had turned her head away, holding back a sob that tore at her heart.

"Look at him!" Maximus blustered. "You wanted to see him, look at him!" He took her chin and jerked it upward, whirling her face forward toward Bruce. "The man your foolish heart yearns for. Look well! Because he will stand trial in Panama for treason. A most lamentable fate, Señorita."

"Only a coward mocks before a chained tiger," said Bruce. "Or torments a woman, and then boasts of courage and honor. You want to boast, then release these chains and face me as a man!"

Maximus' white teeth showed brilliant in his tanned face. His strong hand came up and gave his short dark beard a musing tug. "A consideration, Bruce Anthony. I may have other plans for a half-English dog-of-a-son who has shamed me!" His hard mouth turned. "As you have honored the Valentin name, I tell you in good faith, so I will honor you. Unless I do something to stop Harro Andres, you will die."

Devora's eyes rushed to Maximus, hope flaring. Was he hinting that he would intervene?

"Do not beg him, Devora! That is what he wants."

"And before we leave Panama, I may have what I want."

Bruce made a slight move toward him, but the guard stepped forward, and Maximus simply turned his back and strode away, leaving Devora standing there, as though he did not fear their moment together, as though in the end he was in full control and would do as he wished.

Bruce looked down at her, his dark hair moving in the wind, his handsome features undiminished by the inhuman treatment he had suffered since his capture. Her heart went out to him and her cool hand touched the cut on his lip, but to her surprise he turned his head away from her touch. His gray-green eyes heated.

"You play right into his trap! Can't you see he wants you to plead with him? To grovel?"

"And if I did, Bruce," she whispered, "for your life, for *us,* would it be such a shame to you? Would it not be evidence of my love for you?"

Bruce made a frustrated attempt to snatch her hands. "No, do you hear me? I would rather die with honor than see you under his mastery, in his arms!"

"How can I leave you to torture, to certain death in the end? If I can stop it, I shall try! Do not ask me not to!"

His eyes narrowed into burning slits. "What has he promised for your cooperation? My release? He lies."

Her eyes, like gems in the fairness of her face, lifted to his suddenly. "No, he has offered me nothing, not yet. . . ."

"Not yet! He will promise anything, then walk away. What has he done?" he demanded.

"Now it is you who allow yourself to walk into his trap! My heart belongs to you. Is that not enough?"

"No, it is not enough. I demand you refuse him. Is that clear?"

"You sound like him. Arrogant, even in chains —" she stopped as she saw his anguish.

"You have pledged me more than your heart," he gritted. "I would see us both dead before you became his bride!"

Despite her heartache she hoped to reason with him. "Is he that diabolical, Bruce? Is there no way for you to make peace with him?" For a moment he looked more angry than she had yet seen him.

"So he has deceived you already?"

"No . . ."

"Maybe I misunderstood — maybe you have suddenly decided being the wife of the viceroy holds certain charms after all. Are you becoming like all the other señoritas who mince about him hoping for his favor? If so, I have agonized and prayed for your protection for nothing!"

She sucked in her breath. Pain, sharp as any knife, slashed across her heart. She slapped him. Then her hand rushed to her mouth, startled by her reaction. Tears came to her eyes. She turned away from him, and as she did saw the startled look on Maximus' face. He stood across the deck with the commander and general. Every head was turned in their direction, surprise written across all faces. Devora, already ashamed, felt she had no dignity left. She had hurt the one man she wanted, and even Maximus looked shocked. She fled across the deck, past a frowning Tobias, and up the steps to her cabin.

What had she done? Everything was in shambles. The Caribbean sun rose higher in the hot blue sky, but hope and love had died.

❧ 10 ❧

The Beginning of Reconciliation

Portobello was the site of the annual fair, the largest on the Spanish Main, coinciding with the arrival of the treasure fleet. Once news of the sighting of the convoy spread abroad, the colonists came from as far away as Vera Cruz to buy and sell.

The day after Bruce's departure from the ship, Devora was escorted off the *Santa Rosa* to meet her mother, Countess Catherina, and Doña Sybella who were already ashore from the *Valencia*. They would stay the night while preparations were made for the treacherous land route across the isthmus to Panama.

The wharf and surrounding streets were thronged with merchants and slaves. Devora scanned the crowd, hoping for some sign that Tobias may have been successful in whatever plans he had to contact Bruce's allies. Tobias had left the galleon before dawn to visit the Franciscan monastery, so he had said, and none of the soldiers on guard had questioned his departure. Upon arising that morning and finding Tobias gone, Maximus had rebuked the soldiers, but by then it was too late. Devora had heard a soldier pleading for understanding: "How was I to know, Excellency? No word was given me to stop him. He is a friar, a good man, and he went off to visit the Brothers."

In the end, the matter was forgotten, or seemed to be, but Devora's heart beat with expectation. Would he succeed in contacting friends to try to rescue Bruce?

Although she was guarded on all sides by Maximus, Favian, and soldiers, Devora was caught up in the throng of merchants and buyers crowding the short, narrow streets. Booths lined the walkway, piled with goods of all sorts. There were mule trains arriving from over the isthmus, carrying sugar, cacao, tobacco, indigo, emeralds, pearls, gold, silver, copper, and tin.

The viceroy had friends in Portobello, and while Maximus rode off without explanation, Favian brought her to a hacienda called the Casa Grande, fortress-like with thick walls, large cool rooms furnished with carved furniture of Brazilian woods, and luxuries from Spain.

"Where did Don Maximus go?" she asked Favian casually, fearful he may have gone off to hunt down Tobias.

"To make sure the soldiers have everything ready for the journey tomorrow." Favian's eyes glinted. "Did you fear he went off to locate Tobias?"

She showed nothing. "Why should I think so?"

He settled his hat with a smirk. "Come, come, Señorita, we both know my uncle hopes to free Nicklas before we reach Panama. Maximus suspects too, so there will be a double guard around him day and night. He will stand trial in Panama, and he will be condemned and shipped off to the inquisitors in Spain."

She turned on him angrily. "Why do you hate your brother so? You've no cause to be envious of him now. Maximus will make you heir of all his lands and wealth. Can you not at least allow Nicklas to escape with his life?"

Favian's smile was wiped clean. His black eyes were grave. "I do not hate him. But Nicklas' fate rests more with himself than it does with either Maximus or the magistrates."

"What do you mean? He is in chains."

"His heart has been bound long before he

was taken prisoner. Even if I were to free him one night and let him escape, do you think he would go and begin a new life? He and Maximus have a destiny. They are doomed to destroy one another." He turned and walked away.

Doña Sybella and Countess Catherina Radburn had been brought to the hacienda from the *Valencia* two days earlier and were already settled into their chambers when Devora arrived with Don Favian. Favian had gone out onto the patio to see Sybella immediately upon arriving, and Devora was escorted to her mother's chamber. As she entered, Catherina was propped up in a chair waiting for her.

"Mother!" Devora's eyes widened in alarm. She hurried towards her, scarcely recognizing the frail woman. Catherina was no longer the well-fed, earthy woman she had been, even in Cartagena. She had not only lost weight, but there was an unhealthy pallor to her skin. A depressed mood, like a tidal wave of defeat, seemed ready to sweep her away. Greenish circles surrounded her eyes.

"Mother — what have they done to you?"

Catherina tried to smile and reached out a pale hand. "Hello darling. . . . It's not what they have done, but what I have done to myself."

Devora sank to the side of her chair. "Where are Isabel and Luis?" she asked of the serving woman and her husband who had accompanied her mother from Spain. "Why haven't they looked after you?"

The countess wrinkled her nose. "Like nasty little mice scurrying from a sinking ship, the two have fled, knowing I have little to offer them now that Robert's been arrested."

"Mother —"

"That aged wench stole my jewels! And Luis came back to take Nicklas' pistol. As he was creeping up to my bed I — I shot him with it."

"Mother!"

"He staggered — I hit his arm I think. Served the scoundrel right. I don't know what happened to either of them. After that I was brought aboard the *Valencia*. I was never so happy to get out of Cartagena. We'll be going by mule across the isthmus. I know I shall probably succumb to mosquitoes along the way. Either that, or be attacked by leopards."

"Mother — I am so sorry about Robert being arrested."

The countess' mouth trembled. Tears wet her eyes. "Robert will hang. And there's nothing to be done about it. If I return I'll be arrested too. All my dreams have turned to dust, Devora. There's nothing left — nothing at all. Except you. Now Maximus will take you away from me too. It's all the harvest of my own beastly folly. Oh that I had stayed in London! That I'd been content to stay married to your father, Warren!"

It was the first time she had witnessed her mother's brokenness and Devora found herself crying too. Not because she understood her mother's fears, but out of compassion for the once gay and beautiful woman who appeared to have grown old and defeated before her eyes.

The tears spilled from the corners of Catherina's beautiful eyes — eyes that she had once labored over with paint and dye, that had once flirted and captivated her dozens of admirers from English lords to Spanish dons.

The salty tears trailed down the wrinkles of her now sallow skin. The once plump red lips were cracked from heat and fever, and there was no trace of powder on her skin, no scent of expensive French perfume, but only the smell of illness. All of her lovers and admirers had slipped through her fingers as time left its mark and took away the youthful past. She had used up her life selfishly; flittered away like a butterfly on the first frosty night of autumn. Little remained for her mother of the entertainments and pleasures she had given her waking hours to attain. The court balls and dinners at St. James Palace in London, the boat rides on the Thames, the romantic strolls in the orange-scented courtyards of Seville and Madrid — these much-sought-after treasures had faded, never to return.

Without yielding our hearts to the Savior, there is no hope, Devora thought, bringing her mother's hand to her cheek, and looking at her with compassion. All the bitterness she had harbored for so long melted away as she realized how brief were the days when two people could love one another, their hearts in fellowship, interacting with the joys and sorrows of life. As death waited to take her mother away from her the hurts and slights, Devora's disappointments and resentments, that had once been like mountains, dwindled to tiny grains of sand slipping through her fingers. Devora clung to her mother as if to hold onto her for a short time longer, and cried into her thin breast, though she knew she looked into the face of a near stranger. What may have been no longer mattered.

"Don't die and leave me now . . . you're all

I have, Mother, we've only just now found each other . . . even Bruce is gone forever . . ." she sobbed, weary, afraid, feeling hopeless.

Her mother's frail hand grasped her, stroking her hair. "If . . . if you mean that . . . if you've forgiven me . . ."

"Oh yes, Mother, of course I have. Christ in His grace has forgiven me of so much, how could I not forgive you?"

The countess cried too, but even as she did a new light appeared to glow in her eyes. She tried to sit up, still holding Devora's hand. "What a foolish woman I've been. To have let a daughter like you get so far from me. You're worth all the silver of any ancient Inca tomb!" She tried to laugh at herself. "Even the jewels I had were stolen by Isabel. What would I have done with bars of silver too heavy to carry through the mosquito-infested jungles of Peru?"

"There must be a—a doctor in Portobello," Devora sniffed, grabbing a handkerchief to blow her nose. "I'll find him. I'll go to Sybella —"

Catherina held her hand to keep her there. "They have done all they could. I was bled again last night. A little more rest is all I need, dear . . . I'll try — I'll try hard to get better."

They looked at each other and smiled like two friends who had met again after lost years. Then the countess seemed to remember something that brought tension to her tired face.

"Then Maximus didn't tell you of your stepfather?" came the quiet question.

"Maximus has told me nothing. He's tormented me with the enslavement of Bruce."

"The beast! Where is he being held now? Do you know?"

"Not exactly, except he's with the other prisoners to be transported by land to Panama. What about Robert? Why was he arrested?" Devora lowered her voice, and glanced toward the door. "For spying?"

"Yes — spying. And it was I who told him to do it. I'm to blame."

Devora shook her head. "You did not control his heart. Your suggestions may have tempted him, but they didn't force him to obey. He had a free will and he chose the path he took."

"The silver at Cuzco, the Inca tomb that Maximus promised to show Robert — all was vain. All the bright silver dreams we so carefully laid and built our desires upon have awakened to the glare of judgment. Though I had a chest of silver beneath my bed, what good would it do me? Without

Robert, without my health, without the freedom to return to England, it might as well be a chest of rocks!"

"Oh Mother, all our earthly dreams fade and die, even as each one of us must fade as a leaf. Whether the king of Spain or England, or the slaves who wait upon them. Life is more than silver, beauty, and pleasure. We were created by God to know and love Him. Any life lived apart from that divine purpose will end in disillusionment — whether a thief, a murderer, or an archbishop, if his heart is far from truth and faith. The Lord Jesus said it best: 'What does it profit a man if he gains the whole world, and loses his soul?' "

Her mother groaned, both palms going to her ashen face. "I fear that I have lost it."

"It need not be! But rather grace and forgiveness for justice, heaven for perdition, if we choose Him. His arms are stretched out still to welcome you, to make you His pure child. For He is gracious to all who call upon His name, Jesus, Savior, Emmanuel — God with us."

Catherina's eyes suddenly widened as she stared not at Devora, but toward the chamber door.

Devora, in her concern for her mother, had not heard the door open. Seeing

Catherina's expression of alarm, she turned her head, still clasping her mother's hand between her own. Maximus and Archbishop Harro Andres stood there.

Maximus' handsome face was hard and shadowed, his dark eyes screened. Andres, on the other hand, looked at Devora with musing gravity.

"I did not know we had a follower of Martin Luther in Portobello," Andres stated to Maximus.

"No," whispered Catherina. "My daughter was — was only trying to comfort me — the Ashby family of England has always been loyal to Rome . . . why . . . we fled with King Charles into France when that evil Oliver Cromwell usurped power in England. Tell him, Maximus!"

Maximus lifted a hand, frowning. "Do not bestir yourself, Catherina. No harm befalls any I have taken under my roof for safety. Andres knows this. He cannot help himself. He likes to see the sparks of fear."

Andres looked at him with a twisted smile. "Your flattery has poisonous arrows, Maximus. You and I have much to discuss about Nicklas. Let's not declare ourselves enemies yet."

Maximus gave a short laugh. "No? I thought we already were." He looked over at

Catherina. "The good Andres has merely come to speak to you about your poor husband languishing in the Bridgetown jail." His gaze swerved to Devora, his eyes warning her to silence. "And you, my ministering angel, will have plenty of time to comfort your ailing mother on the journey to Lima."

Maximus took her arm and led her out the door. "I wish to speak with you in the patio," he said flatly.

Devora followed him into the enclosed garden walled in with adobe and thick, cool greenery. He led her to a fountain splashing over smooth stones.

"How many times must I warn you to silence?"

"I have not yet grown accustomed to men barging into a woman's private chamber. The words I spoke to my mother were for her ears only."

Maximus smiled unpleasantly. "I stand rebuked."

She bowed her head. "I am overwhelmed, Don Maximus."

"Except for your insolence toward Nicklas," he snatched up her hand and studied her palm, "your behavior yesterday is not something I will stand for."

Devora already felt ashamed, but was

troubled even more about hurting Bruce's feelings. "There was not much he could do in chains."

He dropped her hand. "He would have accepted it anyway. He was always more gallant than his father." His searing gaze held hers. "You know the story of his mother."

She turned her back and looked at the water bubbling and singing pleasantly beneath the hot shade of the pepper tree. "Lady Lillian explained well enough."

"There are two sides to every tale. Someday I hope you will permit me to give mine."

She looked at him coolly. "I don't see how you could cast the tale in any light to give it dignity."

"Then you are as bigoted as Lillian and Nicklas!" he snapped. "I did not force her!"

Devora flushed and turned away. "If you brought me here to discuss his mother, I'd rather not."

"I did not force her," he repeated. "But Nicklas is bull-headed and will not believe otherwise. Lillian filled his mind from the time he was a child with lies about me."

"If that is true it was your duty as a father to make certain he knew and understood the truth. You left him thinking it was true. He spent his rejected childhood nursing

193

such thoughts. How can you expect him to feel differently? And now! What kind of a father keeps a son he has any kind of love for in chains?"

"I only do so," he gritted, "because the discipline is good for his rebellious nature."

"Oh," she said with a bitter laugh. "You believe in discipline do you? The whip, the chain, the inquisitors perhaps?"

He grabbed her, jerking her to him. "I could break every bone in your body!"

"And that would make you a happy man, Don Maximus?"

His eyes were suddenly raw with torture. He reached a hand and smoothed her hair, turning her face toward his. "No."

She struggled, and he abruptly released her.

Her face was hot and she backed away toward the fountain. She turned to flee.

"Wait!"

She stopped, her trembling hands clutching her skirts, but kept her back to him.

"What did you do with the forbidden book? Did you burn it as I ordered?"

She let out a breath. "No," she confessed quietly. "Such a treasure cannot be burned, Don Maximus."

He walked up behind her, took her arm

and turned her toward him. "Will it be the book, or you?"

She shuddered beneath his concern.

"Think carefully. If you persist in your doings, not even I will be able to save you." His fingers tightened around her forearm as he drew her closer toward him, though she stiffened. He lifted her chin in a gesture oddly mingled with gentleness and strength. "I think of you often. I could care about you, Devora, deeply. You are a good woman . . . like Marian . . ."

"Please, Maximus, don't — I don't want to hurt you, I don't want to hurt anyone. I am in love with Bruce."

"Bruce? My scoundrel of a son?"

Her eyes dropped to the white ruffle of his shirt and tensed as she saw his heartbeat throbbing in his chest.

He drew her closer. "You and I must come to a bargain over him."

"Bargain?" she whispered.

"Yes. That's what you want, isn't it? His life?"

"Yes. . . ."

His eyes registered his emotions as he studied her face, her eyes, her lips. "My price will prove high, Señorita."

She paled, feeling her heart quaver. He apparently realized her anguish and a

195

muscle in his jaw flexed angrily with hurt pride.

"We will wait to discuss it at Lima."

"Father, the captain wishes to —" Favian stopped in the archway when he saw them standing close together. A smile tugged at his thin lips.

Maximus released her with restrained emotion. Devora brushed past him, avoiding Favian's gaze, and walked quickly into the hacienda. Tears filled her eyes as she climbed the stone steps to her chamber.

Favian petted his thin mustache as he sauntered into the patio, the polished high heels of his red boots clicking on the tan flagstones. "A fair choice of woman, my Father. If it is Nicklas you wish to show your revenge upon, making Doña Ashby your bride will do it."

"I did not ask your opinion, you who are wax in the hands of Sybella."

"I care for my Father. Hear me out this once."

Maximus glowered. "Speak."

"If you intend to have her, you had best come to the hard decision to see him hang. If you leave him alive, you will be sparing a man-eating leopard. If you thought he despised you before, take Devora and there is no remedy. He will stalk you to the death."

Maximus considered, frowning. He went past him and out the front door to where his stallion waited. A small slave boy came running, handing him the reins, then lifted his wide sombrero. "Buenos dios, Excellency!"

Maximus mounted the intricately carved leather saddle and rode through the gate, miserable.

Was there not enough hate between him and Nicklas? Must they now want the same woman?

🌿 11 🌿

The Journey to Panama

The next day they set out for Panama. Devora was hoping to see Bruce but was denied any glimpse of him or the other prisoners since they and the bulk of the soldiers were half a day ahead preparing the route for easier travel. Devora knew Maximus was keeping her away from Sybella as well, because he did not trust either of them where Bruce was concerned. Indeed, Devora would not have slipped away even if she could have after seeing the dark, treacherous, looming jungle. Sybella remained sullen and uncooperative under Don Favian's close guard. Occasionally Devora could hear them arguing. Sometimes Sybella was not angry but pleading, and then Favian appeared to be worn out before the evening fire, and looked as though he had been hard pressed not to surrender to her. Devora could only guess what it was about, but she was certain that it had to do with Bruce. Did Sybella want Favian to help him escape?

Now and then Devora saw Sybella watching her with restrained sympathy. Perhaps she regretted her selfish actions in Cartagena, and was feeling responsible for Bruce's imprisonment.

As for Bruce, she had not seen him since their encounter on the deck of the *Santa Rosa*. Nor had she been able to speak alone with Tobias since he'd gone into Portobello. She remembered what Bruce had told her about Kitt Bonnor coming to the Isle of Pines from Tortuga, but he was not to have arrived yet. Had Tobias been able to hire some friend to bring a message to Tortuga about Bruce? If so, Kitt might arrange to come sooner. If Bruce was sentenced at Panama for imprisonment in Spain, might not Kitt and some of the buccaneering ships be able to attack the Spanish vessel before it could leave Caribbean waters?

A hundred different plans came and went in her mind, yet when the day closed and the first stars appeared in a lavender-blue sky, Bruce yet remained a prisoner with his pirate crew and she was still under the brooding eye of Don Maximus.

Devora's main fears were not for herself, however. Her mother was not improving as she had hoped, and was carried in a litter slung between two strong slaves. Yet she too remained watchful of Maximus, not trusting him around Devora. That night when the camp fires glowed a quarter mile from the Chagres river bank, the smell of roast wild pig wafted on the breeze. Devora looked about for Sybella but did not see her.

"I'm going for your supper," Devora told her mother. "It's just down the road. The soldiers and prisoners are being fed. I'm hoping to see Bruce."

Catherina did not look pleased. "Where's Tobias?"

"I don't know. I haven't seen him since before we stopped this afternoon. If he can get near Bruce, he'd be there."

Catherina drew her closer. "The pistol belonging to Nicklas is under my pillow. It will do us little good now. I've been debating whether to give it to Tobias. Perhaps you should take it."

Devora glanced over her shoulder and saw that the guard had turned his back and was looking off toward the distant campfire, interested in when he'd get supper. She reached beneath the pillow and her fingers touched Bruce's gun. If only she could get it to him! But how? His hands were in chains now and he would have no freedom to conceal it anyway. Perhaps a time would come.

"It is better with you — Maximus may

discover it on me. I'll know where to find it. Don't worry, I'll be all right. I believe Maximus has marriage on his mind, Favian only has eyes for Sybella, and the soldiers are all so afraid of Maximus they seldom even look in my direction."

"That is a blessing indeed. Very well, I'll keep it. We'll look for some way to get it to Nicklas. If not now, perhaps in Panama."

Devora left her and walked the narrow road along the Chagres toward the cook, who, with some others, was dishing out the roasted meat.

The moonlight reflected off the river with its rank smell, illuminating the wild bamboo and palm trees.

Here was country the like of which she had never seen before. Sweltering jungle growth through which the prisoners and soldiers had to hack a path with machete and brush hook. Devora slapped at a cloud of mosquitoes and quickened her steps in the direction of the fire. She had recently learned that the biting insects did not like the smoke.

She stopped. The prisoners were ahead, herded in close to the river's edge where it was known to be a place for alligators. They were back in chains for the night after laboring all day hacking the brush. Her anger climbed when she saw that they were not being fed. The Spanish soldiers were some feet away gorging themselves on the roast pig. She saw Bruce and her anger was such that she started walking in his direction. Immediately a guard intercepted her.

"Why are these prisoners not fed?" she demanded.

Many of the soldiers turned their dark eyes to look toward her. The captain walked forward, removing his hat.

"The General Alfonso de Aviles' orders, Señorita."

"Then he is inhuman. They have worked harder than any of you beneath the broiling sun. How do you expect them to continue to do such work when you treat them worse than the beasts?"

"I'm sorry, Señorita, but —"

"Did you feed your mules and horses?"

"Yes, Señorita." He looked toward the cook. Some of the loitering soldiers began to smile.

"Has the illustrious General Alfonso de Aviles eaten his supper?" Devora demanded wryly.

"Oh yes, Señorita."

"And he now drinks from a bottle of Madeira wine, no doubt, with his Excellency the viceroy!"

"Perhaps, Señorita."

"Bring them food at once, Capitan. If you and your men do not — then I will!"

"Oh no, Señorita, you cannot do such a thing. It is the orders of the general the pirates get no food tonight, only a portion of water."

"They will be fed. And if you try to stop me, I'll call Don Maximus."

She went past him toward the fire and the soldiers moved out of her way, some smiling and eying her with appreciation now that the viceroy was not in sight. They spoke to each other in Spanish, not realizing she understood. The cook looked at her with a grin as she took over his utensils and began to cut and stack the meat onto tin plates. The heat and smoke were dreadful, causing her eyes to smart and her throat to become dry. She burned her fingers on the hot grill, but at last had chunks of roast pork, brown and crisp.

"Help me carry it to the prisoners," she ordered.

They shook their heads. "We cannot, Señorita. We are under orders. If we disobey, we too will be in chains. If you wish to feed the heretics, you feed the heretics."

"I will!" and lifting her chin, defying the stares of dusty soldiers who continued to grin, she gathered several plates, and began carrying them over toward the condemned crew of the *Revenge*.

The men stood quickly to meet her, and with chains clanking they struggled to grasp the hot pork.

"To be sure, Miss, ye be an angel."

"God bless you, Señorita!"

"Har, Missy, ye got more courage than all them rat-toothed Spaniards! When I'm free, ye just whistle and ye gots yerself a bodyguard fer life!"

Quickly she went back for more plates, piling them high, and bringing them to the crew. Despite their hunger they had waited politely, each thanking her before devouring the meat.

Where is Bruce? Her eyes glanced about until she saw him again. He stood by himself, allowing the others to go first. What was left of his shirt was in rags and there were gashes and welts all over his muscled chest and arms from insects and jungle vines. She caught up a double portion and walked over to him. She could feel her face flush as his sultry green eyes swept over her.

"You're very brave . . . Are you all right? No trouble with Maximus, or am I foolish to ask such a question?"

"Never mind Maximus. It's you I'm worried about. Here, eat, before someone comes from General Aviles."

He took the plate. "I'd rather have water now, and your company for a few minutes."

She smiled, tearing her eyes from his. "You can have both. I'll be back."

She made several trips in order to give them all a portion, then returned to Bruce with a large cup of water from which he drank vigorously. As he did she watched him, remembering the joy of being in his arms.

"Tobias was able to slip away for a while at Portobello," she whispered, glancing over her shoulder. The soldiers looked on, holding their weapons, but did nothing to stop her from interacting with the prisoners.

"He may be able to send a friend to Tortuga to warn Kitt our plans have gone awry, but that will do us little good now. There's almost no chance of an attack by the Brotherhood until I get shipped to Seville. If they can take the galleon . . ."

"What if Maximus changes his mind?"

His eyes hardened into stone. "You mean send me to the mines?"

"Yes. Tobias tried to convince him aboard the *Santa Rosa* that such a fate would be most appropriate."

She wondered at his slight smile. "Being

sent to Lima would be the best thing that could happen. There would still be a chance my plans could be enacted."

"How can you even suggest such a thing after what's happened?" she breathed, exasperated. "Why can't you just be content to escape?"

"Content?" His brow lifted as he raised his chained hands. "When I dream of holding you and can't? When I know Maximus plans to have you?" He clumsily took hold of her hand, his grip warm and strong.

"I have your pistol," she whispered, "but I can't get it to you yet."

"Where is it?"

"With my mother, under her pillow. That's the safest place right now."

"Good. Keep it. Use it if you must."

"I won't need it . . . not with Maximus around."

Her voice was so soft he looked at her, alert.

"He acts as though he wants to marry me, Bruce."

For a moment his breath stopped. He stared at her, and she was almost afraid she'd made her worst mistake by telling him.

"That doesn't surprise me," was all he said.

She looked up at him and his eyes softened, but there was anger in their depths as well. "In some ways my father and I are alike," he admitted, nothing in his voice.

"You are gallant," she whispered. "He is ruthless. There is a great difference. Even when he loves, it is ruthless. See how he treats you, though he still cares down deep in his heart."

"Has he held you, kissed you?"

"No," she said, and tried to change the subject, but his eyes narrowed and his hand tightened on hers. "Tobias has promised me he'll get you back to Barbados one way or another. As soon as this business at Panama is over."

"Bruce?"

He looked at her and her anxious gaze searched his. "I — I can save you if you'll let me."

A tiny flame burned in the depths of his eyes. "By promising him you'll marry him?"

Her gaze lowered, and she nodded.

"And I suppose he told you he'd turn me loose if you did?"

"He's hinted he would. Perhaps he could make some excuse to the viceroy of Panama. What could they prove against him?"

He was silent, watching her evenly. She could not bear the warmth in his gaze and lowered her eyes again, staring at the chains on his wrist. She touched them and they clinked, a sound of certainty, of doom.

"You . . . could escape to Tortuga to Kitt, your friends . . . Tobias could go with you. My mother is dying . . . so she would not know about my future. And Sybella must marry Favian . . . I suppose Sybella and I could solace each other that we both lost the one man we loved. She must bear the pain of her betrayal, but I could sleep well knowing you were free, alive, and, one day, perhaps, even happy."

He lifted her chin, causing her to look up at him. His eyes held hers. "You would do that for me, marry Maximus?"

She swallowed, her heart surging with pain, not because she would be the wife of Maximus, but because she would forever lose Bruce. "Yes," she whispered. "To spare you from Spain, from death and torture, yes I would."

He reached a hand and touched her cheek softly with his fingers, then her lips. "You have it all backwards, Señorita. It is the prince who gives up everything and sacrifices himself for the bride he adores. Even as Christ left heaven and suffered for His Church. I could never walk away free and leave you bound to Maximus."

Tears filled her eyes. He leaned over and sought her lips. She took hold of him and kissed him as if she would never let him go.

"Vow to me you'll refuse him to the end, no matter what he promises, no matter what he threatens."

"I promise," she whispered.

"I'll get free some way. We must be patient. And you must go now, before we are found together."

"How angelic of you, Devora," Maximus said from the darkness of the road. "You have come to feed and water Hawkins' crew of cutthroat pirates."

She felt the angry tension harden the muscles in Bruce's body. Quickly she rose to her feet and walked toward Maximus, hoping to avert further trouble.

"It is a long journey to Panama. I suppose you had your horse fed and watered, and even rubbed with ointment to keep the insects from its flesh. It is only logical to quench the thirst of those who clear our path for travel."

A muscle in his square jaw flexed as he looked down at her. "This must not happen again."

"Only if you promise you will speak to General Aviles about adequate food and water."

Maximus suddenly smirked. "Fear not.

209

Nicklas will get his rations. Now, go back to Catherina," he ordered. "Do not wander about without an escort. There are wild animals in the brush, and poisonous vipers on the trees."

She turned away, anxious to leave his presence and, after getting food for herself and her mother, returned to their camp near the river. Sybella was there and she walked up, her dark eyes reflecting the stars.

"You are courageous to contest Uncle Maximus. You may yet get Nicklas free after all. But be careful. Maximus is equal to anything Nicklas may have planned. They are more alike than either of them will dare admit to themselves. Maximus may yet make his escape possible, but he will not let you go with him. I am sure of that now. I think he is in love with you." She laughed. "It's amusing. Who would ever have thought Maximus would fall prey to the English Señorita! The very one he had so cleverly chosen for his son!"

Devora felt sick. "I don't think it amusing. I find no wicked pleasure in hurting him."

Sybella arched her sleek black brow and scanned her. "If I did not know Nicklas, I'd almost think you were falling for Maximus."

Devora flushed and turned away, hearing Sybella's soft laughter.

She brought her mother her supper, but Catherina looked at the now cold piece of pork and made a gagging sound in her throat. "My stomach turns looking at it. Take it away, darling, I've no appetite for such food. Oh for a glass of Madeira," she sighed mockingly. "I wonder if Maximus has any."

"Mother, you promised me you'd start giving it up."

"Yes, so I did. Sybella tells me you were able to see Nicklas. How is he holding up, poor handsome darling. Or need I ask. He's strong enough to take the rigors, I'm sure."

"Yes, and he's living on anger as well. I made a promise to him tonight, one I begin to feel I shouldn't have." She explained about Maximus, and what Bruce had asked of her.

"Don Nicklas is a man of honor," Catherina said. "That makes things more dangerous for him."

The next day they started out at dawn. Tobias pointed out the solitary 1,700-foot mountain of Pilon de Miguel de la Borda near the mouth of the Chagres River where the great fortress, the Castle of San Lorenzo, guarded the river's mouth. Devora looked up at the huge stone walls and saw the bastion's powerful guns staring down in isolated grandeur.

"Panama, the heart of Spain's New World. It's queen of the treasure, the citadel on the isthmus of the Pacific Coast. Sir Francis Drake dreamed of taking it, but not even *El Dragon* could steal this prize."

At San Lorenzo they started upriver in shallow-draft sloops and about forty riverboats and many canoes, until they faced trouble.

"What is it, Tobias?" the countess asked.

"The rainy season's at an end. The Chagres is low."

Now the soldiers had to join Bruce and the buccaneers in the struggle forward. At least seven times they were forced to haul the boats overland, until the decision was finally made to set out on foot. To worsen matters for Devora, her mother's health deteriorated daily, and the torturous journey added to her misery. Nearly every agonizing step of the way was left for Bruce and the buccaneers to hack out with machetes. Devora had never seen such a jungle of overlapping trees, thickets of bamboo, and fetid swamp lands swarming with mosquitoes and other insects. Tangled vines, stinging thorns, and swamps of decaying vegetation fought their progress, but it was the snakes that frightened her. As Devora walked along she suddenly screamed. Bruce was far ahead, but he turned and started back toward her pushing past the soldier. Devora stood, wet with perspiration, her hair sticking to her throat, pointing with a trembling hand at the venomous bushwhacker slithering its deadly, curving body through the undergrowth toward her, its venom able to kill within minutes.

Bruce struck the bushwhacker with his machete as Favian hurried up. Bruce held her as she nearly fainted from fear and exhaustion. Maximus stormed over to them.

"What are you doing here? Get back up to the front!"

"Can't you see she's exhausted? If we are to continue the rest of the day she will need to be carried. For a man who boasts of his interest in a woman, you seem not to care!"

Maximus drew his whip, his eyes blazing with weariness.

"Just try it, Father!" gritted Bruce.

He was without chains since he'd been clearing the path through the jungle. The word "Father" seemed to shock Maximus. He became as still as a statue and looked at Bruce as though coming awake from a trance. The soldiers too looked at Maximus. He slowly lowered his whip.

Bruce led Devora past Maximus to the soldiers guarding Sybella. Sybella brought

Devora to a litter where she lay down. The mosquitoes buzzed and Sybella lowered the netting over the litter. Within a few minutes the procession was moving forward again but Devora remembered nothing more until they camped that night.

It was 25 miles from the mouth of the Chagres to the village of Venta de Cruces, but the bends and twists of the serpentine river lengthened the journey. At last they came to the village, and spent the night there refreshing themselves. Two days later they came out of the jungle onto a broad savanna where Devora was thankful the prisoners no longer had to do the slow and sweltering work of clearing vegetation. After the procession climbed a hill, she looked for the first time upon the waters of the Pacific, as blue as lapis lazuli, with the sun streaming down upon the city of Panama beside the wide bay. She saw ships waiting in the Gulf of Panama which would take them on the Pacific side of the Indies to Callao Harbor near Lima.

She watched the weary pack mules with their large burdens as they endured the last stretch of their journey into the city. She took courage at the refreshing breeze coming in from the Pacific as well as at the sight of palm trees, and thanked the Lord that despite the hardships and an uncertain tomorrow, He had brought them thus far. *Commit tomorrow to the Lord,* she reminded herself once again, *walk forward trusting in Him.*

❧ 12 ❧

The Judgment of the Viceroy

The sun sank behind the mountains creating purple-blue shadows among a series of rounded hills rising just beyond Panama City. Fort Natividad was built in the northerly end of the town defending the one bridge over the Algarroda River. Devora gazed upon the white walls of the monastery of the kindly Franciscan monks and prayed that Bruce might fall into their hands instead of the legalistic Dominicans. There were three great and beautiful plazas in the city, each shaded with coconut palms. As she rode with Tobias to the Casa Royal, the great tower of the cathedral stood guard over the city. She was struck by the beauty of great pearl shells that were set in the cupola, shimmering silvery-white in the last rays of the sun.

The *mercado* was filled with shops of all kinds. A fish market was selling everything from crabs and mackerel to cuchas and mullets. There were colorful dried gourds for sale too, filled with oil extracted from young pelicans. Tobias told her they used the oil on leather. Panama offered a sense of opulence, of lazy indifference to danger. As they rode by she saw green coconuts being sold on the cobbled street from decorative pushcarts, and people were drinking the somewhat sweet milk.

Next to the fish market, the *carcel* stood like a grim outline of judgment. Here, criminals of all ranks, enemies of his Most Catholic Majesty the king of Spain and his Church, were judged.

Devora arrived with Tobias shortly before the final rays of the sun faded into twilight darkness. Maximus had arrived first, followed by Favian and Sybella. Here in the Casa Royal under the presiding authority of Don Juan Perez de Guzman, both governor and viceroy, Maximus confronted the opposing viewpoint of Archbishop Harro Andres as they discussed and debated the fate of Bruce and the prisoners. The archbishop was addressing the viceroy.

"Perhaps I am overly concerned, Don de Guzman, but I have spent the night thinking about Henry Morgan's attack on Granada. I have profound concern over the possibility of a second attack by these hellish pirates, not at Granada, but elsewhere near at hand. May I remind us all that Don Nicklas was there on Granada," Andres looked at Maximus with a wry apology, "or rather, I should say, 'Captain Hawkins' was there with Morgan, since the viceroy of Lima denies any connection between himself and his wayward son."

"Nicklas has spat upon the proud Valentin name," Maximus snapped impatiently. "It was his choice to abandon it for the cursed name of Hawkins. So what do you mean to say, Lord Bishop? Apparently Nicklas was with Morgan, and it appears he was with the cur many times before Granada. The province was caught off guard, asleep in complacency. Who would have expected so daring an undertaking that far inland?"

Don de Guzman listened to both men. He stroked his tawny pointed beard. He stood and came around the long table. "It grieves me deeply, Maximus, that your son has unmasked himself as an English ally, but you understand I have no other choice but to side with the Lord Bishop when it comes to sending Nicklas to Holy Seville. How can you sit in judgment on your son?"

Maximus' nostrils flared. "You know as I do that it's not Andres' sole right to decide this. You forget that I am first of all a viceroy, secondly an aggrieved father. Spain has, and always will, come first in my legal judgments."

Archbishop Andres looked at him as if he wondered, but de Guzman sighed and shook his head sadly. "I simply do not understand what made Nicklas turn like this. Are you most certain he is guilty of treason?"

"We have delivered to you the official letter from St. Augustine," Andres said with a trace of impatience. "It was sent by the governor of Florida to Seville. Had it not been intercepted by —"

"Pardon, Lord Bishop," came Favian's smooth voice. He stood with a bow. "But when I intercepted the letter in Seville, I had no idea what was in it. I was told it was for Don Maximus, my father."

Devora glanced at him. So he preferred to protect Sybella. The lovely Spanish beauty made no move to correct his statement, nor did she show any gratitude in her eyes for Favian's assistance. She fanned herself languidly, but a closer inspection might have shown that her dark eyes were solemn with fear. Devora thought that alarm was more over the fate of Nicklas than Favian.

Maximus waved an arm. "Never mind

that, get on with what ails you, Andres."

Favian sat down, glancing smugly at Sybella, who ignored him.

"It is my opinion that another daring raid by Morgan is highly probable," Andres explained. "If so, Hawkins would know of it."

Devora clenched her shaking hands and pressed them into her lap to keep them from showing. Did he know about the silver mule train? She refrained from glancing at Tobias, who tapped his broad chin as if considering his superior's every wise word.

"You have proof?" Maximus growled.

"I have no proof yet. An attack on the galleon bringing him to Lima is likely. These pirates have formed a brotherhood, from which they ban together in a sworn deposition to come to the aid of the other in need. Can either of you honestly believe they will not seek to free Hawkins?"

Don de Guzman looked concerned, even if Maximus appeared disdainful of the alarm. "What do you think, Maximus?"

"His worries are not new, Don de Guzman. We both know the pirates are always laying new plans to sack a Spanish city or capture a ship. I am sure we will hear much of Morgan in the future. But any attack to free Hawkins will fail. The voyage to Lima will be well guarded with several caravels protecting the galleons. I remind you, my good caballeros, the pirates do not attack the Indies from the Pacific side, but from the Caribbean."

"Consider Drake," protested Andres. "Did the fiend not sail right into Callao Harbor? He sank every ship there and took a ransom of silver before sailing out as free as you like. Morgan is just such a dog. He does not bark until he is ready to lunge."

"Morgan is not a seamen but a soldier — a land-pirate if you please, who attacks by marching men hundreds of miles inland, even as he did at Granada. To attack Lima he would need sail around Vera Cruz. He doesn't have the ships yet." He turned. "Tobias? Your opinion?"

"Morgan will never come to Lima, my brother, for the very reasons you just mentioned. I believe he has smaller boats right now, sloops with canoes. He would need ships like Drake had to attack Callao."

Maximus waved a hand. "He speaks well. If Morgan attacks at all, it will be Portobello, amigos, and perhaps, eventually, Panama!"

"Diablo," breathed de Guzman. "Panama? Such a thought. . . ."

"I respectfully disagree with you, Maximus," Andres insisted shortly. "I am sure there is some mission planned for

Lima. Though I admit I do not know what it may be as yet. Therefore I fear it is a grave mistake to take chances. Transporting Hawkins and his crew there for trial is inviting more trouble than you may be able to handle. I have heard how other pirates prowling in this area are as bold as Morgan. If they somehow were allied in some undiscovered plan —"

"Plan! There is no way they could know that Nicklas has been unmasked and brought to Lima. We, ourselves, would not yet know who the rogue is, if the English ambassador had not been arrested in Bridgetown by Lord Anthony," Maximus scoffed. "I am not worried about lurking pirates in canoes."

"There have been other attacks on our strongholds!"

"While a Frenchman did sack Portobello in the not too distant past, Nicklas' allies are likely to be nesting at Tortuga, the breeding ground for the worst of pirates."

"So we know," the archbishop said. "But I was thinking of another of Nicklas' allies."

"Half his crew is dead. The others sweat in Panama's dungeons awaiting trial."

"Ah? But I speak of Kitt Bonnor."

"That dog," Maximus said with a frown, as if remembering.

Devora recalled how Maximus had sent Favian to the Isle of Pearls to bring Kitt from the dungeon to Cartagena for trial, but Bruce had rescued him, foiling his father's success.

"I'd give anything to have that slippery shark in chains! But Kitt is likely to have gone straight to Tortuga after bring freed."

"If Kitt learns Nicklas is a prisoner, I wouldn't put it past him to try a surprise attack."

Maximus watched him. "Who is there to inform him?"

"I cannot answer that. Nevertheless, I suggest carefulness, Maximus. Remember! Lady Lillian Bruce is on her way to Barbados. Nicklas has an English uncle there, her son, who is the man who holds Earl Robert. She most certainly will inform Lord Anthony of Nicklas' dilemma."

I'd forgotten that! thought Devora, hopes rising. Devora fanned herself, keeping her eyes straight ahead. Tobias had managed to send someone to warn Kitt of Bruce's capture. Archbishop Andres was far closer to the truth than Maximus.

"After your grave error at Cartagena in regard to the prisoners, we cannot afford yet another blunder in these pirate-infested waters."

223

Viceroy de Guzman's brows lifted as he looked at Maximus for an explanation, since he apparently had not been told.

Maximus' eyes turned midnight black. " 'Another blunder,' you say? Of what do you mean to accuse me! Do you suggest I knew aforehand of the ruse? That I somehow approved or covered Nicklas' masquerade?"

The archbishop refused a look of apology for his hasty words. "What blunder? Have you forgotten so quickly? Your intervention at Cartagena when Hawkins' crew was brought ashore for interrogation. You refused me those prisoners and sided with Nicklas."

"I did not yet know that my son was Hawkins!"

"Then your decision must have been a blunder. You cannot have it both ways, Maximus. Had it not been that Nicklas had transferred his crew to the brigantine, making his escape impossible when blockaded by your galleons in the Boca Chica, he would have escaped with his entire pack of pirates."

"I stopped him!" Maximus roared.

"You stopped him, Excellency, with the loss of your flagship, the *Santa Maria*, and the death of twelve prisoners."

"Nevertheless I captured him and he is in chains, which is proof of my justice."

"One might ask, for how long?"

"Enough of your ranting! If you question my loyalties to his Majesty, make your accusation now before Don de Guzman."

"I make no accusation. Not to the authorities. Not yet."

"Not yet!"

De Guzman raised a hand for peace. "Honorable caballeros, I ask for patience. Maximus, I had not heard of this action of yours in Cartagena. It must be written up and sent to Holy Seville."

The archbishop turned away from Maximus and looked at de Guzman. "Excellency, it is clear to me that despite his sea-roving ventures of treason and piracy, Don Nicklas — or 'Hawkins' as we now know him to be — remains Maximus' son. As such, Maximus is hardly in the position to see to his son's trial. Even if he is as unbiased as he claims, is it fair? Imagine passing the death penalty upon your own son."

Maximus' eyes heated like black coals of fire. He strode toward Andres, but de Guzman came between them.

"No son of Don Maximus Valentin is an English heretic pirate — and if that is what Hawkins is, he is not my heir. He will stand trial!"

The archbishop remained cool. "You

225

must admit, agreeing with Nicklas in Cartagena that his crew be sent to the mines looks rather suspicious for you."

Maximus was ruddy with anger. "In saying thus you defame my honor and loyalty to the Spanish throne. Do not forget that I hold the office of the Viceroyalty of Peru! My authority is not to be taken lightly. I would think again before threatening me."

Andres smiled wearily. "Threaten you, my son Maximus? Nay! I find it my religious duty to warn you."

"Warn me! Of what!"

"Just this — regardless of Nicklas' ruse in coming to the Indies, we know the reason his Majesty sent him here. It is you, Maximus, and not Nicklas, who will be held responsible should His Most Royal Majesty not receive the increase in silver bouillon expected from the treasure fleet. Though Nicklas hangs in Lima, this will in no way free you from being called back to Seville to answer before the throne."

Devora saw a sober look steal across Maximus' face. The archbishop had succeeded in frightening him.

"The king will want to know why you permitted Nicklas to remove members of his crew from my interrogation in Cartagena — when it may have unearthed the identity of your son long before he sought to escape with his men."

Maximus looked at him with nostrils flaring. "You still imply I knew he was Hawkins? That I cooperated with his scheme?"

The archbishop's face lost some of its hardness. "No, Maximus. I know your pride well enough. You would have preferred to see him dead rather than shame the Valentin name."

Maximus appeared slightly mollified. "Then what do you suggest?"

"Just this — when the treasure fleet arrives, there had better be enough silver to please Seville. If not, it will be the surest sign it was your intention all along to work with Nicklas to pirate the fleet. You will answer with your son for piracy."

This was the first time Devora had seen Maximus afraid. Sweat dotted his forehead. He stood with one hand gripping his scabbard. "The mule train will bring double silver to the treasure galleons when they arrive. I have ordered another shipload of slaves from Portobello to be brought to the mines. They will arrive in time to reinforce Nicklas and his pirate crew. You have no need to worry."

"Let us hope so, Don Maximus."

Don de Guzman sank into a high-back chair, looking as concerned as the archbishop. "Under the circumstances, Maximus, I think you had best let me transfer Nicklas to the first galleon sailing for Seville. If you have slaves arriving, you will not need Nicklas. The less you are involved with your son, the safer it will be for you."

Devora's heart fell like stone.

Maximus, however, took to pacing. "No, Juan, I'll not allow it. I have jurisdiction over the prisoners regardless of Andres' concerns." He stopped and turned toward both men. "I may have more slaves coming, but if the king expects the silver production to be increased, there is only one way to assure success. I'll need every man I can get."

Andres' eyes widened. "Do you mean to suggest you will bring Nicklas to the Peruvian mines?"

"Does Seville want silver? Does the Lord Bishop think I can produce it without increased manpower? Years of hard labor in the mines is a fitting end for a pirate who expected to rob the galleons," Maximus said heavily.

Devora wondered if Maximus realized he had fallen into Tobias' trap. He had spoken the very words of Tobias. Though the mines were a death trap, there was perhaps a chance of escape, but being sent to Seville meant certain death.

"I need those prisoners," Maximus stated again, looking at de Guzman.

"If anything goes wrong, Maximus, I will be the first to join ranks against you before the court of the ecclesiastics."

"Nothing will go wrong. I will see to this task myself, though I first intended to turn the production over to Don Favian."

Favian frowned, apparently unhappy at losing the position.

"When the treasure fleet arrives, the treasure house of Portobello will be bulging with bars of silver. I vow my position as viceroy upon it."

"You may also be risking your head," de Guzman said wryly. He looked over at the archbishop, as did Maximus. "Well, Lord Bishop?"

Andres appeared to reconsider after Maximus' passionate vow. "Let it be noted on official paper that I disagree with this decision. But if Don Maximus insists, and you are willing to allow for it, then I will not contest further." He looked at Maximus. "The success or failure of this mission rests entirely on your shoulders. As does your hope to receive the title Count of the Realm.

Hawkins and his crew of pirates are in your hand. I suggest, however, that they be sentenced tomorrow for the record."

Devora's tension slowly released from her body, leaving her weak. Bruce had at least escaped the inquisitors. There was much to give thanks to God for. A brief glance between her and Tobias convinced her he also was far from being disappointed.

The next day at the *carcel*, Tobias watched the prisoners file out for judgment, flanked fore and aft by helmeted and cuirassed soldiers. Bruce was ragged, his face growing a beard, his body covered with dried smears of blood. He and the others contrasted sharply with the haughtily garbed viceroy of Panama, Don Perez de Guzman, and members of his *oidores*. Even so, Tobias was proud of Bruce. Despite his condition he looked every inch a knighted warrior. He could tell from Maximus' scowl that he knew it as well, and was undoubtedly pleased over his decision to refuse Devora access to the sentencing. There was nothing about the undaunted "Hawkins" that would repulse any woman attracted to the courage of a buccaneer.

"So you are Hawkins?"

"I am Don Nicklas Valentin. The Spaniard who sired me by forcing my mother against her will is this man — your esteemed viceroy."

Maximus stood up, his voice as cold and sharp as steel. "Gag him!"

A soldier rushed over and stuffed a cloth in his mouth.

Maximus sat down again on the dais and straightened his white judicial wig, avoiding Bruce's even stare.

The soldiers and officers in the *carcel* turned to look at Bruce with shock since many had not realized Maximus was his father.

"He is 'Don Nicklas Valentin?'" squeaked the judge, astounded, and turned to look at Archbishop Andres for an answer. Andres' mouth twisted, and he said nothing.

"Your Excellency! Surely this pirate should be lashed here and now for such mocking words to your face —"

"He speaks the truth," Maximus admitted flatly. "This scoundrel, this traitor to Spain, this *pirate* was unfortunately sired by me. He is my 'son,'" Maximus stated.

Bruce held his eyes so long that Maximus turned an ugly color beneath his tanned skin.

"And I refuse to turn this wild jackal over

to anyone other than my own lawful jurisdiction as head of the viceroyalty of Peru. It
is I who will teach him a lesson. But lest you
think I shall coddle him — look, and see!
Nor will he be granted favor in the future. I
will see he pays tenfold for his crimes! He
will be sent to the Peruvian mines."

Tobias listened, his throat aching and dry
with emotion as Maximus sentenced Bruce
to seven years of hard labor. His crew received six years for following his orders.

Seven years, Tobias thought, devastated.
No man could survive so long in the mines.
His gaze darted toward Bruce. He con-
tinued to stare evenly at Maximus.

"Take him away," Maximus said. "I want
them aboard ship tonight. Tomorrow we sail
for Lima."

❧ 13 ❧

Lima

From the Gulf of Panama the viceroy's flagship and two accompanying Spanish war vessels, well equipped with guns and soldiers, transported the prisoners southward along the coast toward the mines of Peru.

As their voyage brought them toward Quito the coastline was now coming plainly in view for the first time since leaving Panama. Though the Pacific waters off the shores of South America were blue, the shallower shoal waters had emerald-green tints. Thick palms fringed the shoreline and farther inland was jungle. As the ships occasionally came closer to the coast Devora could see flocks of birds with plumage the colors of maize-yellow, scarlet, and topaz. She was even able to hear their screeching and singing which, filling her spirit, caused it to bloom with the joy and hope of their music. Man's fallen world still revealed so much of the beauty of God's handiwork.

Nor could uncertainty and danger destroy her reason to hope, to pray, to look up and trust. The hymn of the songbirds was clear: He who took such care with the birds was surely mindful of her dilemma. The bright feathers were like a living rainbow after the storm. *God,* she thought, *will always have a rainbow for us if we look for it.*

As the days passed the galleons continued to sail southward and, after crossing the equator, the warm tropical sea breezes suddenly turned cold. Amazed at the change, Devora came out on deck to find Sybella and Favian standing together. He placed a shawl around Sybella's shoulders and they stood near each other. She turned and walked to the other side of the ship, not wishing to interrupt a relationship that had seemed to make peace in the last few days.

She saw Tobias reading a small black book and occasionally looking off toward the distant Pacific Ocean. He saw her, and smiled a welcome. She walked up, drawing her shawl about her.

"The steaming tropical forest has vanished," she said. "I see little but dwarfed scrub trees and gray skies. It looks like rain."

Tobias pointed toward the arid, grim, dry land that wandered southward in stark beauty. "Ah, this section is like the Arabian desert for all the moisture it receives."

"But the clouds!" she protested.

He shook his head. "Clouds without water. There is naught but sand and rock. Seven-year droughts oft come to Peru. But the rainless clouds still hang by the mountains, promising, yet delivering nothing. Like the empty promises of false prophets! See those distant mountains? The mists settle upon them and the Lord sends what the Indians call *loma*. So the Lord keeps the cattle and llamas alive. He is good. He is the God of the tropics and the Shepherd of the dry desert. He gives to all food and drink."

She smiled and breathed in the air deeply, leaning against the ship's side. "I'm anxious to see your llamas. Catherina told me of them. She says they are like the desert camels. They can go for miles without water."

"Llamas are the wonder animals of Peru. We wouldn't know what to do without them. Tomorrow we will see the cormorants. We will be sailing through their nesting and breeding grounds. They are so without number that they blot out the sun."

She could hardly imagine that many, but Tobias' description proved true. She awoke the next morning and found her mother standing by the port window clutching her cloak about her as she stared transfixed. Devora heard the cry of the birds and the thundering and beating of thousands of strong wings.

"Let us go up and see," Catherina said, a sudden excitement in her voice. "It makes me feel adventurous again."

She helped her mother to the deck where they stood together, locked arm in arm looking up with great wonder. Birds! More than anyone could number, darkening the sky with their wings and filling the ear with their cry.

"Look!" Her mother pointed.

Over the port bow Devora recognized pelicans with their sacked beaks. Tobias came and pointed out other species: albatross, frigate birds, man-of-war birds, terns, and plovers.

"How many are there?" the countess asked him, amazed.

"The capitan has said that for the next twenty-five miles we will see birds riding the waves."

Devora laughed. "At last! There is enough of something good. Come, Mother, you must rest now and I'll bring us some breakfast. Tobias tells me that we shall be in Lima tomorrow."

The next morning Tobias pointed out the

island of San Lorenzo, and beyond it, the harbor of Callao. The ship slid into harbor, and on the wharf soldiers unloaded the prisoners to transport them inland to the mines.

Devora did not see Bruce, but watched an officer approach Maximus with a letter. A short time later Tobias informed her that Don Maximus would of necessity be riding on to the province of Alto Peru. The Audiencia, she had previously learned in Cartagena, was a legislative body headed by a president appointed by the king to administer affairs under the direction of the viceroy. In this case the president was Maximus' older brother, Don Roman. Among the Audiencia were the *odiores,* lawyers, who made up the viceroy's privy council.

"The president has asked him to come at once over some pressing problem they are facing there at the mines."

Maximus left with a guard of soldiers, and Favian assumed leadership over the general and his soldiers who were bringing the prisoners to Cuzco. Meanwhile, Tobias would escort Devora, the countess, and Sybella to the palace of the viceroy in Lima.

"I cannot stay on in Lima," Tobias told Favian. "I go to the old adobe house where I raised Nicklas. It's my God-given duty to minister to the Indians and anyone else I can aid there."

Favian showed displeasure. "Beware, my Uncle. You know what Maximus has said about a crusading spirit. He will not be sympathetic with the problems your religious convictions may unleash over the conditions at the mines."

Tobias smiled at him. "You tend to the work Maximus gave you, my son. Let me worry about the work I feel Christ has entrusted to me."

Favian shrugged, flipped his reins and rode over to Sybella. He said something to her but she lifted her chin and turned her head away. He frowned, then rode down the wharf to where the soldiers were lining up the chained prisoners for the march to Cuzco. Devora was shading her eyes, trying to pick Bruce out of the prisoners, but he appeared to be nowhere in sight.

Tobias' eyes flashed. "Maximus, Favian, and the general — they all expect these prisoners to work like beasts. Then they deplete their strength with a forced march through rugged terrain. And they withhold adequate nourishment. It is madness."

Devora's spirits were vexed over her own inability to help Bruce. How could the Valentins expect her to live in peace in Lima knowing he was in the mines? But at least Bruce was where he had wanted to be, and while not free to carry through his earlier plans at the mines, at least he was not on a ship sailing to the courts of inquisition.

"Oh Tobias, what hope do we have for Bruce? Is there any?"

He smiled wearily and patted her arm. "Our great God is the Father of mercies, and the God of all hope and comfort. We will plod on. That Bruce is being sent to Cuzco is no small victory."

"At the mines yes, though not as commander, but in chains," Devora whispered in a moment of discouragement. "How can any of us ever be free? Maximus holds all the weapons. Everything is to his advantage."

"No, not everything. As he will learn before too many weeks pass."

"What do you mean?" she whispered, but Tobias would not explain.

"We must wait patiently. Any rash move by me or Bruce will bring the authorities down upon us before we are able to defend ourselves."

His confidence, however mysterious, renewed her willingness to hope. Surely Tobias was moving behind the scenes to accomplish Bruce's orders. What they were, she did not know, and perhaps that was best.

Once again committing their needs to the Lord in prayer, she turned her attention to what might lie ahead for herself in Lima. At least Don Maximus would be away.

An ornamented, gilt-work coach drawn by some of the most majestic horses she had ever seen waited with African slaves to bring them the eight miles from Callao to Lima.

The horses followed the Rimac River. As Devora peered out the window at the strange new world into which she had come, she saw Indians in bright colored serapes and rebozos of brown, blue, white, and green walking the dusty road with their herds of shaggy llamas. She noted the thatched adobe huts and wondered if they were like the house that Bruce had been all but abandoned to as a child.

"The Indians, are they the Incas?"

Tobias looked genuinely troubled. "They are descendants of the ancient royal Incas. The language they speak is the Quechuan tongue. Cuzco was their royal city."

"Please, Uncle Tobias, let's not get into a lament over the evils done to the Indians," sighed Sybella, fanning her face.

"I thought Lima was the royal city," Devora said, surprised.

"Lima is fully a Spanish city, built by the first conquistadors after the Incas mistakenly told them about the Mountains of Silver. After that, it was like turning a wolf loose among lambs. The greed and cruelty of the conquistadors is indisputable. God will surely hold us accountable."

Sybella shrugged. "I will not stay at the palace long. I want to go to Cuzco, to the family hacienda. I want to ride the horses." She smiled at Devora for the first time, as though she might try to develop a friendship, as both of them were caught in ill-favored circumstances. "I was born at the hacienda. I love it there . . . it is peaceful. The mountains, the wind — the horses, they race like the wind. Nicklas used to —" she stopped, as though catching herself and looked out the window.

Tobias watched her sadly, then tapped his chin thoughtfully.

Except for asking questions about Lima, Devora preferred the silence. She drew her mind away from Bruce and wondered what would befall all of them in the months between now and the time for the mule train to bring the silver down the mountain to Portobello. She wished Maximus could be delayed indefinitely at Alto Peru!

Lima, City of the Kings, greeted her with its somber magnificence. She saw the spires of one of several cathedrals, the *cabildo,* the government building, and the *Casa Royal*, or the royal plaza where courts were often held. The climate, she noted, was warm and soft, and the first thing she thought of was Bruce working in the mines. But the mines were in the mountains. Would they be cool or hot?

The streets were crowded with hundreds of Indians with prized llamas. Soon the dirt streets gave way to avenues paved with stone. There were great, beautiful houses with barred and shuttered windows, such as the one she had stayed in at Cartagena.

Sybella began to talk, coming out of her sullen mood. Her liveliness had returned as though she had come home at last.

"Lima is no dull city. There is much grand pageantry. Parades, masked balls, much flirting. Ah, the handsome caballeros on their fine steeds dress in velvets with embroidery. They are not like the dull soldiers aboard the galleons."

"If Favian hears you speak so he will become jealous," Tobias teased his niece.

She sighed and fanned herself. "Favian is a burden. One I wish I did not have." She looked at Devora with a faint show of remorse in her eyes. "I should truly have gone back to Spain when I had the opportunity. Instead I deceived you and Nicklas. And where has it gotten me? As Uncle Tobias says, we reap what we sow."

"Does this sad confession mean you will lie no more but make the best of the life God has given you?" Tobias asked gently.

Sybella pursed her lips and stared at her black lace fan. She snapped it shut, then opened it again. "I do not intend to marry Favian no matter what Uncle Maximus says."

Devora preferred to look out the window. In the plaza square she saw the *charros* Sybella had told her about. They sat tall in their silver-inlaid saddles, with broad-brimmed hats also edged with silver. There was gold lace on their fancy jackets, some trimmed with fur, and all were embroidered handsomely. She tried to imagine Bruce in his teens growing up in Lima and Cuzco, handsomely riding fine horses in his Spanish garb. No wonder Sybella had fallen in love with him when they were young.

The men wore what looked to Devora like silver-buttoned leather leggings, and silver stirrups with spurs — everything was lavishly made of silver, as though the precious metal was as abundant as iron!

"Here in Lima, jewels are as common on hat bands as rhinestones," Sybella bragged. "Mere shop keepers wear pearls from San

Lorenzo and the Pearl Islands. Even the zambos wear belts of silver, and their skirts are fine cloth with ornaments. Oh how the nasty brood of pirates would delight to sack Lima! But alas, we are far from the Caribbean coast!"

"Zambos?" Devora asked.

"They are half Indian and half African."

The palace of the viceroy gleamed with carved silver ornamentation. Devora was overwhelmed by spacious salons holding large pieces of carved furniture in rosewood and jacaranda. The thick walls were tiled, and Spanish tapestries were displayed. There were great wooden portals, studded with iron, which opened into large stone courts surrounded by more galleries. In some places the balconies overhung the street under wide roof eaves, and again, all the windows were barred with iron grillwork.

Devora's chamber was on the second floor and she put her ailing mother to bed as soon as soldiers carried her up on the sedan chair. When they were alone in the cool shadowed room the countess allowed her anguish to reflect in her eyes. She held Devora's hand weakly.

"Lima, at last. I once dreamed of coming here with Robert to visit the royal Inca tomb

. . . now that I'm here, I would give anything to be in England with you. I've lived to taste the bitterness of my ways. In my self-sufficiency I imagined myself to be above defeat, otherwise I wouldn't have brought you so far into Spanish territory. Now I face man's most feared enemy, death." Fear surfaced from the depths of her eyes. "How it interrupts our vaunted plans! And Robert — how I depended on him! Folly! I was so confident he would return. Now, like Lady Marian, I will die here and be buried here. I shall never see beloved England again. Worst of all, Robert and I will leave you here alone in the heart of Spanish territory to the plans of Maximus. I had anticipated you would be the bride of the handsome Don Nicklas I met in Seville."

Devora could not endure the thought of marriage to Maximus. Yet she had already forgiven her mother's selfish plans. She was now cast upon the mercy of God, and what better place to find herself?

Devora tried to smile as she stroked her mother's feeble hand. "Don't you remember the stories of Moses and Joseph? How they were placed into circumstances they had no control over? Yet God had plans for them. Naturally I'm not as important as they, but He cares for the smallest of His own. Let us lay the past to rest once and for all, Mother. You may have planned all this for silver and political gain, but God is sovereign in His purposes. He overrules in the lives of those who worship Him for good."

"I have no such confidence, my dear."

"Nor have I, much of the time," Devora whispered honestly. "Sometimes I tremble in fear as circumstances seem overwhelming, yet Scripture encourages me to stand firm in faith. And you can do the same. His word is the source of peace and strength, telling us God's good plan for our lives is never frustrated by the magnitude of circumstances. If I'm here at this time — I choose to believe it is part of His overall plan for me. There are lessons to be learned, faith to be tested so it can grow stronger, so that in the end I might understand more fully His faithfulness."

Devora spoke these words, and her heart believed them, yet her flesh was weak and fears of all sorts mocked her from the shadows of her mind. *You speak as a hypocrite. Do you truly believe God brought you here? Why, if He did, would He allow all this to happen to you? Why are so many others living happier lives than you? And Bruce! Do you actually think your prayers are going to set him free? He will die, just like your mother. And then*

246

you will be left here, alone. Just like Bruce's mother and . . .

Within a few hours of her arrival in Lima, Devora discovered that Maximus had guards watching her every move. The countess lifted the pistol from beneath her robe. "Take this and keep it near you . . . Nicklas would approve."

Devora had no idea how long she would be under guard, or just when Maximus would return to resume their social life. Sybella boasted of the spectacle-loving Limians whose lifestyle was indolent and carefree, with slaves attending to their every need. "Some are so lazy that slaves carry them in sedan chairs wherever they wish to go. Another slave walks beside her mistress carrying a parasol for shade."

"I wouldn't want to live like that," said Devora.

"Nor I, but I do want to attend the festivities. It is a shame we must wait for Maximus."

During the day Devora heard the frequent ringing of bells and learned that they were a call to Mass, to prayers, to saintly festivals, and they were also used at the close of the day to indicate when the Angelus was to be recited.

"The miraculous doings of the saints become legends," Tobias had told her. "The legends are passed on from mouth to mouth among the people of Lima. I fear much of their zeal is also colored with superstition. They see saints appearing in the clouds to give aid in any trouble; they believe in relics of saints and in the spells of sorcerers."

But all was not grave. Sybella explained how Spanish ladies went out onto the streets, their costumes designed to shield them from the eyes of men, "but we make of it a provocative disguise. We only show our feet below our silken skirts —" and she produced a skirt, laying it on the bed for Devora to see.

Devora gasped. "But . . . it's narrow! It shows our hips and stomach —"

Sybella smiled, and sighed. "Yes, our curves. And from head to waist we wear a black silk manto."

Devora examined it curiously. "There's only a small hole for one eye to look through."

Sybella laughed. "An inviting, flirtatious eye peeps out. In this disguise we go to Mass —"

"You're not serious, to church?"

"Yes, of course. And at church we exchange secretive glances with the handsomest young caballeros lounging in the church portals. We sometimes go to balls in the costume too, so that no one knows who we are. The disguised señoritas and señoras are called *tapadas*."

"Meaning?" Devora asked, smiling.

"Meaning 'wrapped up.' Ah yes, we used to have such a merry time in spite of the restrictions imposed by the men of our families. Every day we used to get a chance to escape confinement from behind the closed balconies. We go out for the afternoon *paseo*, a dear Spanish custom from the mother country. We are permitted to go out in carriages, or sedan chairs, just as long as we are swathed in mantillas. Then we're paraded through the Plaza park. Sometimes groups of young men wait for us on the other side of the bridge over the Rimac River." A far off glow came to her eyes. "Once, years ago, Nicklas met me there. . . ."

Devora's smiled faded. She refused the bait, and instead, picked up the manto and placed it over her head. She peered at herself in the mirror and saw one violet-blue eye looking out.

"If Maximus were here we could attend the theater," Sybella continued. "The theater is always attended by the viceroy. It's expected of him. Your English Shakespeare is nothing. Wait until you see the stately dramas of Calderon de la Barca, Spain's great playwright. And all the lords, dons, and doñas dressed in costumes and jewels." She looked at Devora and suddenly asked bluntly: "Maximus wants you to marry him. I know — I can tell by the way he looks at you. What will you do?"

Devora laid the manto back on the bed. "I love one man. I will refuse Don Maximus."

"He may not permit you to refuse. But think of how powerful and rich you will become."

Thinking instead of Bruce, Devora walked sadly to the latticed balcony and looked out on the street as a cavalcade of handsomely dressed Spanish gentlemen rode by on white horses. "No matter what Maximus may give me, if he takes away Bruce, I shall be a pauper."

"Tobias is working to bring about Nicklas' escape."

Devora looked at her. Sybella shook her head. "You needn't worry. I'd never betray Nicklas. What has happened to him came from my mistake, but I never intended to harm him."

"But you threatened his grandmother and me with that letter."

"Yes, but I don't suppose Favian has told you that he was there that night, that he overheard everything. You had no sooner been taken to the *Magdalena* when he confronted me in the house. He learned about the letter and told Archbishop Andres. So you see, it was not I that betrayed Nicklas." She walked to the door to leave, the manto on her arm. She looked back.

"I should like to make a trip to Cuzco to the mines. I would like to see Nicklas . . . if I go, would you make the trip with me?"

"You know I would go in a moment, but what will Maximus do if he finds out?"

She smiled wryly. "He will be very angry, but he is still in Alto Peru with his brother."

"You mean Don Roman?"

"Yes, he was there that night in Cartagena after Nicklas first arrived. He is the new president of the Audiencia, under the authority of Maximus. Together they will do mostly what pleases them in Cuzco. I shall make plans for a trip to the hacienda next week. Unless," she said dourly, "Uncle Maximus returns first to stop me."

Favian remained at the mines and his absence would of necessity be extended. Devora was kept further in the dark when Tobias also disappeared. She believed he was searching for some way to give Bruce the opportunity to escape. Tobias had allies throughout Lima and among the Inca Indians, as did Bruce, who was in favorable territory having grown up near Cuzco in the adobe hut. The idea caused Devora's heart to beat faster. Perhaps all was not lost after all as long as Tobias remained at liberty and Sybella wanted Bruce released from his chains. The Incas, for the most part, disliked the dominating Valentin family, even as they loathed the conquistadors who had come on ships and taken their kingdom by deceit and cruelty.

Sybella, however, was less free than she had anticipated. "Uncle Maximus seems to have the upper hand," Sybella complained, two days later. "He arrested my personal guards back in Cartagena after Favian told him what happened at Lillian's house. I don't know why Favian would betray me, except perhaps to restrict my activities. But I shall get my way, wait and see."

The next day Sybella started having unrelenting tantrums with the soldiers that Maximus left to guard her and Devora in the palace. Devora heard her shouting at the viceroy's guards.

"I am a Ferdinand! Do you know what that means? In Spain I could have you thrown in the dungeons. I will not be treated with such contempt."

"I am sorry, Señora."

"You will be sorrier still before this is over."

"Yes, Señora."

"If you refuse me my own coach and guards here in Lima, then I will still go to the hacienda at Cuzco. There I will confront the viceroy himself, and Don Favian."

"I am sorry, Señora, but we cannot let you leave the palace. We are under strict orders from his Excellency that you and the English señorita are to remain until he returns."

"Until he returns? And when will that be? A month from now? Two?"

"I do not know, Señora, but you must stay in Lima. If you do not, I lose my head."

As it turned out, it was two months before Maximus returned to Lima. No sooner had he arrived from the Audiencia in Alto Peru, than Tobias also returned. He'd been working with the Indians near Cuzco, he said, and visiting a small native church that he'd first begun when Bruce had been living in the adobe hut about four miles inland from the spacious Valentin hacienda.

Devora didn't doubt Tobias had been about the Lord's work, but she also believed he'd been laying plans for Bruce's escape. She was convinced of this when she was bidden by Maximus to come down and join him on the balcony. When she appeared she walked in on a discussion with Tobias. . . .

✺ 14 ✺

Love's Unending Devotion

"I tell you, Maximus, they all prefer to die rather than exist under the treatment Favian permits."

"Death is preferable to chains? Is that it? Of course, their honor demands it of them," he mocked. "Pirates! Bah, they are fit only for the gallows."

"Chains are but half of their humiliation. Their backs are marked with lashes that do not heal, drawing flies. They are denied adequate food and water. How long will you allow this sin to continue toward the son of your loins?"

Maximus paced, hands on hips, his dark, handsome face showing lines of moodiness. He stopped when he saw Devora standing in the doorway. His impolite gaze whipped over her. "Go back to your chamber. I will call for you again later."

"Let her stay," Tobias said. "She should hear about the conditions which the viceroy permits his soldiers to wreak upon the political and religious prisoners of Spain."

"Am I the king of Spain?" Maximus roared. "Every ordinanza is issued from Seville. I am here to carry them out, not create them!"

"Excuses, Maximus. You are as a sovereign here in Peru. If injustice and cruelty exist, you stand as guilty before God as the king of Spain as you enforce the evil. To do nothing is as wicked as cracking the whip!"

"Harangue! You know the plight I'm in. If I don't get that silver ready for the treasure fleet, it is I who will be called before Holy Seville."

Devora understood that the royal insistence on increasing revenue from the New World inevitably meant more forced labor upon the Indians in the mines, the forests, and at the haciendas. The early laws issued by Spain for protecting the natives would be ignored by the dons and members of the Audencia.

"You err in trusting Favian to get the silver produced. Favian is not up to such a task."

"I will be going to the hacienda myself now that I've finished the work at the Audencia. Favian will answer to me."

"It will be too late by then," Tobias warned.

Something in his tone caused Devora concern as she looked at him. Maximus too gave him thoughtful attention.

"The Indians are sick. The illness spreads throughout Cuzco and Potosi," Tobias said gravely of the primary silver towns with their adjoining mines. "And in protest of Favian's cruelties and indifference to the Incas, Nicklas refuses to order his crew to cooperate with Favian."

For a silent moment Maximus stood there as if flabbergasted. Then a ruddy color flared in his handsome face. " 'Nicklas refuses' to cooperate? 'He refuses' to order 'his' crew to work? He has no freedom to refuse any order by his brother. He has no crew — he is a slave!"

Tobias paced the tiled salon, shaking his head. "You have always underestimated Nicklas. You do so again. He has the allegiance of his old buccaneering crew and there's little anyone can do about it, least of all Favian."

"Favian has my vested authority until I arrive. He can order their death by torture if he so chooses."

Tobias turned sharply. "That is my point — he already has."

Maximus grew so still that Devora could hear his breathing, or was it her own heart thudding so loudly, so painfully? She was ready to plead with Maximus to stop the carnage when Tobias added: "Two men were tortured to death in front of Nicklas, yet he did not relent. An Indian and one of Nicklas' crew from the *Revenge*. Such insanity only hardens his heart and his pirates. I tell you, Maximus, they are angry enough at the cruelty inflicted in the mines to all die before they relent and take up their picks and shovels. If you want that silver you'll need to come to terms with Nicklas."

Maximus' face hardened stubbornly. "He will either submit, or they *will* die, one by one."

"That is wicked and foolish. Will you play games with human life, Maximus? Not even a beast should be put to death without a valid reason! All life is precious. It comes from God. Are you now declaring yourself a god that you would slaughter men who refuse to bow the knee to you?"

Maximus stormed to the balcony and threw open the doors to let in the cooler air. "I will go there. And I will deal with this. But I warn you, Tobias, Nicklas and the prisoners of Spain will work, or every last one of them will die before his eyes."

Tobias stood, his silver hair glinting in the candlelight. "Unless you and he come to agreement, you may need to follow through on that threat."

Maximus' eyes flickered hotly. "Nicklas is a condemned prisoner. The murderous pirate dogs with him are also condemned prisoners. I will make no agreement with 'Captain Hawkins.'"

Tobias analyzed him for a steady moment, then turned to Devora. She held in her despair, but knew she must look pale when sympathy reflected in Tobias' gaze. "A word of advice, little one. Do not go to the Cuzco hacienda, but remain here in Lima."

Maximus strode toward them. "I shall make that decision. I've already decided she will come with me to the Valentin hacienda." He looked at her with a slight challenging smirk. "The lovely señorita wishes to ride horses with Sybella, I am told. Far be it from me to deny her such pleasures. She has been confined to the palace these two months in my absence. It is time for mountain air and sunshine. We must put the rosiness back into her pale cheeks."

Tobias started to protest, but Devora laid a hand on his arm, her eyes pleading with his for peace.

"It is all right, Tobias. I wish to go to Cuzco."

"You see?" Maximus taunted smoothly.

"The young woman approves of my company, Tobias."

That was not the reason of course, and she was sure Maximus knew that, but she said nothing and continued to look at Tobias, trying to keep him from further confrontation.

"Will Sybella be with Devora?" Tobias challenged Maximus, looking at him evenly.

Maximus smiled. "Would I seek to take Devora to the hacienda alone?" He bowed lightly. "I shall even arrange for the countess to come along. And of course, I can depend upon you to be there, my brother, preaching the judgments of God upon my hellish ways."

"You are wrong, Maximus. I have warned you too often. The Lord's Spirit does not always strive with a rebellious man once he has hardened his heart." He spoke quietly as he turned away, "That is the last warning you will get from me."

Devora looked at Maximus and saw the whiteness showing around his tight mouth as he stared after Tobias. The sound of the friar's sandals echoed down the outer hall as he walked away.

His warning must have sobered Maximus, for his arrogance diminished and a look of concern worried his brow. He appeared to forget Devora's presence and walked over to the desk where he took a cigar from a silver box and used a candle to light it.

Devora was still standing by the door when several moments later he became aware of her again.

"I suppose you think I have an iron heart. That I have little capacity for tenderness or mercy."

It would have been easy to toss him a barbed remark, but each rebuttal gave him reasons to unleash further harsh treatment against Bruce. She kept silent.

He poured himself a goblet of wine.

"I should like to go back to my chamber."

"No," he snapped. "I desire your company. Come, sit down."

She tensed, watching him. His gaze fell over her. "You have taken no pains to adorn yourself. Why?" came his blunt question. His eyes showed irritated amusement. "Are you afraid I shall not be able to contain myself?"

"No. But I have no cause to adorn myself since I've been cloistered these last months. Perhaps you thought I would try to escape to Barbados in your absence?"

"I have no concern over that. You are like a lioness easily baited by the scent of her cub. Nicklas is at Cuzco. That is why you consented to go with me to the hacienda. You hope to ride one of the stallions to see him."

That he understood only troubled her the more, but she refused to show concern, and lifted a brow. "You seem to understand so much, Don Maximus, why can you not see the wrong in treating Nicklas this way?"

"You need no answer to that. We both know Nicklas. There is nothing I could do now to win his allegiance to me as a father."

"I don't think that's true. If you really wanted to win him, you —"

"No, it is true. I understand now the bitterness that has grown in his heart toward me since boyhood. He has planned this betrayal for years. He was never loyal to me, to Spain — even when he was knighted by the king in Seville, his plans were all made to reap vengeance."

Her heart ached with frustration. "That may be true, but you made it all so easy for him to turn against you, Maximus. If you had tried to reach out to him at all — when he was at the military school, or even when he arrived in Cartagena — things could have been different. If you had asked him to forgive you it might have begun a healing process. It wouldn't have happened quickly, but it would have been a beginning. It would have been an ointment for the wounds that have lain festering all these years."

"Words! Like Tobias you toss them like rose petals! They are empty and vain. Ask his forgiveness? Nay, never. It is my *son* who has betrayed *me*. He has shamed my name before Spain. And now I am left to cover his tracks to save my own head! He will work, and his crew, or they will wish they had never been born!"

She went to him. "You suggested to me aboard the *Santa Rosa* that you would be lenient with Nicklas, yet you have done nothing to show grace."

"I have spared his life."

"Seven years in the mines. Which of your forced laborers has lived even two years, I wonder? How many die monthly?"

"Enough!"

She could have said more to unveil his cruelties, but she would leave that to Tobias. She turned to walk out but Don Maximus went after her, grabbing her arm and whirling her about, his black eyes blazing. "I am the viceroy! I did not give you permission to turn your haughty back upon me and walk out."

"I did not know I was haughty. But I wish no more of your words, Excellency!"

"Maximus," he gritted. "You will call me by my name."

"You just rebuked me for being haughty. Now you tell me I am not familiar enough."

He grabbed her, pulling her into his arms, this time kissing her roughly.

"So you wish to save his neck do you? Answer me," he insisted when she remained silent.

Her palm itched to slap his arrogant face, but she swallowed back her bitter words.

"Yes."

He waited a moment, satisfied, studying her face.

She stared back gravely, her violet-blue eyes darkened like jewels.

"You are angry because I kissed you. Because unlike Nicklas I did not plead for it, but took it."

"You deceive yourself, Excellency. I willingly kissed him the first time aboard the *Revenge* in his cabin because I was drawn by his character, and now I love him as I will never love another man. No matter how you use your selfish power, your aggrandized glory, I will love him. I will love him though you turn him into a scarred mass of flesh! I will love him though you force me to marry you and bear your unwanted child! There is nothing you can do to my soul nor my body that will destroy my heart's devotion to your son!"

Maximus stared down at her, his hands clenching and unclenching, his face filled with a pain she had not known he could display.

"You were a fool to tell me that, Devora. Now, eventually, when I am through with him at the mines, Nicklas must die."

"Do you think his death would change my love? Love is stronger than death, Don Maximus."

Maximus turned ruddy, then the color of clay. His mouth tightened and she saw his heartbeat throbbing in his muscled neck. As he stared down at her in dangerous silence, Devora turned and, with head high, walked from the salon.

Maximus heard her steps walking away on the tile. This one could not be defeated, he thought savagely, amazed. A mere woman had defeated him. Her honor, her virtue, had left him without armor. She was like Marian. Like Marian who had unwillingly, yet with dignity, given him a son, and to her dying breath had retained her faith in Christ, her love for things holy and good, and had died without cursing him, but praying for him. These were weapons he could not defeat. They frightened him as the hostile words of an opponent never could. It was a strength that defied his own brute power. He might humiliate her and Nicklas, he might even kill him and make her watch the spectacle. But even that, he was sure would not defeat Devora, not any more than chains could defeat his son. No wonder they had been drawn together. She was willing even to marry him to spare Nicklas' life.

Wearily he returned to the desk, refilled his goblet and finished the strong, fiery drink in a few continuous gulps. He stared at the decanter of wine, then hurled it across the room, smashing it against the wall.

❧ 15 ❧

Arrival at Cuzco

The next morning a large mule train waited to leave Lima, their packs piled high with food-stuffs and water, weapons and mining equipment. Myriads of silver bells tinkled musically beneath the blazing Peruvian sky. They had begun the long journey that would bring them up the steep rocky trail into the mountains toward the royal Inca city of Cuzco, conquered by Spain in 1530.

Spain's military invasion of the Indies had depended heavily upon the majestic Spanish horses bred and shipped from Andalusia, Spain. But the conquistadors maintained their conquest and strengthened their economic hold by depending almost entirely upon the mule. It was the mule trains that supplied essential links between Nombre de Dios and Panama, between Lima and Cuzco. Whether transporting silver down the mountains to the waiting treasure fleet or bringing up foodstuffs, without mules they were nearly helpless.

As they plodded along, Devora held the reins and settled her fibrous sunhat, riding just in front of Tobias. The countess was carried by slaves in a sedan chair, and Sybella was ahead near Don Maximus. Devora was curious about Cuzco, not just because Bruce had been raised near the mines, but because of her interest in the great Inca Empire. It was to her enrichment that Tobias knew so much about the Indians, for he had secretly ministered to many of them while Bruce was growing up among them. Did their friendship in any way play into Bruce's plans for escape?

"At Cuzco you will still see the city's ancient Inca flavor. Though many wealthy Spaniards live there, they have not been able to obliterate all their culture. They have built on the foundations of the Inca civilization."

"How did they defeat the Inca warriors?"

"Partly by superior weapons and war horses, and partly by deceit. They promised the Inca king peace, but they broke their word. Yes, they defeated them, and we, the sons and grandsons of the conquistadors, have stayed to make the Indians our servants."

She saw his anger and allowed the moment to settle before asking more questions. She learned that the conquistadors, for the most part, had come from pastoral pursuits, grazing semi-nomadic flocks and herds in the arid uplands of Castile. This was the area of Spain where the Valentins had come from. In the New World they had carried on the mastery of flocks and herds on horseback, receiving large land grants down in the valleys by Seville. These dons then turned their hacienda plantations over to indentured stewards, who used forced labor from the Indian and African slaves to produce sugar and wheat and to raise cattle and sheep.

"The various Indian groups labor under worse conditions than did their forbears who were enslaved by the Incas."

She looked at him, mildly surprised. "By the Incas?"

Tobias pursed his lips. "Yes, they slaughtered and made slaves of the peaceful Indians when they came here. In a way the Incas too were conquistadors. The word 'Inca' means chief or king. Later 'Inca' came to include all the other Indian peoples which they conquered. Greed and cruelty are not symptoms of Spain alone. But that in no way excuses our sin, my child. God holds us both accountable. It is the way of fallen mankind."

"Where did they come from?"

"Most likely Asia, during the eleventh century — the time of Europe's First Crusade to take Jerusalem from the Turks. The first conquistador arrived from Spain in 1520."

"Pizzaro?"

"Yes, he was a Spanish soldier who came in search of gold. He reached Cuzco around 1527. Once he shrewdly determined the amount of wealth available, he returned to Spain to gather an army. He returned around 1533 with soldiers and attacked Cuzco and captured the Inca king, taking him prisoner. The Inca king offered Pizzaro a room full of gold for his freedom."

Tobias lapsed into thoughtful silence.

She frowned, for she could see where the path was leading. "I assume a room full of gold was not enough?"

"Perhaps, but Seville then wanted a room full of gold also, and so did all the other conquistadors. Pizzaro took the gold from the Inca king, but instead of releasing him as he had promised, he killed him."

Devora snapped the reins. "I knew it. And when the gold ran out it was silver."

"And the silver has not yet run out, so

Spain uses Indians and Africans, and all manner of political and religious prisoners, to work the mines and the haciendas. And with each passing year the population shrinks, and the coffers of Seville grow fatter."

"The silver is used to finance the religious wars in Europe?"

"Mostly, though much is kept here by the dons, and spent lavishly in Spain as well."

Devora glanced ahead at Maximus and imagined him as Pizzaro. Yes, he would make a fitting conquistador, she thought. If he could send his son to the mine, he could betray the Inca king for a room full of gold. *What of me?* she found herself wondering. *I do not want a room full of gold, but there are other things in life I want badly. If tempted by my heart's desire, would I too compromise?* Only a month ago she would have said no. Now as she thought of Bruce under the oxhide whip, she frowned. She had already implied to Maximus that she might marry him if he would free Bruce — and she had done this despite Bruce asking her to promise him that she wouldn't. She knew that all fail to live up to the righteous standards of God, each in his or her own way. She thanked God for His grace as she thought of Romans 4:7: "Blessed are they whose iniquities are forgiven, and whose sins are covered." Even Pizzaro's sin could have been forgiven, had he ever been drawn to repent and trust.

"Afterward Spain took control of the Inca Empire," Tobias was saying. "And by the 1570s the Inca Empire's last resistance against Spain died out. Peru became part of the expanding empire of Spain."

As they journeyed toward Cuzco during the days that followed Devora saw Indians living in communal mountain villages farming according to their custom in mountainside terraces, waiting to be commandeered by the Spanish hildagos who could have them rounded up like cattle during harvest time.

"The Audencia allows the use of Indians for service on their valley rancheros. It is supposed to be for the good of Mother Spain, but it is also for the private benefit of the dons."

"But what of their own little farms, their herds?"

"Naturally such selfish actions leave the Indians little recourse but to neglect their own farms. It is left to the women, if they are not also taken. They are put in the weaving shops, called obrajes. The first viceroy of Peru was Mendoza. He introduced the wonderful merino sheep with its fine wool. This created a woolen textile business which earned a sinister reputation for mistreatment of the laborers in the workshops. The women are forced to live and work as slaves. Believe me, Devora, the hildago has brought with him from Spain a disdain for manual labor. If he can get others to do his work, he will. Like Don Favian, they become caballeros in fancy clothes, become experts at sword play, and are quite indolent."

"And the mines . . ." Devora frowned.

"Ah yes, nothing good can be said of the forced labor in the mines. This was called the *mita,* first begun by the Incas themselves. The Indians are taken from their homes to work there under savage conditions. Thousands of Indians have died."

"And now Bruce is there . . ."

"Perhaps not for long," Tobias said quietly, since Maximus was too far away to hear them.

"Can you tell me what you have planned?"

"It is best we do not discuss it. I will only tell you that the labor force of the Indians has become too ill to work . . . perhaps it is typhoid." He looked at her with a wry twinkle in his eyes. From this, she understood that the Indians were not actually sick.

"But what if Maximus and Favian whip them and make them work?"

His slight smile vanished as he looked ahead toward Maximus. "He will not do so. Not if he knows he needs them. They are the only workers he will have to produce the silver for the fleet. Favian is already behind schedule."

Her heart suddenly felt lighter and she actually smiled. "And you had something to do with Favian's difficulties, I assume?"

"Let us hope and pray that Maximus does not think so. I have never done well with a pick!"

As Maximus rode to the side of the trail and waited for them, Devora and Tobias lapsed into silence.

Above her head on the rocky trail were herds of llamas. They indeed did look something like a camel, except they had no humps. Most of them looked to be about four feet tall. They were white, brown, black, or white with black or brown markings.

"The llama is an amazing animal," Tobias said with a chuckle. "They know exactly how much weight they can carry. I once saw a soldier load one of them with too much baggage. It behaved like a mule and refused to budge. When it had become weary of the soldier's stupidity, it showed its feelings by spitting a green fluid in his face. But as soon as the soldier removed but a small part of the poor beast's burden, the llama got to its feet and obediently carried the heavy load over the trail."

Devora smiled and decided she liked llamas. Their whitish wool stood out against the azure sky and bare brown plateaus.

When at last they came up over the ridge to a pinnacle on the trail, she gazed in the far distance at the glorious Andes, crowned with perpetual white.

Along the narrow and steep trail there were plants and wildlife she had never seen in England or Barbados. Tobias, an expert on this area of Peru, told her of mahogany, cedar, and walnut trees, though high in the mountains she saw only pockets of alpine grasses.

"There are jaguar and monkeys in the jungle, but here in the mountains we see puma, llamas, alpacas, chinchilla, rodents, and snakes."

Remembering the vipers she had come across near Panama, she shuddered.

Traveling slowly, a week had passed before they ever came in sight of Cuzco.

274

During this time Maximus, for the most part, avoided her. At night around the campfire she attended her mother. Sybella too, stayed close. Two Quecha Indian women had also been brought along to attend the countess and a complaining Sybella.

"I do not remember the journey from the hacienda down to Lima being this trying."

"You were not as spoiled and hard to please back then as you are now," Maximus said.

At last they arrived at the narrow streets of Cuzco. Devora saw Spanish houses built on top of ancient Inca walls. The mule she rode was jostled by llamas that were being herded by Incas in their colorful serapes. There was a great crowd and some sort of religious celebration was going on at the cathedral.

"We have arrived at the feast of Corpus Christi," Maximus told her, pleased. "We will stop."

The feast was celebrated in the Plaza de Armas where the Incas had once gathered long ago to share in their pagan Feast of the Sun. Devora saw a large crowd gathered and an Inca carrying a glittering image of a Roman saint around the Plaza.

She could see why it might be easy for the

Indians to have exchanged their allegiance from the Inca's worship of the sun to the flashing gold and silver images of the Roman Church.

"In their own minds there is little difference," Maximus told her.

The truth of Christianity is sadly missing, thought Devora. *Superstition and imagery have replaced the knowledge of God.*

Maximus had exchanged his mule for his Andalusian white stallion, which had been brought out from the hacienda and was waiting for him, cared for by a group of Spanish peasant boys. The boys had been sleeping in the street for two weeks waiting for his arrival, they told him in rapid Spanish. The eldest breathlessly informed Maximus how they had nearly lost the horse to a bandit who tried to steal it.

"But we caught him, Don Valentin. He is being held by the mayor."

"Good. We'll hang him." Maximus looked down at Devora, deliberately trying to provoke her. "You will ride with me."

"Thank you, but I prefer the mule."

"Do not vex me," he gritted. "Obey."

Reluctantly she climbed down from the mule and avoided his eyes as she placed her foot in the silver stirrup. He pulled her up to sit in front of the saddle, slipping a strong arm about her waist. He whispered into her hair: "This is where you belong. In my arms."

She stiffened at his touch. He laughed and only tightened his hold. "Do you think your coolness troubles me? Before we ride on to the hacienda, we will first visit the cathedral for good luck. Tobias! Jorge! To the Holy Square!"

Devora was indignant. "You are impossible, Don Maximus. You will attend the festival for 'good luck'?"

"It is a custom. We will not be long."

"That's not what I meant. One does not go to church for good luck. And God does not bless unrighteousness no matter how religious the festival might appear or how many gold and silver statues we carry about."

He laughed. "You amuse me. But do not begin your preaching now. I would think you'd wish to attend. You could light a candle to one of the protective saints to aid your beloved slave who digs my silver."

Again she stiffened, and he reached around and drew her face toward his. The dark burning eyes mocked her, but were irritated as well. "I could show my ownership and intentions right now before everyone by kissing you. Do you dare me?"

She jerked her chin free. "I have already asked God to help your son. And I would never dare you to provocation, your Excellency."

"You are wise. But it will do you no good now. I have made up my mind, my charming violet-eyed señorita. I care for you. I admit it. And anything I want, I take. And so I will take you from my arrogant, buccaneering son."

"If he is arrogant, he gets it from his father."

"You remind me of his mother. That is why I find you fascinating."

"Could it be, Excellency, that it is she that you really love and miss more than you will admit? And so you only transfer your feelings to me?"

"I do not care to trouble my thoughts about it."

"If you told Nicklas that you loved his mother he might change his mind about you."

"I told you in Lima — our relationship was not the way he thinks. His grandmother lied."

"You should tell him so, if that is true."

The balconies of the Spanish houses around the plaza were hung with tapestries and filled with waving people. When they realized that their viceroy had also arrived home to Cuzco, the uproar was hysterical. People ran into the street and surrounded his white horse, trying to kiss his hand, and some fell on their knees. Women wept emotionally.

Devora was dismayed and frightened. The sight sickened her, but Maximus seemed to take it all calmly enough as though he deserved the adoration. He waved at them, and then gestured for the soldiers to clear the narrow street. They moved in at once bringing order and roughing up the people, but they were so hysterical no one seemed to mind the harsh treatment.

Spaniards in their stiff clothes mingled with Indians in the crowd. When Maximus reached the cathedral square, Devora saw an Indian noble in the procession pulling a gilded image of the Virgin in a gold cart.

Tobias rode up beside them, his dusty friar's tunic tossing in the breeze. "You may lose your honor in the Peruvian mud if Nicklas finds out your intentions toward the Señorita."

His face hardened. "We will not discuss that now. Devora, get down, but wait for me by the door of the cathedral. You will join me there."

She climbed down, anxious to get away. She spotted her mother's sedan chair moving beside the procession. She walked alongside of her mother down the narrow stone street toward the cathedral.

"He is like a king in Cuzco," Catherina said worriedly. "Who can deny him? I could almost wish you were not so lovely."

Devora was very worried about her mother. She noticed how the countess was breathing with more difficulty, and that her eyes were hollow, bespeaking a worsening condition. "You should never have come here, Mother."

Catherina tried to smile. "I'll live, if only to see you safely out of here and on your way to Barbados with Tobias. He has promised me you will escape. The question remaining is when? I fear nothing will happen until the treasure fleet arrives. Until the mule train from the mines brings the silver. And that is at least four months from now. Somehow we must see you escape Maximus until then." She sighed. "I've been thinking of the royal Inca tomb Maximus promised me and Robert . . . maybe I shall see it after all."

The so-called Holy Square of the Incas was now called the Plaza de Armas. The Roman cathedral had become the center of Cuzco's religious festivals instead of the

Inca Sun temple called the "Coricancha."

She had no choice but to enter the cathedral on the arm of the viceroy while the citizens of Cuzco gaped and applauded, waving as though they were little gods. Her heart felt sick.

Inside the cathedral things were still as the noise on the plaza was left behind.

"As you can see," he told her in a low but proud voice, "the clergy of the Roman Church has obliterated the memory of the golden sun worship of the Incas. Instead, they built this magnificent cathedral in its place. There are many gilded churches in Cuzco."

Devora remembered the temple of Solomon built in Jerusalem. None of these cathedrals, however beautiful, could compare. Yet God allowed Babylon to come and destroy the temple and bring the people to Babylon. Gold meant nothing to Him when the people's hearts were far from Him; worship was offensive unless the worshipers' hearts were devoted to Him in love and obedience.

She knew Maximus would not understand and remained silent.

They stopped in the aisle. Devora looked about in the silence. She did not sense reverential awe, but the overpowering will of

Maximus. He took her hand in his, and she wondered if he would notice that it was cold and damp from nervousness.

Maximus showed her the altars of pure gold and silver. She gazed upon the rich carvings of gold leaf. The furniture too was carved in rare wood, and the gold and silver images of Rome's religious saints glittered brightly in the light coming from many candles. Outwardly the sight was beautiful. But she knew that the gold and silver had been dug by prisoners under the fierce lash of an oxwhip. Forming the ill-gotten goods into an altar did not make them holy.

"All these saints were brought from Spain," Maximus whispered. "They are now patron saints of the Cuzco churches. England has nothing, compared to Spain," he boasted. "When your Queen Elizabeth I took office she had to hold up a Bible and kiss it."

"You think she did that because she lacked for something better? The queen was saying to all Europe that it was the God of the Bible that made England great. That God had saved England in the war with Spain and France and from those who opposed believers of the Reformed faith."

"England, a great nation?" he mocked. "That small piece of land could be crushed beneath the boot of our king if he wished to bother."

"Indeed? He has tried. King Philip sent the great and magnificent Spanish Armada against Queen Elizabeth's 'small piece of land,' and it was the God of Martin Luther who sent the great wind which destroyed his fleet."

Maximus looked down at her, but he did not become angry. "You are beautiful, Devora, when your eyes gleam like violet gems."

She looked away. She had expected his anger, not his passion.

"Before the mule train loads the silver to carry it down to the treasure fleet in Portobello, we will marry here. You will be with me when I sail to Seville."

Her chest tightened but she wisely said nothing. She had already said too much. She had best put her faith in the God she boasted of, instead of in her resistance to Maximus.

❦ 16 ❦

The Tide Begins to Turn

Bruce had now been at the mines for two months. He lay awake, chained to the other prisoners. The problem of escape occupied his every waking thought. He and Tobias had made plans, but would they work? And if not, what of Devora?

He had some peace because Tobias had been able to let him know that Devora was safe at the Valentin Hacienda. Safe from Maximus, but for how long?

The mines were reached by a steep, mountainous trail that serpentined its way down the sides of the cliffs. Bruce paid close attention to the mule traffic that traversed back and forth, knowing that they came from the silver provinces that lay across the plateaus. This was the route he was familiar with from his boyhood. This was part of the crucial trail used by the famous mule train that brought the silver to Portobello.

He knew the Incas as well, including the primitive and warlike nomads to which the Spaniards gave the general name of Chichimecas, "the wild people." They were not so wild to those who did not plan to exterminate them.

The great Valentin hacienda was some four miles to the east. Less than a mile south of the mine was the small abandoned adobe hut where he'd grown up with his grandmother and Tobias. Memories, bitter-sweet, came to haunt him. He was not beaten yet, though Maximus no longer worried. There was still a slim possibility that the mule train could be attacked on the Gold Road and the silver brought to Holland, but Bruce must first arrive at the Isle of Pines.

When in Portobello, Tobias had been able to send Bruce's message to Kitt that their plans had changed. Unless Bruce showed up, Kitt was not to lie in wait along the Gold Road for the mules. But Tobias had included more in that message to Kitt — strategic information concerning the Dutch slave ship the *Golden Sun* that Maximus was depending on. There were 150 Africans aboard, destined to bolster the labor force working the mine. That cargo of slaves must not reach Lima.

The days at the mine were long and torturous. From the first hint of dawn that blushed while Peruvian stars still glowed in the sky, until late in the evening under the moonlight, Bruce and the prisoners worked the mine. The oxhide whips came often upon their backs, cutting flesh and leaving sores. During the daylight hours they sweated outdoors with picks; during the night, candles were lit and the work continued deep in mine shafts so poorly constructed that cave-ins were always a threat. There were deaths daily. New Indians were brought in.

He hauled ore and moved rock until his body ached continually. He was surrounded by the stench of sweat, filth, and fresh blood from the whips until it filled his breathing and eventually became unnoticeable. He pushed carts of heavy ore over to the smelting ovens with wheels riding awkwardly in poorly laid tracks. The Spanish soldiers impatiently rode guard, cracking the whip to insure he kept moving without a pause. Blessed with strength, he did keep moving, filling his mind with thoughts of freedom, of confronting Maximus face to face, of feeling Devora's lips on his, her cool hands in his hair. All this waited for him on the *Revenge* if he could just survive an hour, a day, a month longer.

There were always new Indians and prisoners to take the place of the dead, or so they foolishly thought. It was on this hope that he was staking everything — that Maximus would finally come to have a shortage of laborers to replenish his workers.

He had already arrived at the conclusion that the soldiers, sweating under their heavy breastplates, were not capable of showing pity. They despised the heretics and African slaves the most, considering them animals to be squandered upon the work for Holy Seville. Half-dead prisoners staggered along beside him, mouths open, flies buzzing, denied adequate water and food receiving only feeble rations at the end of the grueling days. The mules were fed and watered, but not the prisoners who were considered cheaper than mules and certainly not on a par with the magnificent horses. Indians were replaced when they collapsed and died.

Bruce persevered believing that the justice of God demanded that the authority of the dons be defeated in the end. He prayed incessantly for the opportunity to help bring an end to the injustice, and for the fountain of Christ's mercy to overflow to the parched souls of a race of people horribly oppressed by greed and false religious zeal.

Words came to Bruce's mind as he labored with the pick until his muscles burned and cramped, words from Isaiah the prophet that his grandmother had made him memorize. With each whack of the pick they echoed in his mind. "They lavish gold out of the bag, and weigh silver in the balance, and hire a goldsmith; and he maketh it a god; they fall down, yea, they worship. They bear it on their shoulder, they carry it, and set it in place, and it standeth; from its place shall it not move; yea, one shall cry unto it, yet can it not answer, nor save him out of his trouble . . . for I am God, and there is none else; I am God, and there is none like me . . ." (Isaiah 46:6-9).

Bruce looked up at the Peruvian stars glittering in the sky. It was not to an idol of silver he prayed to, but to the Glorious One, the Ancient of Days! *You, O Lord, who heard the groaning of Israel Your people when they were slaves in Egypt, look upon us and bring an empire to an end that tramples people under their feet like dust. This silver belongs to You. Somehow enable me to get it to Holland to strengthen their hands against the oppression of those who would end Your Reformation of truth.*

Now and then Bruce saw Favian and Maximus, but both kept their regal distance. Usually they met in the silver house where a strict accounting was kept. But now and then they rode out to the actual mine and surveyed the prisoners. Maximus had arrived one day with a sullen Favian to upbraid the captain general in charge of the prisoners.

"Is this all they have produced? We are behind schedule!"

"The prisoners are exhausted, Excellency. I am losing at least a slave a day. We need fresh Africans, who are larger and better able to endure the work."

"They should arrive soon. Until then, I will hear no more excuses."

"Yes, Excellency."

Maximus turned to Favian. "You wanted this command, and then are unable to meet the schedule. You will produce the silver, Favian, or you too will be working alongside the worst of these dogs."

"Yes, my Father. I will not fail!"

Maximus saw Bruce, halted for a moment, then clamping his jaw, turned his horse and rode away.

Favian turned to the sullen captain and unleashed his frustration upon him. "If you wish to live, Valdez, you will see to it that your prisoners produce silver enough to please his Excellency."

Favian turned to ride toward the distant silver house, when he, like Maximus, noticed Bruce.

He rode up, dust flying. "You do not deceive me. What is this deviltry you're doing?"

"Deviltry?" Bruce asked innocently.

"Yes! Maximus does not yet know the truth, but he will if you do not call off the scheme."

"Do you speak of the Indians' fear?"

Favian glared. "They fear to work because they claim the spirits of the Inca gods are disturbed. What have you told them?"

"What ails you, my brother? Perhaps it is you who fear."

"Me! Fear? I could have you whipped now if I wished."

"But you do not. Why? Not because of brotherly affection, to be sure."

Favian's mouth formed a tight line.

"Shall I inform you of why you do not, Favian? It is not what I have told them that forces them to cease their work, but what you in your folly have done. That folly is what you are keeping from Maximus and the captain-general."

Bruce saw tiny beads of sweat forming on Favian's narrow forehead. "Of what do you mean to accuse me?" Favian asked in a low voice.

Bruce smiled. "Thievery — of the worst sort. But it is what you have done to *hide* your thievery that has the Indians upset."

Favian's mouth slipped open as he realized Bruce knew his secret and wondered how it was possible.

Bruce said quietly, "And now Favian, you will do something for me — unless you wish Maximus to discover what you have been up to these last two months."

"You speak in riddles."

"Do I? Then I shall make it plain, so that you fully grasp my threat."

"Threat? You, a slave? Threaten *me?*"

"Yes, you. Your position of power totters. It will fall as soon as Maximus learns you have been stealing silver. But as I said, what ails the Indians is where you are hiding it. In a sacred Inca burial tomb, sealed until you opened it a month ago."

Favian turned pale. He stared down at Bruce for a long moment as though wondering if deviltry was possible.

"You forget I have friends among the Incas, while you and the Spanish guards are despised. A 'friend' has been watching you from the rocks — a friend who did not take lightly to your desecrating the burial tomb of an Inca forefather. He trailed you there when you brought the mules with silver."

"So Uncle Tobias has told you!"

"Tobias? Do not be a fool, Favian. Tobias has not seen me since I arrived, thanks to you, but that matter is about to change. That is part of our bargain."

Favian shifted in the saddle, then glanced about them to make sure no one else was nearby to overhear. "How was I to know it was sacred?"

"That's one of your weaknesses, my brother, you should have known. You were born and raised near here, even as I. You do not know what they think, because you do not care what anyone thinks or feels except yourself. Just remember about Tobias. He will come in and out at night to see me, and you will arrange for the captain-general to be elsewhere guzzling his maize beer."

"You expect me to believe that is all you desire? To see Tobias?"

"For now? Yes."

"For that, you will keep silent?"

"Yes."

Favian's eyes narrowed. "I do not believe you."

"You will have to. The 'friend' who was able to get a message to me beneath your very nose has already told Tobias as well. If you suddenly decide I am a threat to your safety, think again. Try anything so foolish and Tobias will bring Maximus to the Inca tomb. But cooperate and your secret is safe. And Sybella will eventually become your devoted wife."

Favian smirked. "Will she? I wonder. All right, you may see Tobias. It is small payment."

He turned and rode away, and Bruce, carrying his pick, went back to work.

Tobias arrived late one night riding a Valentin horse from the direction of the old adobe hut. He frowned when he saw Bruce. "What have they done to you?"

"No more than what they have long done to thousands of others since the first conquistadors have arrived." Bruce smiled. "*You* are as hefty as ever. Perhaps we should change places for a time," he said wryly. "What did you bring me?"

Tobias produced roast meat, pita bread, goat cheese, and a flagon of wine.

As Bruce devoured the food, Tobias attended his injuries.

"And Devora? She is well?"

Tobias was silent a moment too long, and Bruce turned quickly and gave him a searching look.

Tobias hastened, "As well as can be expected. She has wisely and bravely eluded the advances of Maximus so far, but I fear the hour for her continued refusal has come to an end. The countess died two days ago. And Maximus makes bold plans to marry her within weeks. He badgers her, and gives her no peace, even though she is in mourning."

Bruce gritted his anger and stood, chains rattling. The sound stabbed him as painfully as any sharp knife, for the frustrating rattle reminded him again of his inability to act. Bruce thought of his mother, then Devora . . .

"Is that all?" he asked quietly but bluntly.

"She tells me he has behaved the gentleman."

Bruce was surprised, but thankful, but not enough for it to assuage his anger. "It is well for him that he has. I must escape."

Tobias growled his discontent and ran his strong fingers through his silver hair. "Do you think I do not wear my mind out day and night thinking, planning?"

Bruce laid a hand on his shoulder. "Steady. I know your faithfulness, my Uncle."

"Perhaps Favian is our key. That Inca tomb —"

"No, not yet . . . I still need Favian, but I have an idea."

"Perhaps we have the same one."

"That slave ship," whispered Bruce, "have you heard anything yet? By now Kitt could have attacked it."

"He could have, but there is no news yet. I have waited daily in frustration for some word to arrive by messenger from Panama. Silence greets us."

"Then we need to act without certain proof."

"What if Kitt failed to take the ship? Those slaves will arrive at Callao. Maximus intends to go there soon to get news about the slave shipment."

"Then we need to act now. I cannot wait, Tobias! Tell him you have gone to Callao for him. Bring news of the sinking of the ship. Anything to convince him he is dependent upon the prisoners he has now. I will do my part here among the Indians."

"They will cooperate then?"

"After Favian desecrated their sacred tomb they are willing to die if necessary. Tell Tupac to spread the word; the Indians are to say they are too sick to work."

Tobias stood. "I'll leave tomorrow for the hacienda to speak with Maximus."

❦ 17 ❦

The Door of Escape

Devora, dressed in mourning black, sat at the long dining room table at the Valentin hacienda, watching the candlelight flicker in the silver candelabra. The voices of Tobias and Maximus droned on in the background but she was not listening. Her mind was on her mother's sudden death. Two days ago she had gone to her chamber and found Maximus coming out, a grave look on his chiseled features.

"She died in her sleep," he had told her, and Devora had rushed to her bedside to find Catherina no longer breathing. It wasn't until after the funeral that she stopped to consider why Maximus had gone to her mother's room so early in the morning. She lifted her eyes from the gently swaying candle flames and studied his face as he listened to Tobias. She noticed his hard mouth, his determined, even stare as he watched Tobias. But he'd have no reason to hasten the death of Catherina. Had she said anything to him the night before to frighten him? But Maximus was not frightened by threats. What then, might she have told him, if anything? Or was she merely jumping to conclusions because she was so distraught over her mother's death? Devora had known it was coming, but still, it had seemed so sudden.

She thought back to the moment when she had gone up beside her bed, but couldn't recall anything unusual that might show a struggle, or any expression on her face. Her mother had appeared peaceful, her lips turned slightly upward as though she were smiling.

No, Maximus would have no reason to harm Catherina. . . . Then what had brought him to her chamber so early? When she had asked him, he said he thought Devora was there. Devora was not completely satisfied, but there seemed to be no other answer. She feared him now, even more than she had before. She was alone at the hacienda except for Sybella. Even Sybella watched Maximus with a new, thoughtful stare. "He'll insist you marry him soon," Sybella had told her after the funeral. This time, her voice had been sober. When Devora had looked at her, Sybella was frowning. "I am sorry you came here," she had said, but unlike her other emotional tirades, where her dislike of Devora had been so apparent, there had been nothing personal in her tone of voice, leaving Devora to think that Sybella was thinking of Maximus.

Now as she sat at the long table with Sybella and Tobias, Favian entered the rustic dining room and reluctantly took his seat opposite his father. Tobias had arrived last night and Devora had not yet had a chance to speak with him alone, but she had heard Maximus arguing with him late into the night. Then, this afternoon, Favian had arrived, having been called to the hacienda from the mines for a family meeting. Favian looked glum, and Maximus looked impatient as always.

She came alert when she heard Tobias say: "You are sure the authorities in Panama knew of your order for slaves?"

Maximus turned to Favian. There were taut lines around his mouth. "That was your responsibility, Favian. Did you carry it out?" he demanded.

"Of course, my Father. I issued your decree before we sailed from Panama. The ship was the *Golden Sun*. It was on its way to Quito."

"Then that accounts for the blunder,"

Maximus said in a cutting voice, bringing his Venetian wineglass down on the mahogany table. He stood, looking as much on edge as did Favian. "You can do nothing right, Favian. You were jinxed at birth. I should have known better than to trust you to handle this. I should have issued the order myself."

Favian banged his silver fork down. "I tell you I did as you ordered. One hundred and fifty African slaves were due at Callao Harbor a week ago."

"Then where are they?" Maximus shouted. "Tobias just came from Callao and reports that the ship has not been seen since it left Santo Domingo."

"I have no way of knowing, Father. Perhaps it is delayed."

"The royal treasure fleet has left San Luca and is even now on its way to the Indies. We are desperately behind schedule and the Indians and pirates under your supervision are failing to produce the daily quota, though I have warned you of the consequences."

"I tell you there is a conspiracy, Father."

"Conspiracy!" Maximus scoffed. "Too long you have relied on excuses. You pleaded with me to put you in charge of the silver production. I did so wishing my son success in the eyes of the king. And when I return from business with the Audiencia in Alto Peru, what do I find? The silver quota is not being met! Indians are 'suddenly ill' — Indians," he repeated with emphasis, "who have never had a sick day in all their lives. And the English dogs fall under the whiplash like weak women! You expect me to believe this?"

Favian stood from the table, pale, his limpid eyes reflecting the candlelight.

Devora glanced at Tobias and saw that he stared at his glass thoughtfully. She suspected he had something to do with all this.

"What slaves do you speak of, Uncle Maximus?" Sybella asked a moment later.

Maximus looked down at her. "African slaves. The only kind to have. So well do they work that one is worth two Indians. As for the religious prisoners, I am told they succumb within a month."

"Is it any wonder?" Devora stated. "Do not the Spaniards take better care of their mules?"

"If you're worried about Nicklas, then perhaps I should take you to the mine to soothe his wearied brow."

"You need not worry about Nicklas," Favian said. "He is as proud and unyielding as ever."

" 'Proud' doesn't fit him," countered

Sybella. "Nicklas is honorable, in spite of how you and Uncle treat him."

"She is right, Maximus," Tobias said. "You have given Favian free hand to order the soldiers to whip the prisoners and it isn't working. Perhaps you should try another approach."

"And what approach do you suggest?" Maximus asked with a tinge of sarcasm. "Release him from his chains? Send the cook to barbecue for him each evening? Maybe send him my best wine?"

Devora pushed her plate away.

"There is nothing wrong with the ill Indians that a few hangings wouldn't cure! You may mock what I say about intrigue, Father, but Nicklas is behind this pretended illness."

"Nicklas?" Tobias repeated with dismay. "Do you yet fear your brother so that even when he is in chains you blame him for this?"

Favian looked at him suspiciously. "He has won their respect and trust. And he has sent a secret message to the Incas to cease their work."

"Oh Favian," mocked Sybella with a tinkling laugh over her glass. "Are you going to blame every upset on Nicklas?"

Favian flushed, as though he could take

mockery from his father and uncle, but not Sybella. "Perhaps it is Tobias who carries out Nicklas' wishes."

Devora tensed, but Tobias calmly lifted his bushy brows. "Have I turned pirate also? Next you will accuse me of sinking the slave ship."

"No, you are too sympathetic to the slaves to sink the ship. But you may have sent a message to the English pirates who did."

"Enough of this," Maximus rebuked. "We may sit and argue all night while the silver is left in the mines."

"Word should be sent to Panama to learn if Tortuga buccaneers have made an attack at Santo Domingo of late," Favian suggested. "You may find that to be the reason why the slaves have not arrived."

"Perhaps you should saddle a mule and make a 'quick dash' over the isthmus," Maximus said wryly, "if you think that could aid our dilemma."

Favian sat down. There was a moment of awkward silence while he looked at Sybella, then Tobias, as though they were in league to turn Maximus against him.

"You heard what Archbishop Andres warned in Panama," Tobias said. "If the silver is not delivered, our illustrious king will . . ."

"You needn't remind me," Maximus said. "The archbishop is soon due to come to Cuzco to see how matters progress. If there is anything he can fault me for concerning Nicklas and the prisoners, he will do so. He would still like them to stand trial as heretics before the inquisition. But in order to succeed I will see to it that the Indians work, if I must take them one by one and hang them."

Devora looked at Sybella and saw that she too was revolted.

"They will die first. Then what? Without the African slaves, who will replace them? These men are emaciated and weary to the soul — not even fit to work. Promise them all the food they want, and adequate sleep, and it may be that you will be able to turn meat into silver. Nicklas was not far from the truth in Cartagena when he told you that the prisoners were a precious commodity. This is a grievous lesson that Spain has yet to learn. It is common wisdom to grant these men the same care you would extend toward your mules. If they are hungry, feed them. Thirsty? Let them drink. Injured? Attend their wounds."

"This is bribery," mocked Favian.

"They will not work for Favian, but they will for Nicklas."

"Ah! So that's it." Favian jumped to his

feet. "You would release Nicklas from his chains. This is a conspiracy!"

Devora remained outwardly calm and looked over at Maximus to find that he was watching her reaction and paid little attention to Favian's. She was pleased that she showed none.

"Maximus, your objective is to produce silver, not to slaughter prisoners. These men are all needed."

Maximus swept up his glass and emptied it as he walked over to the window, looking out thoughtfully as though he realized his dilemma.

"Conspiracy or not, our tactics are failing miserably."

"You have always been a pragmatic man, Maximus," Tobias said.

Favian walked over to Maximus. "What do you intend to do?"

"That, my son, will not concern you any longer. You have once again failed me. It seems I must depend on Nicklas to save my neck before the king. You are dismissed from your position!"

Favian angrily threw his glass across the room, his lean face full of rage. "You have mocked me once too often!"

Maximus kept his back toward him, giving him an indifferent flick of his hand.

Unexpectedly Sybella got to her feet with a rustle of garments and came around to Favian. She managed a stiff but friendly smile. "I grow bored and lonely. It will be pleasant to have a caballero to keep me company. Come, Favian, forget the awful mines. I want to spend the next few months here at the hacienda riding horses and enjoying all the fiestas — and I will need a dashing escort."

Favian looked as though he hadn't understood her, then ever so slowly his rage drained.

Sybella looped her arm through his, then turned to Maximus, who was as surprised by the change in her as Favian.

"We shall leave the dull business of whips and sick slaves to you and Tobias," Sybella told Maximus.

"Does this mean you have at last released Nicklas to his just fate?" Maximus asked with a barb.

Sybella snapped open her fan, her voice matching his. "Have I a choice? Come, Favian. It is a pleasant evening. I wish to go out in the carriage for a ride."

Devora watched them leave and wondered how much of Sybella's change in behavior was due to Tobias' plans for Bruce.

When they were alone, Maximus looked sharply at Tobias.

"Nicklas is to be placed in command of the silver production, but he is to be guarded day and night. And if this is some trick to save him, Tobias, both of you will live to regret it."

Tobias' mouth curved. He got up from the table and came around to Devora, taking her hand gently. "Come, Señorita, you grieve for the loss of your mother. We will take a stroll and speak of things eternal. That is —" and he looked over at Maximus with a challenge. "If my brother will permit us to pray together?"

Maximus looked displeased with Tobias taking her away, but he said nothing as Devora stood. "I wish for a stroll, Tobias. I would like to visit her resting place again. She is buried here in the Valentin cemetery."

"Then we will go there now before I ride back to the mines."

Once leaving the hacienda they walked quickly across the yard toward the shade trees, silhouetted darkly against the mountain ranges. The wind was cool and crisp.

"We are safe now," Tobias said. "Maximus cannot see us. Let's stop beneath this tree."

"Oh Tobias, I fear that Maximus has done something dreadful . . . I think he may have

— have put something in my mother's cocoa to cause her heart to stop during the night."

She told him how she had found Maximus checking on her mother the next morning. She gripped his sturdy arms and tried not to cry. His eyes were grave and unhappy. "Easy, little one, what makes you think so?"

She told him of an argument Catherina had had with Maximus the day before her unexpected death. "I do not know what they argued about, because they stopped when I came into her room. Not even Catherina would explain to me later. Then I found him coming from her chamber early the next morning."

He sighed deeply and glanced back toward the rambling adobe hacienda. "It may be. They may have argued over you. Maximus is determined to marry you."

"I will never agree to that. We must escape while we have the opportunity!"

"We will. Bruce has been planning, but it will be dangerous. Maximus may improve Bruce's situation temporarily, but he is suspicious and watchful, as is Favian, but Sybella will at least distract him. But now, this matter of the countess is very disturbing." His silver brows drew together as he looked off again toward the house. "If Bruce knew what you had just told me he would not want you staying here, and I cannot remain to guard you."

"I do not believe I need to be guarded, but when can I see Bruce? When can we escape?"

"Soon. I will arrange for a meeting between the two of you out at the old adobe hut near the mines. I will come back for you in two days. You are not afraid of staying here?"

"No, Sybella is with me. If I give Maximus nothing to worry about, he will treat me well enough."

"Then say nothing more to him about Catherina's death. You do not want him to think you suspect him."

She shivered and nodded, her heart lighter at the same time. Bruce would be released from his chains. Bruce would soon be free. The door of escape was creaking open at last. But what of the silver that Bruce had intended to confiscate and bring to Holland? She desperately hoped he would forget all about those cumbersome plans. They must flee from Maximus while they had opportunity.

Tobias prayed with her, then told her once more to be cautious and that he would arrange for her to meet Bruce at the old adobe hut. " 'Hasta la vista,' " he whispered, then strode away to his horse.

That night Devora could hardly sleep, such was her excitement. Bruce . . . she drifted off to sleep dreaming that he held her in his arms safely aboard the *Revenge*, and that they were sailing over the blue Caribbean toward English Barbados.

But two weeks passed and she did not hear from Tobias. A message arrived for Maximus telling him that Archbishop Andres had arrived and wanted to meet him in Cuzco. Maximus saddled his horse and rode away into town. He had no sooner left when Tobias arrived.

On their ride out to the old adobe hut Tobias told her that the work at the mine was progressing so well that the captain-general no longer concerned himself with Bruce.

"That Maximus had removed Favian and placed Bruce in charge has given some of the soldiers reason to suspect there may have been some error in his arrest. We've made use of that and spread the story that evidence has surfaced that may prove Bruce innocent. Now they are worried, and while no one will come out and say anything, they are all secretly doing their best to show him they trust him." Tobias chuckled.

Devora felt great relief, yet knew they were far from being out of danger. "And his crew?"

"Ah, Bruce has seen to that. Tupac arrived with two mules laden with food and wine, and chica — maize beer. The friendly Incas entertained the hard working soldiers."

She looked at him, wondering, and saw his wry smile.

"While the soldiers enjoyed the wine, the Incas played their musical instruments."

"What kind of instruments?" she asked curiously.

"Oh, panpipes made of reeds of different lengths tied together with fiber. The quena flute — a rather shrill wail — I don't think you'd like it. Whistling pots, gourds filled with seeds, cattle horns, and a *charango* — something like a mandolin from Bolivia. It's made from an armadillo shell. Between the hypnotic music, the wine, and maize beer Bruce was able to release Lieutenant Hakewell, who then set free all the members of his crew."

"They are actually free!"

"Yes, in hiding with Tupac."

"Tupac — the Indian on board the *Revenge*?"

"Yes. He's been with Bruce since they be-friended each other as small boys. Tupac's family was burned alive by the Spaniards, and Bruce had few friends in the Valentin family. So they made a brotherly pact. They've been 'warriors of the heart' ever since."

Her excitement mounted when they ar-rived at the old adobe hut. Freedom blew in the wind that fluttered her dark, ankle-length skirt as she got down from the horse.

Tobias assured her that Bruce would come to meet her before sunset. She would be safe since Maximus never came here. Tobias had been living here and carrying out his plans from this location for the last two-and-a-half months since they arrived. He rode off to locate Tupac, and Devora stood on the warm earth, turning toward the sun-worn, chipped adobe hut. She tried to imagine the man she loved living here as a dark-haired boy taming horses, all the while his young heart hardening toward Maximus. He had resolved to prove himself to one who had openly rejected him. Tears came to her eyes as she envisioned the de-meaning voice of Maximus shouting at him and his grandmother. And now . . . the mis-understanding, the bitterness — and yes, though she didn't want to speak the word, the hate — was coming to an ugly climax.

She grieved that the relationship had turned out this badly, but there seemed no way to tear down the structure and rebuild. Neither Maximus nor Bruce would relent and ask the other's forgiveness. But was she being too simplistic? Asking forgiveness would not change the bitter past, but where was the end of the road?

She looked down at the hard soil and saw the cracks. She was reminded that she could not change them. But God could mend. He had taken the initiative and His grace had found a way for many lost sons and daughters to be restored to fellowship with Him. A door stood open in heaven and the Heavenly Father stood smiling, with open arms to embrace the returning prodigal.

She blinked hard. Yes, the Father understood broken relationships and how to heal them. Restoration and forgiveness had cost Him dearly. His beloved Son had left heaven for earth to seek and to save that which was lost. He had overcome sin and defeated Satan, because He was willing to pay an unfathomable price. Before her mother's death, Catherine and Devora had had their own shattered relationship restored.

But Maximus was not like the Heavenly Father! He was proud, selfish, cruel, and vindictive. What could soften his heart toward Bruce?

And Bruce, did he even want restoration?

She walked slowly toward the low adobe house, her shoes crunching over the parched dirt. She looked at the empty yard, dry and cracked beneath the sun, then opened the door and stepped inside the cool, shadowed room. The old furniture was dusty and faded except where Tobias had cleared a space for his living. There were Inca Indian carvings here and there, some hammered tin pots and pans, and chipped earthen vessels. The wind blew and whistled softly through the open windows, breaking the noon silence.

Footsteps sounded in the next room. Startled, she turned quickly and stared at the figure in the doorway.

❦ 18 ❦

Safe in His Embrace

"Bruce!"

He wore a handsome, but rugged, suit of Spanish design that Tobias must have brought him. A brace of pistols crossed his leather vest, and he wore a scabbard with a sword.

"Bruce . . ." she started toward him. He was actually here, free again, within reach of her hand. They were escaping together. Nothing could stop them now.

He came toward her and in a few steps she was in his arms. Her heart pounded as his warm gray-green eyes took her in, his look of desire mingled with the tenderness that had always been absent from the ruthless gaze of Maximus.

His hands caressed her hair, her face, as if wondering if she were real. She felt his kiss brushing against her eyelids, drifting to her temples, sending everything from her mind but the reality of his nearness.

Outside the wind blew, sending granules against the adobe walls. But they were alone in a world that, for now at least, had become a refuge from all that was dangerous and cruel.

His lips came to hers, causing her to melt. She cherished the strength of his arms about her, the feel of his rough jacket and leather vest beneath her fingers.

"You're everything I remembered," he whispered, his cheek against hers. "You've filled my dreams and every waking moment these past months. I love you so much that if anything happened to you . . ."

"When can we escape, Bruce? Let us go quickly while we have the moment!"

He held her away from him, and though for her sake he restrained his emotions, she could see his frustration. "We must wait for nightfall when Tupac and the others join us."

Her eyes searched his. "But what of the silver mule train? Of your plans to deny Seville the bounty?"

His eyes glinted as he seemed to think about it. "I haven't forgotten. That is the reason I returned to Lima, confronting such risk. It is two months before the mules leave for Portobello. I cannot take the chance of having you at the hacienda with Maximus.

We will escape tonight with Tupac. Yet, there may still be an opportunity to follow through on my plan, but that must wait. You are more important to me now, Devora. First of all I want you with Kitt on the *Revenge*."

Kitt! Escape! Her excitement flared like fire. Yet she knew it was far too soon to think they had managed to successfully elude Maximus and the soldiers. It was a long journey across the Isthmus of Panama. The very thought of passing through the jungle and river again was almost enough to quell her happiness, though at the end of the long journey she would become his bride.

"How can we reach him? What if he doesn't come soon?"

"He will come, but if something should go wrong we will find some other way to avoid the Spaniards until we can get a ship to Barbados."

"Bruce, hold me. I want to think everything will be all right."

"We are together at last. This time, if God wills, we'll never be torn apart again."

"But if Maximus finds us —" she trembled. "He would delight to take me from you, Bruce."

He sobered, his eyes holding hers for a long moment. He cupped her face into his hands and kissed her gently. "There is a way to stop him now."

She held onto him tightly, her eyes pleading, thinking she knew what he meant. "No! Do not go and search for him. He has all the soldiers behind him. Stay with me until nightfall, when we leave."

He ran his fingers through her hair, twisting a honey-colored lock around his hand thoughtfully. "I meant if Tobias married us now, we would defeat Maximus."

Her heart seemed to stop beating, then suddenly began pounding, taking her breath away.

"You mean here?" she whispered.

He held her gaze, then brought her fingers to his lips. "Yes, here. Now. Before anything else can go wrong. Before Maximus tries to stop me from leaving."

"Yes," she whispered. "Yes, I love you."

He kissed her lips, drawing her closer until her trembling ceased within the safety of his loving embrace.

He gently released her and walked to the window to look out across the hard-packed dirt. She followed, her knees feeling a little weak. There was no one in sight. He reached into his bandoleer and removed a pistol.

"I'll go for him. It shouldn't take long. Take this, just in case."

"I have your pistol in my cloak. My mother returned it to me at Lima. Oh Bruce, be careful!"

He smiled at her, then slipped out the back door as silently as he had come. Devora stood there, dazed over the sudden change of events. She began to pace, rushing to look out the window each time she heard a slight noise, fearing that she would see Don Maximus riding up, or Favian.

The time crept by with painful agony. What if he couldn't find Tobias? Or . . . what if he found him, but Maximus arrested them again?

She sank into an old wooden chair, knotting her hand into a fist. If Bruce was caught again she wouldn't be able to stand it. If Don Maximus walked through the door she knew she would scream.

But as the stillness of the hot day crept onward, Maximus did not appear. She continued to pace restlessly. Several times she stopped, startled, and contemplated that she would soon marry Bruce. Here in the adobe hut where he'd been raised!

Finally she heard footsteps and low voices approaching from the back, and stood stiffly waiting. In a moment they were there. Bruce and Friar Tobias. Tobias removed a small

Bible from his leather satchel and Bruce took her hand in his and brought her before his uncle.

Tobias' eyes shone with pleasure as he looked from Devora to Bruce. He opened the Scriptures and read, then soberly put the question to them both. Bruce turned her toward him and placed a small silver cross on a chain around her neck. He looked down at her tenderly, kissed her, and the words of Tobias echoed in her heart.

"I now pronounce you married in His sight. May His grace and blessing rest upon your holy union."

She hardly heard Tobias leave as she stood gazing up at Bruce. In the distance she dimly heard the sound of horse hooves dying away, but love was growing in her heart, a love she was confident would never ebb.

Bruce drew her into his arms. "Maximus cannot have you now. Whatever happens in the future, we belong to each other always."

She clung to him, swept away in the passion of his kiss.

❦ 19 ❦

Maximus is Defeated

Sybella cried softly into her handkerchief as she stood in the courtyard at the hacienda.

"So," Favian mocked in a bitter tone, "you break my heart, querida. Your tears betray you. Your love has flown away with his English dove, leaving a poor mourning dove behind. Leaving you behind to weep into your handkerchief. Poor Sybella."

She whirled, hot cutting words on the tip of her tongue. This time, however, she held them back. She drew in a breath to steady herself and tried to swallow the ache in her throat.

Favian stood inside the adobe wall near the open gate. He walked toward her across the patio, his boots sounding harshly upon the stone. He stopped before her, a cynical look in his eyes. "Tears over a man do not become the great Doña Sybella Valentin Ferdinand."

Sybella knotted her handkerchief and kept silent.

"Where is Uncle Tobias? He has helped them escape, hasn't he!"

When she said nothing he grabbed her arm. "Tell me!"

"Let me loose. How dare you!"

Her rebuke penetrated his emotions and he dropped his hand, sighing as he turned away. "I am sorry — I am upset."

"I can see that," she snapped.

"Maximus will hold me responsible for Nicklas' escape. But he will be more angry over the loss of the señorita when he learns that Devora has fled with him."

"By now she is his bride," Sybella's dull voice stated.

Favian sucked in his breath. "And you said nothing of this? Do you not realize what Maximus will do? I never thought he could care for a woman as much as he does for Devora."

"He does not love her," she said. "He remembers Nicklas' mother."

"Try to tell him that. I hate to think what he will do." He looked at her, his eyes stirring with unrest. "You've been foolish, Sybella. You knew about this two weeks ago when Tobias came to talk to Maximus, yet you did not tell him. You think you can make amends to Nicklas for what happened at Cartagena."

"Yes, it is the least I can do after all the suffering Maximus put him through. He loves her . . . and I would see him have what he wants this time. But you! You have spied on me again," she gritted.

"No, the Indian woman in the kitchen told my bodyguard she saw Devora leaving with Tobias. And she saw you watching them leave, after Tobias warned you to say nothing."

Sybella jerked her shoulder and turned her back toward him. "And now that you know, I suppose you won't have the strength to contain yourself."

"No," he whispered. "I fear for you, Sybella, just as much as for myself. Maximus will learn of this — he always does. Do you think the wench will not tell him if he but threatens her?"

"He has no cause to question her, nor your bodyguard. It is too late to catch them now."

"No, Maximus can still overtake them if you tell me where they have gone."

She turned, her eyes desperate, taking hold of his. "Don't be a fool, Favian. Let them go! What does it matter to us now?"

"It mattered to you in Cartagena when you sent her away. Why not now? Nothing has changed."

"Everything has changed," she said wearily. "Nicklas is in love with Devora. I cannot have a man who dreams of another woman."

"He is a fool. He could have had you and everything else."

She smiled. "If you let him go, you will become Maximus' heir. *You* will have everything."

He looked at her moodily. "Everything? Will I have you, Sybella? If you were in my arms, I would never want for another."

She watched him alertly. "That may not be as impossible as it once was, Favian," she said softly. She took a step toward him. "Let Nicklas go free, say nothing to Maximus, and I will not contest the marriage he has arranged for us."

Favian watched her cautiously, as though trying to determine if he could trust her.

She walked toward him, all pretense gone. "I tell you the truth. I will marry you soon if you truly want me."

"You mean this?" he whispered.

"Yes. I have learned we cannot always have what we want in this life, but a little happiness is better than none at all. We are alike, Favian, willing to do most anything to get what we want. Uncle Tobias was right today when he told me that I was not suited for Nicklas. I hated to hear it at first — it stung my pride — but the more I thought about it, the more I realized it is so. He and Devora belong together. They even share the same faith. I have learned that Nicklas believes like Martin Luther and that heretic John Calvin."

Favian's expression was suddenly altered. She knew why when the formidable figure of Don Maximus moved out from the shadows and walked slowly toward her. Fear tore across her heart. "So, you knew they would escape together, didn't you?"

Favian came between them. "It is my fault, Father. Leave her alone."

"All of you are to blame. You've been plotting together to betray me. You, Sybella, Tobias — and Nicklas. I shall kill him for this."

He pushed Favian aside and took hold of Sybella, shaking her. "Where have they gone, where!"

"To . . . to the old adobe hut . . . but it is too late. By now they are married. Tobias went there — to perform the vows."

Stunned, Maximus stood still. Slowly his handsome features turned livid with rage as he appeared to realize that Nicklas had foiled him.

"Fool," he whispered to himself. "So

simple a tactic never dawned on me." Sweat appeared on his brow and he wiped it on the back of his arm, looking off toward the gate as though his thoughts thundered out of control like wild horses.

"I'll find him. I'll kill him for this. I will thrust the Valentin sword through his treacherous heart."

Sybella came to him. "No, Uncle Maximus — please. You will only hurt yourself . . ."

He pushed her aside and strode toward the lighted hacienda shouting for his captain.

"Yes, Excellency!"

"Mount up soldiers. Quickly! Favian! You will come with me!"

"Yes, Father."

Maximus went inside, presumably to dress for travel and gather his weapons, and Favian began to follow, but Sybella grabbed him, her eyes holding his.

"You must warn Nicklas."

His face was grave, his eyes like dark coals. "I cannot warn him. By now they have escaped from Cuzco into the mountains."

"But Maximus will track him down."

"Nicklas knows these mountains as well as Maximus, perhaps better. If they get to Callao first, they may have a slim chance of getting to the Bay of Panama ahead of him. But knowing Maximus, he will trail him and Devora all the way across the isthmus!"

The evening breeze, sighing its secret song about the adobe hut, made Devora drowsy. She laid the side of her face against Bruce's chest, listening to his quiet heart-beat. He held her, running his fingers through her hair.

"What if Maximus comes here?" she whispered.

"He won't."

She lifted her head. "How can you be so certain?" He sat up and reached for his shirt, slipping into it as he stood. It was dark and they had taken no chances by lighting the candle, but golden moonlight shone in through the small window.

"I know my father better than even Favian. Favian is too close to him. He experiences the fire of the dragon's breath. But I have watched him from afar and know what the old dragon will do."

"I am glad you are so confident," she murmured wryly, "because I wait for the horrible sound of horse hooves thundering into the dirt courtyard."

"Worry no more, my violet-eyed angel. Simply trust your devoted husband and submit sweetly to his every request," he teased.

She smiled. "Your unwarranted confidence will lead you back to the silver mines."

"Never again, my sweet. My next destination will put me in command of the *Revenge*. If Kitt arrives, my plans to take the mule train may yet prove successful."

He reached down and caught her hand, pulling her lightly to her feet and then into his arms. "Come, get your things. We need to meet Tobias and Tupac."

As she put on her shoes, Bruce went to the window and looked out.

"By now, like a wounded jaguar, Maximus will be determined to track down the hunter. If I know him as I think I do, he's stunned, wondering how he could have been fool enough not to realize I would marry you beneath his very nose."

He leaned looking out, musing. She watched him, hoping he was right. Maximus continued to worry her.

Bruce smiled thoughtfully. "He expects me to take you and make a run for it, catching a ship at Callao for Panama. Naturally, he will have the faster vessel and thinks he will overtake us along the way. He'll threaten to blast the ship to pieces, killing all aboard if I do not surrender."

Devora shuddered. "Please, Bruce, let us go quickly. What if you are wrong and he does come here?"

"He will never take the time to ride this far. By now he will be on his way down to Cuzco. If I didn't think so, I would never have told Tobias to bring you here to the house."

"But if he's on the trail to Cuzco, how will we be able to pass through town?"

"We are not traveling that route. That would be as foolish as walking into a trap. While he rushes ahead with a band of soldiers to Callao, Tupac will lead us over the mountain on an Inca trail older than the arrival of the first conquistador."

So that was his plan! Growing up here with an Indian friend was to his advantage. A good escape route was better than all the silver in the mine. Her relief was so great that she laughed. Then they didn't need to board a ship at Callao where Maximus would be waiting for them.

He belted on his scabbard. "We will board a ship at the Gulf of Guayaquil, and eventually follow the old tracks of the mule train to Nombre de Dios." He again looked out the window. "If things go as planned, we will proceed to the Isle of Pines to wait for Kitt."

"Why do you keep looking out the window if you are certain Maximus will not come here?"

"I'm watching for a signal from Tobias. He is above the road with a lamp. There it is — all is clear. Our opportunity waits. Come, we must hurry."

Devora snatched up her riding cloak and Bruce ushered her out the door and across the yard to where two magnificent horses were hidden in the brush. Bruce helped her into the saddle, then mounted quickly. They rode toward the mountains where Tobias waited, and the lamp continued its glowing welcome. Even so, Devora was tense. She was afraid that it would be Maximus or Favian who stepped out from behind the brush with a satisfied leer.

Her fears were unfounded. When they reached the lamp, Tobias greeted them. "All goes well." He mounted his horse and soon they were racing away from the adobe hut.

After what seemed an hour of riding they came across a serape-clad Inca Indian in what appeared to Devora to be the middle of nowhere. Tupac wasted no time. He lifted a hand without a word and rode ahead, leading the way. They followed in silence beneath the moonlight. When they neared some rocks, Tupac stopped. A small mountain creek tumbled and splashed behind them. Devora was surprised to see at the water's edge at least twenty men, all in Inca clothing, ponchos, and leather breeches. As they came out and surrounded Bruce's horse, they reached to grab his hands and give a sturdy shake. Laughter filled the crisp mountain air.

She was sure they weren't Indians. Then one spoke up: "Har, Capt'n, ye got our hides outta that Romish fire, to be sure. Ye ain't never going to have a more thankful crew of pirates then wot's ye got now."

The buccaneer lieutenant she remembered as Hakewell came forward and grinned. "Can't wait to feel the wind off Tortuga, Capt'n! Sooner we depart Spanish soil, the easier I'll be sleeping."

Tupac wore a smile on his olive-brown face, his lean muscled body looking like a panther.

"Devora, you remember Tupac," Bruce introduced. "Everything I know about horses and trails I've learned from him."

"And everything bad I learn from him," Tupac said with a twinkle in his eyes, pointing at Bruce.

The others laughed, still looking much like Incas. Tupac tossed Bruce a poncho and a wide-brimmed hat. "Make yourself like peacock for your new wife," he teased.

"New wife?" Bruce mocked, as he settled his hat. "Bad English, Tupac. You imply I have exchanged my old wife for this pretty new one."

"Ho!" warned Tobias.

Devora laughed along with the rest and wondered why it was so easy to have tears come to her eyes. She looked at the happy faces of the crew of the *Revenge* and her beloved, and glanced up thankfully toward the winking stars.

The moon had set. They rode by starlight well into the night guided by Tupac along the trail, which was sometimes no wider than a footpath. At times Bruce and Tupac stopped to speak quietly, and Bruce would help her down, telling her it was too risky. They would then walk, leading their mounts down the slope where small rocks and loose dirt tumbled into the valley. The horses followed well and seemed to be accustomed to the terrain.

Maximus sat straight in his saddle staring out at the blue waters of Callao Harbor as the gentle swells rippled. He did not move. His white-knuckled fist rested on his leather-breeched thigh. He had ordered a search of every inch of the harbor and its boats, including his flagship. General Alfonso de Aviles had just ridden up to him from the fortress and reported that a careful search revealed nothing of consequence.

"We have interrogated every soldier and fisherman in the area, Excellency. They all have the same story. On pain of death they swear to the saints that no one has seen Don Nicklas."

"What of the English señorita and Tobias?"

"Nothing, Excellency!"

Maximus' sharp gaze fixed upon the small ships flitting in from seaports down the coast, some bringing gold and silver from the mountains of Alto Peru to be stored at the treasure house until the king's bounty would be brought to Panama.

His tanned face was like granite, reflecting the decision of his heart. His flagship, well equipped with guns and men, lay close below the cannon of the harbor fortress, with smaller gunboats moving through the water to huddle about her at his order, making certain Nicklas could not attempt to capture his ship. Nicklas had managed to slip through his grasp.

"He must not have come this way," Favian told him. "We would have found evidence by now."

Archbishop Andres sat astride a horse on the quay between Maximus and Favian. Now that it appeared certain he would not interrogate Nicklas and his crew at a new trial, he made a sound of wearied disdain beneath his breath. "Unlike you, Maximus, I believe I am wise enough to know when we have been outsmarted. Since you have bred such a clever rogue, I wash my hands of Don Nicklas — unless by chance I happen to meet up with the rascal somewhere on the Main — which I doubt."

Maximus shot him a glance.

The archbishop turned the reins to ride back to his ecclesiastical quarters in Lima. "Perhaps it is just as well he escaped with the young lady. I scarcely believe you had the heart to hang him, or turn him over to the inquisitors."

"What do you mean to suggest?" snapped Maximus. "That I could forget his betrayal? Nay, never."

"I suggest, Excellency," he said wearily, "that you concentrate your energies on producing the load of silver for his Majesty. The royal fleet arrives from the Windward Passage in two months. If not, you may need to join the pirates on Tortuga to escape being sent to Seville." With a bored flick of his reins he turned his horse and rode back toward Lima.

Maximus made a growl as he looked after him.

"The archbishop has a sense of humor, my Father," Favian said wryly.

"I admit he is right. Nicklas did not come here with Devora and Tobias. The rogue outfoxed me. And I suppose the officials in Lima will suspect I have permitted his escape."

Favian turned his head and gave him a searching look.

Maximus shaded his eyes, gazing off toward the Peruvian coastline. "He must have traveled by land . . . by horse no doubt . . . and he will try to board a vessel for Panama at one of the smaller ports farther down the coastline . . . but which one?"

Favian shifted in his saddle, the wind blowing the plume in his hat. "If we go in search of them we will lose weeks of valuable time at the mines. Forget him, Father. He will meet his end one day among the diablo pirates he befriends. For your sake, let us return to Cuzco and ready the silver for his Majesty. You heard the archbishop. The fleet is even now on its way from Seville."

Maximus stared at the ships moored to their heavy rings. A hundred thoughts gnawed at him, strange thoughts; anger, yet grief as well. He would never have another son like Nicklas . . . no, never.

Maximus stirred from his thoughts, coming alert. He had noticed a ship. What appeared to be a galleon came into view. Curious, he lifted the telescope to scan the shoreline.

"What is it, my Father?" came Favian's anxious question.

Maximus' heart surged with anticipation. He saw the ship's tattered canvas and what appeared as broken rigging. He could just make out its flag.

"Providence has intervened."

"The *Golden Sun*?" breathed Favian.

"Yes, we have our new slaves to work the mines. She looks to have survived a storm." He handed the telescope to Favian, who focused it on the vessel with excitement.

"We have our work ahead of us," Maximus said, "but we may be able to bring the silver by mule train after all."

Favian was right; and the archbishop. He must forget . . . and ready the silver, lest he be required to report to Holy Seville to answer for his son's folly by paying with his own life.

Defeated. His rogue son had made a fool of him more than once. His pride smarted, smoldering in his chest, but he was also wise enough to know when it was time to turn his back. He must set his mind upon the work that would redeem his tarnished honor before the king. He must safeguard his position as viceroy. Power was the important thing he must maintain, as well as fear in those he ruled. Nicklas had not feared him — secretly he admired him for it. And Devora. Ah yes, he would always remember her. How much she was like Nicklas' English mother.

He had lost them all. All, except —

Maximus turned his head and looked at Favian. He saw his sullen expression, the lines of weariness on his face, and the far off look in his eyes that told Maximus he might also be losing Favian. Favian and Sybella. Was it too late?

"I am proud of you, Favian."

Favian's head turned sharply. He stared at his father.

"You have done your best," Maximus said gruffly. "It is enough." He turned his horse and rode back toward Lima.

Favian sat still upon his horse, surprise written on his face. He looked after his father. After a moment he flicked the reins and rode to catch up.

🌿 20 🌿

The Mule Train

They traveled at night and slept during the daylight hours. From the trail Devora could see the distant blue Pacific but had no idea where they were except somewhere near the Peruvian coastline.

Then one morning, after nine days of travel, they rode toward a small fishing village. The sun had climbed high by the time Hakewell rode back from scouting to tell Bruce they had spied a brigantine anchored offshore. A group of soldiers from a small inland garrison farther east were on the beach cooking over a campfire. Bruce took out his telescope and rode with him into the trees ahead. When he returned, she heard him tell Tobias and the others they would soon have a ship.

Devora remained with Tobias. All of her whispered questions were to no avail. Then, as the sun reached its zenith and the stinging insects were becoming unbearable,

Bruce and the others returned. Even Tupac was now garbed as a Spanish soldier and was admiring his wide-brimmed hat adorned with silver pesos. He blew on them and shined them with a yellow scarf.

Bruce walked up carrying a Spanish jacket gleaming with medals.

"The Spaniards resisted lending us uniforms," he explained with a slight smile. "We had to insist." He handed her a ruffled dress of black lace and mango-colored satin. "Better put this on before we board the brigantine as passengers."

Devora's brow arched as she scanned the dress. "I assume the señorita this belonged to 'resisted' also?"

Bruce's mouth tipped downward. "No, she donated it from her trunk after being assured of her safety." He started to lead her toward the privacy of a clump of bushes.

"I don't need any help," she said, smiling up at him.

"There may be snakes, ants, and insects of all sizes, including three-inch long roaches."

"On second thought — I will need you desperately."

The horses were left to find their way to the village to what Devora was certain would be squeals of delight from the poor peasants, and Bruce became the new capitan of the military brigantine. By afternoon the sails were billowing in the wind and the *Saint Sophia* was following the coastline in the direction of Darien, Panama.

Devora joined Bruce at the whipstaff, enjoying the warm tropical sea breeze that tossed her hair and billowed her Spanish skirts. She smiled at him and placed her arms tightly about him.

They landed in the Gulf of Darien, which lapped the east coast of the Isthmus of Panama. "Sir Francis Drake named this place Port Pheasant for the flocks of wild fowl he saw in the jungle," Bruce told her. Hakewell found that fishing in the bay was bountiful, and Devora and Tobias noticed an abundance of fruit and game.

Here in the secluded bay with jungle that sloped to the edge of the beach, they set up a small camp and Bruce and Tobias made contact with the friendly Cimaroons.

"Indians?" she asked Bruce.

"No, Africans. Slaves who escaped captivity. It's to our advantage they hate Spain. They know the 500-mile coastline between Cartagena, Portobello, and Nombre de Dios better than many Spaniards do. If Kitt and the *Revenge* are anywhere in this area the Cimaroons will spot them and bring word."

Two weeks later, Devora was near the shore where the sparkling waves rolled in on the beach in the moonlight. The trees waved gracefully in the warm wind. She heard a stealthy footfall, whirled, and saw a huge figure crouching in the trees. Her scream froze as he stepped out in a leopard skin cape wearing a woven headband decorated with feathers. The whites of his eyes glowed and his teeth showed in a smile.

Devora let out a sigh of relief. He spoke to her in broken Spanish. "News for Capitan Bruce. Friend Kitt here now."

Kitt had arrived! Devora raced across the beach calling for Bruce. He came running, pistol drawn as though he thought she were in trouble. She grabbed him, laughing with excitement. "Kitt's here!"

Kitt Bonnor and the *Revenge* were on a small island some 75 miles from Nombre de Dios, the isthmus port near the Gold Road where the mule train had once brought the silver to the treasure fleet until it was changed to Portobello, not many miles away. It seemed to Devora that the last great adventure was about to begin. She knew Bruce wanted that mule train — and now that his ally was here, there would be no stopping him. Still, she had to try.

"But if we left now," she protested, "we

340

could forget all that's happened and begin a new life. If not in Barbados, then in the colony you mentioned named Virginia. Oh Bruce, why must you take this risk when we could escape now? If something goes wrong —"

He silenced her with a kiss, his arms sliding about her waist, drawing her beside him. The little waves lapped gently at their feet. The breeze tugged and played in their hair. Beneath the silvery moonlight a sonata of love intertwined their hearts.

Drake had named the little island near Nombre de Dios the "Isle of Pines," for its thick forestation. There, three days later, they arrived to meet Kitt, hiding the brigantine in a sheltered cove where Devora laid eyes on Bruce's English buccaneering ship, the *Revenge*. Leaving a few men to warn of any Spanish sightings, they disembarked in pinnaces toward shore.

Kitt Bonnor was waiting for him, with a crew of at least thirty English and French buccaneers, all armed with cutlasses and boarding pistols, their swarthy faces grinning at Bruce and Hakewell and the other men. When Bruce introduced her the men lapsed into gaping silence.

"Put your eyes back in your head," he told them. "And the first jackanape who so much as winks at her will have his innards washing along the shore."

Devora tensed, waiting for trouble, but the men threw back their heads and laughed with pleasure. She realized he was expected to speak thus, and remembered the rowdy pack of pirates she had done unpleasant business with on the Isle of Pearls the night she had first met Bruce. He had taken her captive aboard the *Revenge* intending, so he had said, to bring her to Tortuga. How long ago that adventure seemed now!

Kitt Bonnor came forward and showed himself equal to the manners of any English lord. He swept off his plumed hat, bowed low, and kissed her hand.

"M'lady, the pleasure is all mine, to be sure." He straightened, his eyes twinkling. "We first met, I believe, at Governor Toledo's residence on the Isle of Pearls."

"Yes," she said with a smile. "The night Bruce attacked with his buccaneers and freed you from the dungeon."

"And now you are his bride. Ah, love!"

She looked at Bruce and he smiled, then turned to Kitt. "Enough of your fair words. Come, we have much to discuss."

"You will be delighted to know," said Kitt as they walked to a council meeting on the beach, "that we spotted the treasure fleet beating its way from Cartagena to Portobello. They must be most anxious to load the Peruvian silver for his Majesty."

"I'm afraid His Most Illustrious Catholic Majesty must be content this time to count his beads; there will be no silver from Cuzco if this heretic can stop it."

Within a fortnight all the critical plans had been made and gone over several times until every man knew exactly what he was to do. Because every buccaneer was needed in the attack, Devora would either need to stay by herself aboard the *Revenge* or go with them on the inland march.

Bruce frowned as he paced. She knew he had never intended to bring her here. Kitt had left the captain's cabin aboard the *Revenge*, and she and Bruce had moved in.

"This is one situation that has troubled me for months," he admitted. "What to do with you."

She smiled, and teasingly took over his captain's chair behind the desk. "You can't get rid of me now. I'm here to stay."

He scanned her and, coming behind the desk, pulled her to her feet and into his arms. "I like that. Until death do us part."

"Bruce, I must go with you," and she explained her scare with the Cimaroon that night when he'd come out from behind the bushes. "I know they are your friends and you trust them. And I'm grateful for all they've done to help you, but all it takes is one out of a hundred for something to end very badly."

"Yes," he said softly, his hold tightening as though the thought tormented him. "I've been kept awake at night thinking of what could go wrong by leaving you here. You'll have to come with us. But I don't like it. I'll make certain you stay back from the fighting with Tobias." He cradled her head between his hands, looking warmly into her eyes. "I'm sorry about this. When it's over we will leave and never come back. I promised you I'd settle down in one of the colonies and I meant it."

"I understand what drives you, Bruce," she said worriedly. "But even if you take the silver, how will it be delivered to Holland to aid the army against Spain?"

"At first I intended to bring it myself, but that was before I met you. I can trust Kitt to bring it to Holland. I don't think you have any interest in a long voyage to the Netherlands aboard a heavily loaded and cramped ship."

"Are you sure your desire is to aid Holland rather than to wreak vengeance upon Maximus?"

He frowned and walked away from her.

He began to ready himself to go ashore in the pinnace. "Let's not ruin things by talking about Maximus."

Devora watched him, deeply troubled. She had been praying for weeks that Bruce could let go of the past and release his father to the Lord, knowing that in the end it was God alone who was worthy to make final judgments on the injustices of life. *We are either too lenient, or too harsh,* she thought, *but almost always unforgiving.*

Not that she could blame Bruce — not after what she had seen of Don Maximus Valentin! She had little pity left for him herself.

The Cimaroons arrived in camp with the news Bruce and Kitt had been waiting for. The treasure fleet had docked at Portobello.

"The mules," Tobias told her, "will soon be coming across the spine of the isthmus."

They climbed into the high elevations and Devora found the rain forest cool and shady after the heat of the lower jungle. She had never seen such tall trees, and colorful macaws and parrots were everywhere. But she worried about leopards and jaguars, and huge vipers in the branches. She found herself always glancing up, never knowing what to expect.

Bruce had them walking in the early mornings before the heat was at its worst, stopping at noon for a siesta during the hottest part of the day, then walking again until making camp for the night. He made her a palmetto hut, a skill that he'd learned from the Cimaroons.

At the beginning of each day they listened for the distant tinkling of the Peruvian silver bells on the mules.

Some days later they arrived at a great summit and here Bruce deliberately stopped. "I want to show you something," he told her, and taking her arm he led her to a great tree that towered above them like a wide, strong giant. Devora saw footholds carved into the tree and when she looked up she saw a high platform in its branches.

She climbed upward with Bruce behind her. When they reached the top, she looked out, startled.

Bruce explained. "We are on the summit of the ridge that bisects the isthmus. Twenty-five miles to the south the Pacific rolls to one horizon — and there" he pointed in the opposite direction, "is the Atlantic.

"The Cimaroon Chief brought Sir Francis Drake here long ago. Drake was so taken by the discovery that he fell to his knees. It's said he looked at the Pacific and asked the Lord to let him sail once in an English ship in that ocean. He did so, and went beyond the Philippines and circumvented the world. Before he left he gave the Cimaroons a priceless gift — he taught them the Lord's Prayer. Even to this day many can repeat it."

Within a week they had reached their desired destination. Tupac was sent into town dressed as a slave to learn when the mule train would be leaving for Portobello.

From the hilltop Devora could see the Bay of Panama with its many ships and smaller boats. The last time they had been in Panama Bruce had stood trial before Viceroy de Guzman and Maximus. She shuddered, remembering, and looked over at him, worried. He was on the ridge looking off toward the golden city through a telescope. Tupac was returning and Bruce and Kitt went to meet him as he climbed up the hill. The news was welcome; the mule train was coming from Panama that night for the journey to Portobello over the isthmus.

"But all news is not good. Favian is with the mule train. So is Viceroy Maximus."

Devora felt her chest tighten. Her gaze swerved to Bruce. She recognized the set of his jaw, the smoldering green that heated his eyes. "It could not be more perfect. I shall take every last bar of silver and leave him holding the wind!" He turned to his men. "Remember, keep your wits. Do not act until I give the signal. Remember Robert Pike!"

The buccaneers, all brandishing double boarding pistols, swords, or cutlasses, smirked at the name of Robert Pike. They looked at each other as if to warn his fellow that he'd pay dearly if he followed Pike's example. Every buccaneer knew the tale of Drake's English crewman, Pike. Pike had lost his wits just as the mule train was approaching where Drake had hidden his men on the Gold Road. Pike had become too excited and leaped up from his hiding place before Drake had given the signal. It wasn't the mule train coming but a lone Spaniard on a horse on his way to Panama. As he rode by, Pike jumped up. A Cimaroon grabbed Pike's shirttail to pull him down, but it was too late. The Spaniard had seen him and galloped down to Panama to warn the captain of the mule train that was approaching. The captain had returned the mules to Panama and instead had sent a second mule train with bags filled not with silver but food. After the bitter disappointment Drake had had to withdraw and wait months before a second try was successfully enacted.

"We have but one opportunity," Bruce told them. "If we fail and are captured, you can be sure this time we will all hang."

Sir Francis Drake's plan was meticulously followed. Drake's bold plan was just the sort that appealed to Bruce. He and Kitt would lead the attack on the mule train at the northern end of the Gold Road, just outside Nombre de Dios, where Maximus, having already passed safely through the isthmus jungle, would think his soldiers had nothing more to fear. He knew Maximus would be unsuspecting once the mules neared their final destination of Portobello and the treasure galleons.

They came to the mouth of the Rio Francisco, where they had concealed the pinnaces that would transport them and the bounty to the brigantine a quarter mile ahead in a small scalloped inlet where trees and thick jungle vine grew to the edge of the beach. Bruce had left the Spanish flag smartly in place should any sloop happen to venture past and see it. Devora waited there out of sight with Tobias.

Once at the Rio Francisco they marched silently down river near the harbor. Bruce assigned each buccaneer his position and lined them along both sides of the Gold

Road, outside of town. Here, just below the road in the underbrush they lay in wait with weapons in hand, waiting for Bruce's signal. Like Drake nearly a hundred years earlier, they were so close to the harbor that they could hear the noise aboard the Spanish ships at anchor.

Tupac and a Cimaroon scout returned from the inland trail and signaled him and Kitt. A hasty meeting occurred under the jungle vine near the final point of the Gold Road.

"There are 200 mules, Capt'n," Tupac said with a grin, sweat dotting his face. "That many to carry it all. Not silver only — but gold, emeralds, and pearls."

"How many soldiers?"

"Fifty, all heavily armed."

"And Don Maximus?"

"He rides white horse, soldier carries flag of Spain. Don Favian just behind."

"Well done, Tupac. Take your position."

"Aye, Capt'n."

Bruce looked at Kitt. Without a word they went to their place to lead the divided group of buccaneers. The moon was bright, silvery-blue above the Caribbean water. The jungle leaves brushed against each other and trembled in the hot, sultry night. Bruce looked at his palms; they sweated. He frowned. He'd given orders that neither his father nor his brother were to be killed —

His father. His brother.

They were not family! *Do not get weak and sentimental now,* he rebuked himself. *Remember your chains aboard the* Santa Rosa. *Your father made you a galley slave. And what about the mines! Do not you still feel the whip lashes? If he catches you tonight he'll just as soon hang you as look at you. Besides, the silver is going for a good cause — Protestant Holland.*

Still, he frowned, and wiped the sweat from his palms on his leather breeches. Soon it would all be over . . . Devora waited, the American colony of Virginia waited. He would forever turn his back on Spain and —

Bruce heard the trill of treetoads and the calls of nightbirds, then, after what seemed hours, he heard the faint tinkle of the silver bells on the mules.

The tinkle grew louder until he could hear the weary hooves of the mules, the snorting of sweating horses, the faint jangle of Spanish spurs, the creak of saddle leather, the low murmur of Spanish voices. The sounds merged as one. The mules plodded along the road where the ambush was waiting. Bruce squinted and saw the silhouetted outline of soldiers. He saw Maximus on his white horse — an easy target, but one that all the buccaneers knew was off limits! Favian rode a length behind.

Bruce sounded the alarm and sprang forward with a shout. Pandemonium broke loose. Horses neighed, mules brayed, pistol shots flashed tiny flames, swords and cutlasses rang, steel smashing steel.

The Spanish soldiers put up a fight but were surprised by the aggressive attack of the buccaneers. Outnumbered, the soldiers were soon overcome, and those still alive when the skirmish was over were bound and gagged and left along side of the Gold Road.

Maximus and Favian were unhurt but stripped of their weapons and their wrists were bound behind them.

Kitt was smiling at Maximus, waving his sword under his nose. "I believe, Don Maximus, that you and I had an appointment to meet back at the Isle of Pearls. Alas, you did not show up."

Bruce walked forward, sword in hand, and looked at his father. Maximus saw him and his eyes spat fire. "No, I did not show, dog," he growled, "but this halfbreed English jackal did show and set you free."

"Leave us," Bruce told Kitt.

Before he could comply, Hakewell ran up. "Capt'n! We gotta get outta here fast. Them shots was heard in town."

"Start loading the boats."

"Aye, Capt'n!"

Bruce looked at Favian, who stood in sullen silence refusing to meet his gaze, but Maximus glared hotly.

Bruce offered a mocking bow.

"Thank you for bringing this great bounty that we have worked for so long at the mines, my Father! We've been waiting patiently. Justice demands wages for all we've been through!" He turned his dark head, his green eyes full of malicious satisfaction. "How much did the viceroy bring us, Kitt?"

"Enough to soothe your scars, Bruce! Gold, silver bars, emeralds, and pearls."

"You have been generous, Don Maximus," Bruce said airly. He laughed. "You will be pleased to know what we intend to do with it. You see, we are here to 'collect' from Spain what is due to our Holland brothers! This wealth will buy more food and weapons to fight the inhumane Spanish Inquisition in the Netherlands!"

"Har, Capt'n," said Deever with a laugh. "When ye puts it like that, our work in the mines were worth it after all!"

Maximus stared evenly at Bruce. "Show the honor of a soldier! If you plan to shoot me, be done with it."

"I think I heard those words before, only

it was I who spoke them when you boarded the brigantine at Cartagena. Perhaps my answer to you should be the same as you gave to me. A galley slave, perhaps?" His smile disappeared. "Or maybe seven years as a slave in Holland."

"You insolent jackal!"

"Ah well . . . I have learned much from you about how to treat prisoners — especially how a father treats a son."

Maximus' mouth twitched. "You were never a son!"

Bruce's eyes burned. "Nor you a father. I never meant anything to you until you believed I could bring glory to the Valentin name. Only then did you accept me as a son. I had to earn your love, which is not love at all. And now I must leave. Hasta la vista."

"You had best kill me, Nicklas. If not, I will come after you."

"Nicklas, no!" breathed Favian. "Please, my brother, please — do not leave us to these pirates to torture and kill us."

Bruce looked at him soberly. "You mistake me, Favian. I am neither a Dominican nor a full-blooded Valentin. Fear not." He bowed, and looking one last time at Maximus' ruddy face, turned his back on them and walked down to the Rio Francisco where the caches of treasure were being loaded onto the pinnaces.

Maximus shouted after him: "My life is worth nothing now. If you take this silver I shall be called before the king!"

"You will not succeed, Nicklas. The galleons will be after you before you ever leave Spanish waters."

Bruce did not look back.

"Nicklas! Come back, Nicklas! It is not too late —"

Bruce clamped his jaw and kept walking. He saw Kitt watching him uncertainly, but Bruce stepped into the pinnace. "Shove off," he ordered. Kitt, without expression, gestured to the Cimaroons, who pushed the boat from shore and then jumped in and picked up the oars. In a moment they were sliding down the river beneath the silvery-blue moon.

❦ 21 ❦

Laying Aside the Iron Mask of Pride

Two days later the *Revenge* was far out on the Caribbean, its hold stashed with silver and emeralds. The Spanish brigantine under Kitt, renamed the *Victory*, followed in close pursuit.

Bruce stood with the wind blowing against him, his shirt sleeves billowing while he looked out across the limpid green water.

Devora came up beside him. She studied the handsome outline of his face, seeing more than physical weariness troubling him. She slipped an understanding hand into his, and though he said nothing, the gentle pressure of his responsive squeeze assured her that he was aware of her, that he loved her, that he knew she understood his sober heart.

"You lost only one crewman and we're all free. Hakewell says your name will soon be acclaimed throughout the Tortuga Brotherhood. No one has managed to attack the mule train since Sir Francis Drake."

He continued to look out at the horizon.

She went to the side of the ship and held the rail, frowning to herself. She knew that Bruce didn't care to admit it even to himself, but the satisfaction of taking revenge upon Maximus wasn't that sweet after all. "The matter over Maximus burdens you."

"I do not regret confiscating the silver for Holland. There is a religious war in Europe and we've aligned ourselves on the side of the Netherlands, believing it to be just. The Reformation must continue," he said firmly. "And nations must be free to choose and establish their rule without the lordship of Rome. But . . . you're right about Maximus."

He joined her at the ship's rail, leaning there. "Forcing him to sample the cup of defeat he has long made others drink hasn't brought me the freedom I always told myself it would. Since I was a boy I convinced myself he was a giant that must be disarmed. Now that I've done so, I've seen him for what he is, just a man. A man enslaved by his own sins. I wasn't the only prisoner. He was one too, dominated by character flaws that he couldn't tame. He behaved as he did not because he was strong, but because he was weak. In exposing the giant I discovered a man who needs the mercy of Christ just as much as I do."

She held him in silent understanding. They looked out toward the sea and drew comfort from each other. "I have your love," he said, "it's enough."

After a moment she said quietly, "There is something I haven't told you. Tobias knows, but neither of us have any proof."

It was difficult to say, but she finally got the words out. "I think Maximus may be to blame for my mother's death."

He took her by the arms, turning her to face him. His gray-green eyes searched hers. "Go on."

She explained about the morning when she had found him coming from her mother's chamber. "I think she was poisoned, though the physician would not admit it to me. He behaved strangely."

"Did he? Was she on a drug?"

"Yes . . ."

"Might she have taken too much by mistake?"

She hesitated. She didn't want to believe it of her, yet it was true that Catherina had been taking stronger doses. "But Maximus was the first to come out of her chamber that morning."

They held each other as though some force might still arise to tear them permanently apart.

"I'm glad you shared your suspicions with me," he told her. "I know you did so trying to ease my conscience. I suppose I always knew it would end this way. That once I gained victory over Maximus, the satisfaction would be short-lived. Tobias was right. He always warned me that vengeance can never satisfy the man who chooses to walk with God."

With the dawn the shrill blast from the boatswain's whistle sent an unexpected alarm throughout the ship. Bruce came out the cabin door and looked over the taffrail into the waist.

"Trouble, sir," his boatswain called. "A Spanish warship. And she's bearing down on us fast! Her aims don't look pretty for us."

A Spanish galleon? Bruce knew who it was even before he looked through the telescope. He remained calm. "Signal Kitt on the *Victory*."

"Aye, Capt'n!"

Bruce came back into the cabin, grabbing a cool cotton shirt and slipping into it while Devora scrambled over the foot of the bed and hurried to him. "What is it? What's wrong? Pirates?"

He gave an unamused laugh. "Perhaps the biggest one of all."

"Who?" she cried.

"There's only one man determined enough to follow me into English waters to take my ship."

She turned pale. "Don Maximus!"

"Yes," came his grave tone. "I should have expected this. I, who claim to know better than anyone else what manner of man he is. I've risked you, and my crewmen, while bemoaning my melancholy mood."

"You mustn't blame yourself. This shows he hasn't changed at all. Bruce — if he does manage to take this ship —" her voice trailed off.

"Yes, I know," he stated, nothing in his voice but cold determination. "That's why I've got to stop that galleon." He snatched his baldric from the peg. "One thing is certain. My father won't be nursing a guilty conscience should he succeed in blowing us out of the water."

"Blowing us out of . . ." her eyes widened. "Oh Bruce! I can't swim."

He halted and looked at her, and despite everything, amusement reflected in his eyes. He smiled, then cupped her chin and planted a kiss on her lips. "Don't worry." He flung open the cabin door and hurried out, calling back over his shoulder: "Stay in the cabin."

On deck, Bruce called orders to his crew. His lieutenant was waiting for him and passed Bruce the telescope, a frown on his scarred forehead.

"It's him, to be sure, Capt'n," he said in a low voice. "It's the viceroy."

Bruce snatched the telescope and leveled it out to sea. He studied the warship, recognizing her elegant lines, her cannons, and the flag of Castile. A smaller flag, but easily visible, was also recognizable, the Valentin family heraldic: the stallion of Andalusia.

"He must'a been gaining on us all night," complained Hakewell. "Whilst we was lolling about enjoying our victory, he was sailing after us."

"That's a good lesson to be remembered. Never depend on yesterday's victories. Not when the foe is only half defeated."

Tobias walked up. "And I'd say the wounded bull is even more dangerous now. How far away?"

"About three miles."

"We spotted him soon as the day's light broke," Hakewell said. "He's coming on strong and bristles with cannon, sir."

"I'm well aware of that ship, Tom. You should be too." He handed him the telescope. "Better look again."

Hakewell sucked in his breath. "That's her all right. The *Our Lady of Madrid*."

Bruce looked at Tobias. "My flagship when I arrived in Cartagena."

"You can be sure Maximus has not overlooked the irony of that," Tobias murmured.

"Do you think he wants a fight, Capt'n?"

"As certain as he steers to cross our path."

"Then will ye give him one?" urged Hakewell. "The *Revenge* is up to her stuff, Capt'n."

Bruce considered. They might try to make a run for it to windward, since the breeze was holding, but the cargo was heavy and even with the canvas spread the galleon would gain on him in time.

He glanced below to his navigator. "Thurman! How far to the nearest safe port?"

" 'Bout two hundred miles to Hispaniola in the north, or Curacao in the southeast, Captain!"

Two hundred miles! Bruce looked at Tobias. Tobias rubbed his chin and looked out toward Maximus' ship. "There's Devora to think of, my son."

Bruce turned to Hakewell, who stood

tensely by waiting for the captain's decision. "He'll be determined to take us, so we'll give him a fight." He stepped to the rail and called a sharp order to the quartermaster at the whipstaff to turn starboard on a heading to intercept the galleon. The bow pitched and her keel came on even to face the *Our Lady of Madrid.*

"Signal Kitt to alter his course!"

"He's following in pursuit, sir!"

Bruce lifted the telescope again and studied his father's vessel, then called orders. The shrill blast of the boatswain's whistle sent the buccaneers running to their stations. Another order to Rohan, his master gunner, and the ship shuddered as the big guns were run out and made secure for battle. Bruce lifted the telescope to check on Kitt. To his satisfaction he saw his loyal friend bring the smaller brigantine into fighting line. It would not be easy for Kitt, but he knew him well enough to know that he was clever and cool in tight conflict.

By midmorning the galleon was within range, its open ports swinging broadside. But Bruce was on the offensive. He would not wait to yield any advantage.

"Fire!"

The forty-pound cannons thundered in unison. The *Revenge* shuddered from the force of her guns. Explosions of fire, smoke, and metal ripped into the *Our Lady of Madrid.*

"Hold course, Rohan!" and the *Revenge* held steady, giving Kitt's brigantine an opening to let go her eight guns and demi-culverain while the *Revenge* had slipped by the galleon and was turning, now presenting her larboard guns. "Fire!" The second volley ripped into the galleon, followed by yet another from Kitt.

The galleon swung broadside and the big guns fired upon the *Revenge.* Bruce grasped the bulwark as the ship staggered under the vicious pounding.

Fire raced along the deck and the crew rushed to beat it out, rolling and emptying barrels of water with cutlass and machete.

The *Revenge*'s forecastle was smashed, but Bruce knew that if they could board the galleon in hand-to-hand fighting, they'd have a chance against Maximus.

"Thurston! Straight toward the galleon! Give their gunners the narrowest target!"

Before the new heading was reached, the *Revenge* plunged ahead to grapple with the galleon. The galleon's starboard guns blasted a second broadside at close quarters. Bruce looked up at the rending of timbers and the shouts of the buccaneers. The *Revenge* plunged into the cloud of smoke that masked the galleon, but soon the Spanish vessel was looming just ahead. Bruce took heart. He saw Maximus in full military garb shouting desperate orders to running soldiers.

Bruce did the same, shouting a crisp order to his trumpeter. The rallying call sounded across the Caribbean to Kitt who had already set a course to grapple with the galleon.

"Stand by to board!" Bruce shouted to his English and French buccaneers. "Digges! Prepare the grapnels!"

"Prepared, Capt'n!"

"Rohan! Pass word to the gunner in the prow! Fire as fast as he can load."

"Aye, sir!"

The cook rushed forward at Bruce's command bringing his fighting gear. Bruce tossed aside his plumed hat and took the steel head-piece. But as the cook handed him more ammunition, Bruce saw that it was Devora. Soot from the smoke colored her face with splotches, and a blue pirate's scarf held her honey-colored hair in place. Bruce's green eyes narrowed, but she threw her arms around his neck and kissed him. "God be with you," she managed amid the shouting and explosion of guns.

Their eyes held in wordless devotion, then swiftly he drew her into his arms, kissing her a final time.

"Come back to me, Bruce. You must come back," she called, as Tobias rushed up and drew her to safety.

Bruce moved forward leading his buccaneers, his lieutenant at his left. They stooped for refuge from Spanish guns and fireballs as the two ships came alongside each other. Bruce and the buccaneers gripped their grapnels carefully, then on signal stood and surged forward, hurling them across the small gulf of sea. Over half reached the galleon and stuck fast. At once they surged together, pulling to bond the two vessels together, while the Spanish soldiers blasted at them with muskets. But Kitt's men were already attacking the Spanish soldiers who were trying to dislodge the grapnel irons that held firm.

Bruce, gritting and sweating, pulled with his muscled body until he at last heard the sweet sound of the two ships jarring together with a groan. A shout went up from the buccaneers as the *Revenge* was literally moored to the galleon by the grapnels.

"Board and board!" Bruce shouted. The drums begin to beat with a feverish heart-stopping cadence. The advance guard surged ahead.

Some Spaniards fired their muskets while others rushed forward with swords slashing. Bruce led the buccaneers over the galleon's taffrail. Kitt and his crew now joined in the boarding, and the Spaniards had to turn and meet them. Bruce's sword smashed against his opponent again and again, then rammed through a chink in the armor. As he withdrew his blade, the soldier doubled and fell to the deck. He stepped over him and moved forward, his line of men pressing ahead, steel ringing against steel.

More buccaneers followed until all were aboard the galleon, leaving the *Revenge* practically empty.

Devora continued her endless pacing of the cabin floor, hearing the fighting in the muffled distance. Her stomach hurt and her hands sweated. What if the worst happened, what if —

"I thought I would find you here," Maximus said from the doorway.

She sucked in her breath and whirled, her heart stopping. He stood there, wounded, blood splattered on his shirt, but still gripping his pistol. His dark eyes blazed fever-ishly and sweat ran down the hard lines of his tanned face.

The worst of her sudden fear made her weak and she leaned against the desk. He had killed Bruce.

Maximus' mouth turned as he read her thoughts. "No, I did not kill Nicklas. It was simple to abandon my ship and come here. All the English dogs are aboard the galleon. They are like piranah fish . . . when they are done there is nothing left. . . . It was unwise of Nicklas to leave you unguarded, for if I wished to destroy him . . . I now have the opportunity."

She glanced at the pistol aimed at her heart.

Maximus smirked. "Killing you, Devora, would be the end of this blackhearted scamp who was my undoing. Getting even with him is simple enough. He has already destroyed me, and I could destroy him. But!" He walked unsteadily into the cabin. "Not much is gained by that, is there? Not now. Too late for that."

A strong and heavy man, he staggered on his feet as he sank to a chair.

She made a move toward him, but he raised the pistol.

"You are bleeding profusely, Don Maximus. Please, let me staunch the wound."

He waved her aside wearily. "So that I may have the pleasure of standing trial in Seville? Thank you, no, Señorita — I mean 'Señora'." And he bowed his arrogant dark head. "Again, very clever of my jackal son to steal you from beneath my nose. If I were a younger man, and not on my deathbed, I might yet contest him for you. But you may relax . . . I do not have any such desire. You see, you were right that night at the hacienda when you told me it was not you I really loved, but Marian, his mother. I now know and understand something more of my own heart. You reminded me of her . . . I was trying to relive the past, to make amends for my grave error in treating her as ruthlessly as I did. That was the reason why I would marry you. In my mind, I suppose I was finally offering her that honor — an honor that should indeed have been hers."

"Please, Maximus," she said gently, seeing his torment, "Lie down, wait for Nicklas. You must tell him all this."

A shadow appeared in the doorway and Devora turned to see Tobias. He entered quietly and simply looked down at Maximus, great, heavy sadness on his face. They stared at each other without saying a word. Tobias looked at the pistol, then at Devora, but Maximus lowered it with exhaustion.

"If I had wanted to kill her I would have done so by now." He leaned his head back against the chair, his breathing growing more difficult. He winced as he moved.

"Did you kill Catherina?" Tobias asked.

"Bah . . . I would not waste the effort . . . such a woman . . . she overdosed herself." His gaze swerved to Devora. "I am surprised you did not know . . ."

Know what? she wondered, moving toward him.

". . . know my physician was giving her *coca* plant, a 'divine plant' to all ancient Peruvians." He reached into his jacket and pulled out a small wad of leaves. "Tobias can tell you . . . so can Nicklas . . . when chewed it stimulates one to forget pain . . . your empty-headed mother took too much . . ." he put a wad of leaves in his mouth. "Go for Nicklas, Tobias . . ."

Tobias gave a slight nod of his head, then turned quickly and ran.

It seemed to Devora that an hour had passed before Bruce arrived, yet it could not have been that long. When he entered the cabin, he appeared to be as blood-stained as Maximus, and just as weary and drenched with sweat. He stared down at his father, but Devora could not penetrate his expression.

"Leave . . . us . . ." Maximus rasped to Devora.

She did so, glancing at Bruce with troubled concern as she went past him. Tobias waited outside the cabin door and taking her arm, led her away to the opposite side of the ship, away from the smoldering galleon. She hadn't wanted to, but she couldn't help herself and her heart ached. She began to cry. Tobias held her and patted her shoulder.

He said with a husky voice, "There is no tragedy like the tragedy that need not have taken place. If only the iron mask of pride could have been laid aside from the heart sooner. Who knows?"

Bruce went to Maximus heedless of the pistol that rested on his lap and tore away his armor and opened his shirt, revealing a gaping wound.

Maximus shook his head. "No . . . too late. Better this way."

Bruce groaned and tried to lift him from the chair to haul him over to the bed, but Maximus resisted. "No, no, my son, let me die here Nicklas . . . there is nothing left . . ."

Bruce grasped him by the shoulders, gritting his frustration and rage. "Why did you come after me! Why couldn't you be con-

371

tent to accept defeat! You could have escaped Seville! You might have taken great possessions and gone into Mexico! You could have retired with horses and brought Favian and Sybella with you! You could have had grandchildren and died at a ripe old age! But *no!* You had to bring us to this!"

Maximus' brows lowered angrily, his eyes glazed, then a thin smile tugged at his lip. "You thought I would escape?"

"Yes," Bruce admitted.

Maximus looked at him a long minute. "You have given your heart away, Nicklas . . . you do have feelings for me."

Bruce's eyes filled with tears.

Maximus sighed heavily, his chest rattling. "Always like Marian . . . too sentimental . . . yet brave too — you fought well, Nicklas. As for grandchildren, if you had not betrayed me and Spain, I would have had yours!"

"I detest Spain and all she stands for!"

"Like you detest me?"

"Don't say that now!"

"Better this way," he repeated. "Something I want you to know . . . I am a proud and angry man . . . I didn't tell Marian I loved her, but I did . . . I loved your mother . . . in my own way. But my ways are not yours, or hers . . ."

Loved his mother? Bruce might have scoffed, but something raw and painful in Maximus' eyes convinced him he spoke the truth as he perceived it.

"I do not love Devora . . . but she reminded me of your mother . . . of you too . . . don't know if I would have gone through with the wedding or kept you seven years at the mine . . . too angry to say I was wrong . . . I was afraid of showing weakness."

Bruce stared at him, his pain too deep for words.

"Forgive . . . me . . ."

A sword ripped through Bruce's heart. He resisted, then lowered his dark head against Maximus' heaving chest. "I do forgive you, my Father."

Maximus tried to say something, but could not. A scarred hand lifted to Bruce's shoulder and squeezed with its last bit of strength, then fell to the side of the chair. His breath gasped, then stopped.

Bruce clenched his fist and then let it drop gently to rest against Maximus' arm. He closed his eyes and allowed himself to weep like a little boy.

"Now you tell me, my Father!"

Epilogue

Bruce and Favian buried Don Maximus at sea. Favian, though injured, was released by Bruce to return home to Lima since he would not be held responsible for the mule train.

"Sybella and the family inheritance are yours," Bruce told him.

While they did not part enemies, neither did they part as brothers. Favian was satisfied that Bruce had plans in English territory.

Tobias considered returning to Cuzco to carry on his work among the Indians, but Favian warned him of Archbishop Harro Andres' suspicions that Tobias was of the heretic Reformational belief.

"Perhaps I will settle in St. Augustine," Tobias later told Bruce, but Devora put a quick end to that, knowing how much Bruce cared for his uncle.

"Oh no you don't. There must be someone around to restrain Bruce when he grows weary of plantation life and decides to cast his buccaneering eye toward the Caribbean." She put her arms around him. "We need you, Tobias. We both do. The Lord has been using you in our lives. And Bruce's grandmother will be pleased you've returned with us also."

"Well, if you put it that way . . ." and his brown eyes glinted with new cheer.

"From what I hear of Devora's uncle, he will enjoy a minister at Ashby hall to engage him in theological discussions," Bruce told him.

"Then you intend to settle in Barbados?" Tobias looked from Devora to Bruce. Devora, too, looked at him. She had already told Bruce that wherever he decided to go, she would support him in the venture, even to Holland to deliver the silver for the armies.

"Kitt will be in command of the last journey," he told her. "We will map out our own plans for the future. I've some new ideas other than the colony at Virginia."

The *Revenge* limped into Dutch-held Curacao for repairs before voyaging on to Carlisle Bay, Barbados. The trade winds blew warmly and softly across the blue-green Caribbean. The sky deepened into purple and the silvery moon rose slowly above the low hills. The palm trees glimmered in the moonlight and swayed gently.

"Bruce, are you at peace finally? Or will you never know peace and rest of soul? Can you be content?"

"Too much of my past has been driven by a desire to excel and reap vengeance. That is never the way to peace. I will never again seek vengeance, which only belongs to God." He turned and looked down at her, then drew her into his embrace. In his clear gray-green eyes she saw that which made her heart rest with joyful satisfaction.

Slowly, wordlessly, he drew her closer and kissed her upturned lips, while the trade winds softly entwined them in a moonlight sonata all its own . . . and Devora knew that she had her answer.